BBC
DOCTOR WHO

Dark Horizons

BBC
DOCTOR WHO

Dark Horizons

JENNY T. COLGAN

BBC
BOOKS

1 3 5 7 9 10 8 6 4 2

First published in 2012 by BBC Books, an imprint of Ebury Publishing.
A Random House Group Company

This paperback edition published in 2013.

Doctor Who is a BBC Wales production for BBC One.
Executive producers: Steven Moffat and Faith Penhale

The Random House Group Limited Reg. No. 954009

Addresses for companies within the Random House Group
can be found at www.randomhouse.co.uk

A CIP catalogue record for this book is available
from the British Library.

ISBN 978 1 849 90457 5

MIX
Paper from
responsible sources
FSC
www.fsc.org
FSC® C016897

The Random House Group Limited supports the Forest Stewardship
Council® (FSC®), the leading international forest-certification organisation.
Our books carrying the FSC label are printed on FSC®-certified paper. FSC is
the only forest-certification scheme supported by the leading environmental
organisations, including Greenpeace. Our paper procurement policy can be
found at www.randomhouse.co.uk/environment

Editorial director: Albert DePetrillo
Series consultant: Justin Richards
Project editor: Steve Tribe
Cover design: Lee Binding © Woodlands Books Ltd, 2012
Production: Alex Goddard

Printed and bound in Great Britain
by CPI Group (UK) Ltd, Croydon, CR0 4YY

To buy books by your favourite authors and register for offers,
visit www.randomhouse.co.uk

To my best Wallace.
I am sorry I told you
The Family of Blood
'isn't that scary'.

Chapter
One

The Doctor looked down at the board, sighed and gently knocked over the king with one finger. Lost again. That was the problem with playing chess with yourself. You always lost.

And he wasn't playing Bobby Fischer again. That had gone very wrong. Very wrong indeed. He hated it when people bandied about phrases like 'brought the world to the brink of nuclear war'.

The Doctor frowned to himself. What he really needed was someone to play chess with who wouldn't take it too seriously. Someone who wouldn't get really upset when he beat them.

Henrik and Annar stared hard at the board. They were trying to keep it sheltered high up in the prow, where there was a little space just underneath the dragon's neck that decorated the front of the longship, away from the bosun's prying eyes. If he knew they were playing with his second most precious piece of cargo, there'd be trouble.

But there wasn't much else to do nearly a full moon's turn out from land, once your rowing stint was over and you'd talked about as many girls as you could mention in one breath, and the meat was turning green and you could scarcely remember a world where the horizon didn't move up and down constantly; where your clothes weren't wet from dawn to dusk, and you ate the same dry bread, dry meat and porridge oats every day, like cattle. Henrik glanced over to the hens in cages along the side of the boat. They'd stopped laying. He frowned. That meant harsh weather was coming.

Henrik cast his eyes back to the board. The chess set had been packed up well; it was being taken to Iceland as part of the dowry gift, as the Duke of Trondheim prepared to marry his daughter to Gissar Polvaderson, to cement the bonds between their two lands.

The Duke of Trondheim's daughter, Freydis, had long hair that looked like it was made out of spun gold. Gissar Polvaderson, as everyone knew throughout the world, was the fattest man anyone had ever seen, who dined exclusively on whale blubber and drank hot mead from the second he rolled from his cot in the morning. It had caused plenty of sniggering amongst the sailors.

'Keep your eyes off those chooks,' grunted Annar to Henrik. 'We're not going to be eating roast hen for a long time, so don't think it.'

'If they're not laying…' said Henrik. Suddenly, the idea of a roast chicken, dripping with juices, roasted over a good fire, with the flatbread his mother used to make back on the farm, was the most wonderful thing he could think of. 'I'd trade a kingdom for that,' he said ruefully, looking down at his pieces. They were beautifully carved from walrus ivory, in the Trondheim style; Gissar, proud on his throne, his fat cheeks showing over his beard.

Even though the carvings were small they were still, Henrik thought, flattering. He had seen the King once; he was short, his belly bulged over his leather windings, and his face was covered in old pustules that he tended to fiddle with distractedly whilst giving orders. Henrik had been, on the whole, disappointed. It was the first king he'd ever seen; he'd expected someone a bit more impressive.

And beside him on the board, the carving was of the Princess, Freydis made as queen-in-waiting, her hair curling down over the back of the throne; her expression proud and stern. They had been made over four moons by the finest bone-worker in Trondheim; they were the most precious, beautiful objects Henrik had ever seen. He weighed the heavy piece in his hands. Its cool beauty suggesting luxury and leisure time. Henrik had never owned much more than his sheepskin and cord boots in his entire life. The idea of commissioning these – for hundreds of crowns – was amazing. He hoped they would be appreciated.

'Check,' said Annar.

Henrik cursed. He had been so distracted by the pieces, he'd forgotten to concentrate on the game. He bent his head. But, just as he did so, a sudden, terrible screaming rent the air.

As the men leapt up, startled half out of their wits, hands already halfway to their swords, the beautiful board tipped over, the pieces rattling and scattering all over the deck.

Chapter Two

The Doctor emerged from the TARDIS onto a flat stony shore. There wasn't a tree to be seen, and the low land looked cold and desolate. Ahead was a great scree of pebbles, leading off to a wide long beach, and choppy water the colour of steel. Another island could be seen across the water, on land that looked just as flat and as desolate as where he now stood.

Behind the TARDIS was a springy heath without a sign of human habitation, but several lean-limbed rabbits whipped past as the Doctor bent down.

'Hello, Lepus,' he said, crouching down to watch them bounding about, curious, at his feet. As soon as he crouched down, they scattered like the wind.

'Well, there's someone about, then. Rabbits! Brand new to the twelfth century. Perfect!' he said, looking around. 'Something bad clearly happens to you when you meet something shaped like me. Although I'm not very scary,' he added. 'Well, I can be. But very rarely to rabbits, I promise.'

His voice tailed off as he glanced up at the clouds,

which were flitting faster and faster across a lowering grey sky. On the opposite island, rain was already clearly falling heavily, and on the heath the heather was starting to stir with the gathering wind. The rabbits had all completely vanished.

'Hmm,' said the Doctor to himself as the first drops began to fall. 'Weather. Weather needs… What is it? It is so much easier when someone else is around to tell me this stuff. Extra clothes. Yes.'

He frowned then popped back into the TARDIS, re-emerging wearing exactly the same tweed jacket and bow tie, but with the addition of a very small yellow checked scarf. He licked his finger, stuck it in the air, nearly got blown over then took a sniff of the air and headed off in the opposite direction, bent heavy against the rain and the wind.

The screaming continued; grew louder if anything, accompanied by a furious banging.

The rowing men shouted and cursed as Annar and Henrik rushed to the stern of the boat, where a tiny door was rocking on its hinges. Unusually for longboats, this had a small caged section, barred with wood.

Vikings did not normally take prisoners.

The two men exchanged nervous glances.

'You do it,' said Annar. 'It's your turn.'

Henrik looked agitated. 'Maybe we should…'

'What? Open the door? Have that monster marauding up and down the decks? Have you gone mad?'

Henrik shrugged. 'But she's been shut up there for days.'

'Because she tried to claw out our eyes, remember?'

The screaming and banging continued. 'Let me out! Let me out!'

'The last time we let her out, she bit the captain.'

'That's true, but…'

'And the time before that?'

'The ship's cat,' said Henrik, sadly.

'Don't let her out!'

'But she might really need help this time.'

'LOOK OUT!' The screams grew louder. 'LET ME OUT! NOW!!!'

'You might lose an eye, of course,' said Annar, darkly. 'But it's up to you.'

Henrik kept quiet. He could never admit it publicly, of course. But sometimes when he thought of her… well. He might well have behaved the same way himself, under the circumstances. The banging grew louder, her voice more insistent.

'You HAVE to listen to me. You HAVE to see this.'

But even as she spoke, her words were drowned out by a shouting from the men below decks at the oars.

Oaths and shouting rent the air; many of the men jumping up from their benches and pointing, open mouthed, to the back of the ship.

Henrik followed their pointing fingers, and the desperate howling of the woman locked in the aft. His mouth dropped open, in shock then, instants later, in an awful, dawning terror.

Inside the tiny locked cupboard – little more than a cage on board the great longship – the princess Freydis shrank against the door, still giving it vicious kicks with her foot as she listened to the murmurs and exclamations outside. Well, she was sure they'd listen to the other *men*. The lowliest poxy serf rower – his opinion was still worth more than hers, and she was a princess. And being a princess meant nothing at sea.

She had kept track of time by carving a line out with the nail of her little finger on the left wall of the tiny space that the men had shut her into as soon as it had become clear that she had no intention of going quietly.

The only light came from a tiny gap in the caulking between the planks and she had used that to try and tell when was day and when was night. The three servings of oats a day had added to a sense of time, and she had tried to stretch and move around when she was able; the sailors would no longer let her out, in case she tried to attack them again. Which she would, she swore to herself. Her father may have sold her to the Icelandic King – she'd expected to be married off, that was the way of it. But she hadn't expected to be sold to someone so old, so ugly, the news of whose boils and enormous spilling belly and foul breath had travelled all the way across the great world sea to Trondheim. She had hoped for a young prince from the sweeter Suedan lands, or even a choice in the matter. But the greater peace of their trading kingdoms, as her father had explained in the great hall, in front of the roaring furnace and all the tribes, was more important than her happiness. Surely, as a daughter of Wolvern, she understood that?

She nodded. But vowed to herself – as a daughter of Wolvern, who had united the warring tribes, brought peace to their region, established trading with their neighbours – that she would fight and fight and never give up.

But this. This was something different. She cringed as far back from her tiny look-out as she could, pressing herself as closely as possible against the door.

'LET ME OUT BY ALL THE GODS!!!!' she screamed, her voice deafened by the roaring of the sea, and the helpless shouts of the men above.

Henrik stared. It could not – should not – be possible. But there it was.

A fire was burning above the water. A great line of heat. Through the air, where there was nothing to burn. Witchcraft, whispered someone.

Annar's curiosity got the better of him. Hypnotised by the extraordinary sight, he leant further and further over the side, his brain trying to understand what it was actually seeing.

All of a sudden the boat lurched to one side and he lost his footing, slipped and fell into the icy water. The men dashed to help him but, before they could reach out a hand, the flame suddenly rushed at him like a living thing; like a snake darting forwards.

Flames shot through his body, contorting him. Even his eyes seemed to spark and glow orange. His face took on a hideous rictus grin as the skin burned off his very bones, his last cry dying in his charred throat. A terrible, terrible smell filled the air. The men were too shocked even to scream.

And now, every single oar was on fire.

Chapter
Three

Corc, the village chieftain, scratched his beard. He still didn't know what to make of it. None of them did. For the fourth straight day in a row, he'd had the men gather them all in before they started at the runrigs. Now he was trying to persuade his son, Eoric, to get as much of the unexpected bounty – turtles, seals; some sea birds – salted and put away for the oncoming winter.

Eoric, as usual, was complaining about it. He wanted to go and shoot rabbits with his friends and try out his new bow that had arrived on the last trading ship from the mainland. It was willow, pliable and light to carry, and befitted, he thought, the chieftain's son. Corc had simply grunted at that and said he didn't care if his bow was made of peat as long as it filled their pot.

It wasn't fair, Eoric had thought. Life on Lowith was hard enough, and as the chief's son – and possibly chief himself one day, as Corc never stopped reminding him – he was expected to pull his weight more than the others. He never got to go and have any fun, thought Eoric darkly. Plus, if all the turtles had suddenly decided to start washing themselves up dead on the shore, well then, that was great. Surely it meant *less* work?

The bounty had started half a moon ago, washing up the animals, shoals of them, onto the shore. No fish, just the animals who breathed above water. Dead and, oddly, seemingly half-cooked. Some of the women thought it a gift from the Gods, but Corc wasn't so sure about this, or at least was nervous. When the Gods gave a gift, there was usually a debt to pay. Still, there was more in the sea than he would ever understand, so he was simply grateful nonetheless. But whatever was causing it, the unexpected gifts should be salted and stored for hard times, or traded with the mainland for their wood and tools, he knew that much.

'Now, Eoric!' Corc shouted, but his son had already stormed off.

'Later!' he shouted back, rudely.

Corc sighed. How could he be chief of the village when he couldn't even control his own son? And now the food would go to ruin.

Almost as an afterthought he glanced around for his younger boy, Luag, but he was not in their low, dark homestead; no doubt wandering around in a dream cloud as usual, singing, or drawing or doing something else completely useless. Corc sighed and stared again at the large pile of dead turtles. Hela, the boy's mother, had been a hardworking, quiet woman, and he did miss her, though it would not have done to admit it. He wondered if she would have known how to keep the boys in line.

He missed the first yell, or assumed it was just the young village boys, exuberant for their hunt. Then he heard it again. Then he saw what they were yelling it. He dropped his gutting knife, and ran.

The Doctor smiled to himself as he caught the first hint of smoke over the brow of the low dune in front of him. Smoke meant fire, and fire meant tea, in his experience. Although it might be a bit... primitive. These were early days, after all. He hoped it wasn't musk tea again. Bark tea he could just about handle, as long as you didn't let it steep. But musk was very difficult. Still, a nice fire would be lovely just around now...

He marched over the springy turf. The settlement was small, and basic. Straw roofs were visible, over trench houses dug deep into the earth to keep out of the wind. Openings between the roofs and the deep houses would let some light in, but also the wind, the rain and anything else that came past. Steps were cut into the earth, and some hardy, scrawny goats and sheep were tethered to each end. Chickens squawked and padded through the rough earth pathways from house to house. There was a large communal fire in the middle of the settlement, with a cauldron swinging gently over it, which the Doctor took to be the focal point of the village. The villagers, however, were nowhere to be found. That was peculiar. Fires burning, animals tethered, poultry still roaming… yet not a single human being to be seen.

The Doctor wiped down his dark wet hair and sighed.

'I really, really wanted that cup of tea,' he muttered to himself, removing his sonic screwdriver from his pocket, and trudging on into the tiny settlement.

On board the longship, the cries from the men above were getting louder. But Freydis, her eye pressed against the hole in the caulking, suddenly stopped screaming. 'By the Gods,' she had shouted. Looking at the water, she thought she understood.

A tall plume was emerging from the water – a plume of fire, shooting straight up in the air, metres and metres high, with flames spitting off the side. It was impossible, unbelievable; the fire burned yellow and red – if Freydis had known of such things, she might have thought it looked like a fountain, or a hose shooting straight up through the waves.

It was impossible, and terrifying, and the rowers couldn't seem to move away from it; already ash and cinders were falling on the decks. Freydis could hear the screams of men, hurt. She hardened her heart against them. Not one of them had come to her aid when she had been dragged from her family and friends in Trondheim and put on this prison ship. She had no sympathy now.

And of course, she understood. It was all for her. In

the stories, everyone knew. In the stories of the Gods, Siegfried had protected his lover Brynhild by putting a ring of fire around her. What else could it be, this impossible thing in the ocean, but the Gods coming to save her, a princess? This was exactly the kind of thing they did in stories she had heard since she was a child.

She watched, as the first scent of smoke from the burning mast filled the air and raised her chin. She would not be afraid. She would not scream. She would be safe. The Gods had come to save her.

Hastening past the deserted settlement and down towards the water, something caught the Doctor's eye. It was a piece of flint, hastily thrown to the side of the path. He knelt down and examined it closely. On it was drawn, in a shaky, child's hand, a beautifully articulated outline of a long, low boat. The Doctor checked the flint; it was still powdery. He could imagine instantly what had happened.

A young boy, maybe, lingering by the shore, maybe avoiding chores. There would be a lot of chores in a place like this. Sees something unusual on the horizon, draws it – and shows it to an adult, who would know instantly, terribly, what it meant.

To wake up one morning as usual, then to suddenly find out, without barely a moment to prepare, that Viking raiders were descending, to burn and take everything; to do nothing but plunder and destroy. The Doctor could only imagine the fear and panic it must cause. How could you keep your wife, your children, your few possessions safe from those who would take everything, and slit your throat for a goblet of ale? Who had made the most extraordinary journey across perilous seas with, in fact, no other goal in mind? The Doctor shook his head. Humans. Their abilities to do astonishing feats for ridiculous reasons never ceased to amaze him. They did make other races seem so… simple.

The Doctor placed the flint carefully back on a rock – the drawing was rather lovely in its innocence – then hared down as fast as he could to the shore to see what awaited them.

Corc, and his son, Eoric, stood at the front of the line on the shore. Corc glanced at Eoric. The lad stood taller than his father now, his brown shaggy hair reaching down past his ears, and his whiskers coming in. His son growing up fast made him feel older. He also looked fearless, with his iron blade strapped tight to his side and a fierce expression on his young features. He was ready to fight, had always been desperate to be a man. Not like little blond motherless Luag, who could be found hanging around the village women's skirts as often as not. A dreamer. Liked drawing and walking around with a head full of sodden clouds in Corc's opinion. It wasn't what they needed on the island, anyway. Not with winter setting in. And this.

He cast his eyes to the right. All the islanders had their eyes fixed on the horizon, as the longboat had moved in past the headland, ominously silent except for a faraway plash of oars on the water. Corc swallowed hard and tightened his grip on his spear. If it was a fight they were wanting, they'd get one. Although he felt too old for the fray these days. Thirty-six; an old man. Still, the young men looked fierce enough.

But they didn't remember the other times. Corc as a small boy had watched in horror from behind the pig stalls as they had carried off, screaming, his mother and his sister, their hut alight, the air full of the smells of burning: burning huts, burning hair, blood and muck and slaughtered animals. He had stayed there, frozen with horror cowering behind the squealing animals, all night and into the next day, when hunger had finally driven him out, into a village he hardly recognised, the people who remained feeling almost ashamed. They had shared what food they could with him, but they could not bring his family back. And he did not want to creep in under someone else's hearth, like a stray seal searching for a new litter. That had toughened Corc up for ever. And they would not pass a second time.

But Eoric was shouting now, pointing; and as the boat rounded the headland they saw something astonishing and unbelievable. There was a fire; a fire on the water. It was impossible, incredible, eye-rubbingly absurd, but there it was – a huge burst of flame, emerging from beneath the waves, and spreading now, beginning to encircle the wooden boat, which no longer looked fierce, with its square striped sail and prow in the shape of a wild dragon of the furthest north, but instead small; human; puny against the fire, which was blowing up harsher and harsher into a great wall of terrifying flame. Corc swore by the Beltane Gods; this was what he had wished, fervently, on his enemies these last thirty years. But now it was happening, and even here on the shore he could hear their impassioned shouts even over the roar of the waves and the crackle of the flames, he found something in himself he hadn't even known was there: pity.

On board, the panic was turning the men into animals. They were pushing and shoving over one another to get as far away from the fire as they could, but it was impossible. One man shinned the mast; another ran so far towards the port side of the boat that he tripped and fell overboard. Instantly the wall of flame shot out another ray, and he too was incinerated with an unearthly scream. One boy was huddling underneath the rowing benches, rocking back and forth with his eyes shut, muttering under his breath. The only word comprehensible was 'mother'. Another, the old bosun, had grabbed one of the barrels of mead from the galley area and was gulping down as much of it as he could.

Henrik looked around him in consternation. The flames were licking the stern of the ship now. He grabbed a bucket and started throwing water on the fire, as the captain had already started doing but, to his horror, the water had almost no effect on the flames at all; just like Annar, the flames continued to burn, even when wet. Henrik shook his head. Another man, his eyes wild and glistening with the madness of panic, rushed to the side of the boat and executed a graceful dive into the sea. The flame hit him before he even hit the water; outlining in flickering orange and red his graceful shape, before the skin turned black and crackled and with a final, deafening howl, he was extinguished.

Fully half the boat was crackling now, the flames growing closer and closer. Henrik blinked as the black smoke stung his eyes. He clasped his sword. If only there was something to fight. If he could die a warrior, he could stride through the gates of Valhalla, of heaven, proudly and immediately. But how could you fight this – magic, an impossible thing, a snake – monster made of fire, sent from the Gods themselves? Nonetheless, he drew his sword. Just in case. Then, amongst the commotion and the noise he realised something. Freydis. The woman. She had stopped screaming. Was she dead? Or was she condemned to die this horrible, horrible death locked up, all alone, in a cage?

'Hello hello!'

The Doctor strode cheerfully down to the beach. Even though the weather showed no signs of improving, and he hadn't seen a chess set anywhere yet, the prospect of brokering some kind of reasonable peace deal between some hardworking peaceable island folk and a bunch of marauding Vikings was perking him up no end. Mind you, this was Scotland. A ruckus might be part of the fun. Well. He'd talk them out of it.

When no one from the line of islanders on the beach even so much as turned to look at him, however, he squinted and looked harder.

'Is that ship *on fire*?' he said. 'And no one's going to help them? I mean, I know it's cold, but...'

He instantly started taking off his shoes.

Corc turned round. 'Odin's tongue, who are you?'

'Why don't we do that introductory stuff *after* we've saved all the burning humans?' said the Doctor cheerily, pulling off his shoes, socks and jacket and then charging towards the water. 'Ah!' he said, putting a toe in and almost turning around. 'Next regeneration, I need body fat again,' he muttered to himself.

'Hoi,' said Corc, pointing. The Doctor followed it and saw another sailor, his body illuminated by the shooting finger of flame. The Doctor blinked several times.

'You don't happen' he asked 'to have a Halotron 1 fire extinguisher kicking about, I suppose?'

Corc and Eoric stared at him.

'Nope, never mind, forget I asked.'

And the Doctor plunged into the wild and freezing sea.

The boat was lurching now, as more of the thick timber caught, smoking at first then catching faster and faster. There were minutes left, Henrik knew, if as much as that. He lurched drunkenly back down the shifting deck and, slowly, the smoke and the spray almost rendering him blind, pushed back the heavy wooden bar of the cage.

Henrik didn't know what he was expecting to see in there – possibly nothing, if Freydis too had been incinerated – but not the calm, composed princess, kneeling obediently on the deck. Her face – it was the first time he had seen her when she wasn't screaming or spitting at anyone who crossed her path – was oddly beautiful in the crackling light, and she looked up at him with a dreamy look, as if she had no idea where she was.

'I am saved,' she said, her hand over her mouth.

Henrik winced, almost choking on the thick black smoke. 'Well, I wouldn't be too sure about that,' he said. 'I just…'

Freydis smiled. 'Oh. Not by you,' she said. 'By Odin of course. By the Gods.'

'Oh. Well. Good,' said Henrik, suddenly feeling ridiculous. 'Only I just wanted to…'

But he didn't get to the end of his sentence. Suddenly the mast cracked from the flames and came pounding down on the deck, making a sickening noise as it landed on several sailors. Even Freydis looked momentarily startled.

'Come with me,' said Henrik, barely knowing what he meant. He shot out his hand. And, barely realising what she was doing, Freydis took it, and ducked through the low entrance.

This was no ordinary fire, the Doctor realised, swimming briskly. The flame, if you looked closely, glowed green as well as orange and yellow. No wonder it worked so well on the water. But how... He watched closely, treading water, pained as another man went over the side, then WHOOSH, lit up like a flamethrower. It was an ungodly sight.

He didn't – couldn't – make a move to help in time, so instead, murmuring briefly, 'I'm sorry', he focused fiercely and completely on the process. At one point he ducked his head completely under, to see what was happening underneath the waves. There was nothing at all, except what seemed to be a tiny glimmer of green, far below, which could be a trick of the light. The fire did not seem to exist under the surface, just above it. But where was it coming from? It seemed to erupt from the surface of the ocean itself, but could not survive immersion. Well, that was information he could use.

Before the flames turned on him, he eyed a section of the deck he could still board, then plunged under again, his feet kicking against the waves.

Henrik and Freydis drew closer together as the flames licked higher, the boat now filling with water as its sides burned away. Freydis was shaking like a leaf.

'It will be all right,' she whispered, glancing repeatedly at the sky, as if expecting at any moment the grey clouds to part and the great bridge to Valhalla to open up ahead of her and usher her to heaven.

Henrik swallowed, his mind a jumble of conflicting thoughts at these, his last moments. 'I'm… I'm glad…' he said, stumbling, then felt like an idiot for saying this, then wondered why he was worrying about sounding like an idiot when he was facing certain death. Instead of any more talking, they squeezed hands together more tightly, and closed their eyes as the flames burned higher and higher around them.

'Hallo!' came a loud voice moments later.

Henrik opened one eye. This wasn't exactly what he expected from the famous Valkyrie who should be waiting for him, drinking horn in hand, at the gates of Valhalla. Plus, he could still feel the flames beating against him.

No. This tall, pale, clean-shaven creature crouching in front of him, shivering and gesticulating madly, didn't look like he was welcoming them to anything.

'Now, I don't want to hurry you,' the man continued.

Freydis blinked opened her wide pale eyes. Then she blinked again, as if she had expected to find herself somewhere else, but said nothing.

'No, let me start that again,' said the man. 'I really, really do want to hurry you. So, if we want to get out of here, and I would recommend us definitely, *definitely* doing that, we need to move pretty sharpish.' He moved to the front of the burning ship. 'OK. About here. Here's what we're going to do.' He called over to the remaining, terrified men, most of whom were cowering. 'Right everyone. We have to capsize the ship!'

'Are you crazy? We'll drown as fast as we'll burn,' shouted one man.

'No, no. It's the only way. The flames can't burn you underneath the water. Can't you see? They only catch light above the waves. They need the air to burn. Once they're burning, any part of you that's in air will burn, and jolly well keep on burning. But if we're all under... with some air...'

Henrik blinked. 'For how long though?'

'My good man, could we have one deadly issue to deal with at a time? Thank you,' said the Doctor. 'Now. Everyone. Jump as hard as you can on the starboard side. And for heaven's sake, duck. You want to be *inside* when we go over. I'm not sure I can stress this highly enough. Now. One. Two. Three...'

Stunned into obedience by the chaos all around them, the sailors leapt as one and rocked hard on the unstable surface, which nearly tipped them in, but not quite far enough.

'OK,' said the Doctor, gesticulating to the captain to roll over the barrel of mead to their side of the boat. 'One more time.'

And, as the flames licked ever higher, the tiny group on the diminishing boat in the middle of the wide, cold ocean jumped and pushed as hard as they could, until they felt the boat turn turtle, almost agonisingly slowly, the remains of the mast rolling down first, as they clung to stools and planks. The sky above them, already dark with smoke, became completely dark as the boat creaked over, dunking all of them in the water as they held on as tightly as they could.

'GET UNDER! GET UNDER!' shouted the Doctor. One poor lad was too late and didn't make it with them on time. His screams, as the boat crashed down on them, leaving him outside and exposed to the terrible flames, were piteous to hear, but Freydis and Henrik were already underwater, Freydis plunging down down down into the depths, swirling round and round with the caskets, hammocks, oars, planks, bread, chicken cages, boots and axes as they sank through the freezing dark.

Henrik felt his eyes and ears fill up with the icy water as they plunged in, and fought his instinctive urge to panic; instead, he looked for the way the bubbles were going, as his father had taught him, and felt for the boat above his head. He caught a rowing bench, bolted to the keel, and hauled himself up into the air pocket, taking a huge gulp of air. Instantly, though, looking round, he realised that the long golden braids of Freydis were missing. She was not there.

The Doctor always had to resist the temptation to stay under. It was so beautiful, so new down there, so much to see: it was always hard not to stay too long. But he had a large lung capacity advantage over the others, and he had to use it. He dived as far down as he could – he wanted desperately to find out the source of the fire, but first he had to count the heads.

The blonde hair, never cut, swirled round and round in the wake of the fast-moving water. The Doctor grabbed hold of it, coiled it up around his arm like a mythical beast. Freydis looked astonishingly peaceful, sinking in the water, her arms flowing free, but her legs together, wrapped up in her long gown like a mermaid's tail; her eyes closed, even the faint trace of a smile around her mouth.

'Oh no you don't,' said the Doctor, drawing her to him, wrapping her body gracelessly around his, and shooting them both up as fast as he could from six metres down, aiming for the dark under-body of the longship. 'Not on my watch, please.'

Chapter
Four

In the dark, lapping enclosure, with the hull of the boat overhead, the six surviving men – from an original crew of forty – were staring at one another, wide eyed and panting. Nobody spoke. They could hear the creaking of the wood; the splashing of the waves against the upturned hull… but as the boat had submerged itself in the water, the parts still burning had sheared away and sunk, and the crackling, terrible noise of the fire had gone – at least for now. They panted hard, barely able to believe they were still alive; still too panicky to think beyond, to think of their fellows who had not made it. Except for Henrik. He took a deep breath.

'I'm going down,' he said. 'I have to find her.'

The other men looked at him dimly, without really seeing him. Henrik gulped. He could swim, of course, but he'd learned in the cold, placid fjords, not a wild, endless raging sea when he was already cold and shivering and very, very frightened. He steeled himself… but just as he did so, there was a splashing break in the water and the Doctor popped up, Freydis pale and clasped around his neck.

'Ha ha!' the Doctor exclaimed. 'Here we are! Have you chaps invented the kiss of life yet?' He glanced at the uncomprehending faces. 'Thought not. OK. Watch, and pass it on to your descendants, etcetera. Can you hold her steady, please?'

Henrik found himself trying to tread water and hold up the princess as the strange man did what appeared to be blowing into her mouth. He decided not to argue as, with a stutter and a quick throwing up of what seemed like pints of seawater, Freydis's clear eyes twitched and blinked open in shock.

'There we are,' said the Doctor. 'Great. I hate doing that. Salty.' He instantly turned away. Freydis continued to blink in confusion.

'It's all right' said Henrik, patting her on the hand. Although in the freezing cold and wet darkness, with something outside that could shoot flame, it didn't seem all right at all.

'Now,' said the Doctor. 'First things first. I'm the Doctor, by the way.'

One of the other men, who'd been watching the scene, now put up his hand by way of a greeting. 'Dorcnor.'

'Ragnor,' said a second.

'Terrific!' said the Doctor. 'I love not having to explain my name. Now. Listen. Has anyone noticed that it's a bit cold in here?'

The skin on the men had gone translucently pale. Most of them were trembling, with chattering teeth. Freydis, ominously, was not.

'I see you have. Great. You're way ahead of me. Right, well. Not to spoil your day, but if we don't get out of this water in the next seven minutes, you're probably going to go hypothermic and die. But if we do try and get out of the water, whatever that fire thing is, it's going to go for us. It's clearly sensing motion on the top of the waves, I'm afraid. So. There's only one obvious solution.'

Everyone looked at him blankly.

'We're going to have to make like fish.'

'Under the water?' asked Henrik, stupidly.

'No, flying fish,' snapped the Doctor. 'Yes. Under the water. All the way to shore. Follow the waves. If you absolutely have to breathe, turn on your back and try and stick nothing up further than your nose. At your own risk.'

The men looked at one another.

'It's a long way.'

'It's a long night, death,' mused the Doctor. 'I'll take the girl.'

Surprisingly, Freydis suddenly seemed to wake up a little more.

'You will not lay your hands on me,' she said, her voice weak but absolutely undeniable. 'You will keep your hands off my person.'

'Yes, I'm sorry about that… kissing thing just there. Unavoidable.'

'You should not have saved me,' said Freydis, furiously. 'This is the will of the Gods. They are protecting me. Calling me to them.'

'By killing all those other chaps?' asked the Doctor mildly. 'Nice fellows your Gods, are they?'

'This is meant to be,' persisted Freydis.

'Don't talk to me of things that are meant to be' said the Doctor, more sternly than he had intended. 'Now. Everyone. You have to take as deep breaths as you can. And quickly, before that *thing* realises there are still people in here. Are you ready?'

'Vikings are always ready,' said Ragnor.

'Well, that is excellent. Come on then. Follow me.'

Looking back, Henrik would remember that long passage under water as if it were a dream; the tightness in his chest; following the Doctor's long slim form with the waves ahead of him; feeling his blood pounding his body as he forced his legs to kick, every sinew of him straining to breathe, to lift his head above the waves, to breathe in – water, air, it scarcely mattered – the Doctor occasionally letting them turn over and risk a tiny mouthful of air under the up-turned boat, which ended up a mouthful of saltwater as often as not – and being dimly aware at last, at last, that the water was getting shallower; the waves crashing on the shore; and finally the sea spitting him out up on the cold white beach; he, and his fellows, and a bursting, panting Freydis, washed up with the tide and the detritus from the boat; casks and corks and chess pieces, scattered all around.

The Doctor was the first to stagger to his feet onto the shore; the swim had affected him less than the others. He jumped around to stare out to sea, but there was nothing left; no trace of the proud Viking boat that had been there – the burnt hull was in their arms; her mast, proud sail and goods long gone, along with the men who had sailed her, and the extraordinary plumes of fire that had devoured her.

'Well,' he said, clasping his hands together. 'I do think this calls for a cup of tea.'

He turned round again, and found himself face to face with Corc, chief of the isle of Lowith, standing at the head of a line of village men, swords drawn, faces of stone.

'Here they are!' he said jovially. 'All saved and grateful.'

The Viking survivors were coughing and gasping their way up the beach, the cold taking root in their very bones. They were human flotsam amidst the wreckage washed to shore: odd spears, pieces of charred wood, chess pieces.

Corc shook his head. 'Why?' he said simply. 'Why did you bring them here?'

The Doctor glanced from one group to another, confused. Then he remembered.

'Oh *yes*,' he said. 'Viking raiders, pillage and burning all that stuff. Oh, I wouldn't worry about that. I think they'll be so grateful for a hot cup of tea and perhaps a blanket of some kind...' he added hopefully, pulling his shirt back on, 'that you'll all be best of friends in no time.'

'They came before,' said Corc, not moving. 'I swore they would not come again. Not while I stand.'

'Well, *yes*,' said the Doctor, a hand moving to adjust his bow tie. 'Is this on straight, by the way?'

'Is what on straight?' grunted Corc.

'Um, never mind.'

'Who are you? Are you one of them? The advance party?'

'No,' said the Doctor. 'No, no, no, no. I'm...'

He took out the psychic paper. He looked at it for a long time, but it remained frustratingly blank.

'Runic society. Gah!' he said to himself. The paper apologetically produced a picture of a rabbit. 'Rabbit inspector? I don't think so.' He looked back at the hard man and round at the hard landscape, and reluctantly put the paper away. 'I'm a friend,' he said. 'I just turned up at the same time, that's all. A traveller. I'm a friend who wants to help.'

He turned out to the grey sea. 'Did you see that thing?'

Corc met the Doctor's steady gaze. 'I did.'

'Have you ever seen anything like it before?'

'Fire that moves upon the water?'

It was his pause that gave him away.

'You have.'

Corc blinked. 'I haven't seen it,' he said.

'But?'

'But… well… at first…' he said. 'At first it was the turtles.'

'What about the turtles?'

'More than we had ever seen before. Washed up, dead upon the shore. Ready for eating too. Like a gift from the Gods.' He snorted.

'Interesting,' said the Doctor. 'Creatures that float above the waves. No fish, though?'

Corc shook his head. 'Turtles and seals mostly. Do you think it was a gift from the Gods?'

'So what did you do?' said the Doctor, ignoring the question.

Corc began to feel rather stupid. 'Well, we took it, of course. And left the water God well alone.'

'You just took it and crossed your fingers?' said the Doctor.

Corc didn't understand this, and looked at the Doctor impassively. His hair was dark. Perhaps he came from one of the fabled countries overseas where everything grew and everything could be eaten and life was soft and easy. He had heard of these places. Someone from there could not begin to understand what life was here.

'Do you think…?' asked the Doctor softly, 'Do you think now your water god, or whatever it actually is, has found that he can feed on human flesh, that he will leave your sons alone? Do you think that he is only here to deliver fish now?'

Corc stared at the group of desperate figures on the shore. The Doctor implored him.

'Look. Something is wrong. You know it is. You can feel it. You can see it. The reckoning is here for your free food. And I can help. I can help you figure out what it is, and how to stop it. Altogether. You can do it… but you can't… you really can't, I'm afraid, leave a load of human beings on a beach to die.'

Corc eyed the coughing, shaking men and the figure of the girl lying on the shoreline. The Doctor gave him a long look. There was an even longer pause. Then Corc raised his spear and turned to face his people.

Chapter
Five

'We will save them,' Corc announced loudly to the long row of men and women standing on the shore. There was an audible intake of breath.

'*No!*' came a young voice. It was the sullen Eoric, his son. 'No! We shall not show mercy! They would not do the same for us! They would leave us all for the birds, dead in our beds without thinking about it for a second. They are the animals; the animals of the furthest north.'

'And we are *not* animals' said Corc, turning to face his son. 'The osprey cannot have mercy, but we can.'

'Father, you will build up their strength then they will turn, pounce and kill us all,' said Eoric. Several of the other men of the village were clearly agreeing with him. The Doctor stood poised, unable the leave the negotiations. He caught, though, out of the corner of his eye, a trace of movement, and he smiled.

Corc looked around. He was a hard man – he had to be – but this stranger was right. They needed to find out if there was a threat to them – a threat more serious than the Vikings.

But more than this, he could not be publicly challenged by his son. One day, yes. But not yet.

'*Do it!*' he roared.

Eoric felt his stomach lurch, but he stood firm. He wasn't a child any more, and his father had to realise that. Suddenly, however, one of the women gasped and pointed. Down by the water's edge, a small boy was already darting in and out of the sailors, comforting them and trying to cover them up with his own clothes.

'*Luag!*' roared Corc in disbelief at his younger son. But once Luag had begun the work, the women of the village followed him too, taking off their woven head coverings and long brown and dun-coloured cloaks. The Doctor's lips twitched. Corc gave him a shrewd look. Eoric spat once on the ground and made an unusual pointed gesture with his second and fourth fingers off the tip of his cheekbone that the Doctor had never seen before on Earth, but was nonetheless recognised as profoundly offensive in more than 4,000 cultures in the universe. Eoric then stormed off in a sulk. Several of his buddies followed along behind him.

Well, thought the Doctor, there wasn't time for that now. He grabbed his jacket and wrapped it round Freydis, as the islanders welcomed their sworn enemies, helping them back up to the settlement and added huge mounds of gorse and peat to the fire, which crackled up comfortably high.

The Vikings shot glances at each other – six men, one woman – as gradually they began to rub sensation back into painfully chilled fingers and toes. One of the women brought round a bark tea that they gulped gratefully, and a hot mutton broth with spelt bread that tasted to Henrik better than the sweetest honeyed mead. The captain, Ragnor, could converse a little in their language, which sounded a bit like home and a bit like something else to Henrik, but he mastered the pleases and thank yous easily enough.

Henrik noticed that the tall, oddly dressed stranger – who had taken an enormous gulp of the bark tea, then (obviously believing himself unobserved) spat it out behind a patch of gorse, sighing heavily – sounded completely at home in either language. He wondered who the man was.

What were they going to do now, Henrik thought, once he could feel his fingers again. It could be months before another boat was sent out; King Gissar wasn't expecting them for weeks. Trondheim wouldn't send a boat, it would just assume they'd all died at sea. Which most of them had done. It struck him suddenly that they might never see their homeland again.

The Princess, Freydis, wearing the stranger's jacket, had warmed herself up and drunk a tiny bit of tea but refused the meal and had now taken herself off to sit on a nearby rock, and stare moodily into the middle distance. He had thought that perhaps being rescued from certain death might make her slightly less disagreeable, but clearly that was not the case.

Freydis herself was trying to puzzle it out. She had not seen the great stone bridge to Valhalla open in the sky. And yet... and yet, here she was. Alive, and no longer on the way to marry Gissar. She felt tricked out of what she had felt was her certain fate – and yet her fate had changed nonetheless. She glanced curiously at the tall strangely dressed figure conversing at high speed. Could it be?

Attention had turned to the curious stranger.

'Why do you speak our tongue? Are you a Norseman? You have no beard. Are you a child?'

'I think he's a fish,' grunted Ragnor. 'Did you see the way he swam out there?'

'Well, I...'

'He's our saviour,' said Dorcnor, raising the cup to him. 'Thanks, friend.'

'Well, I...'

'Well, how do you know he didn't start that fire?' said another. 'It had to come from somewhere...'

'Well, I...'

Freydis turned round imperiously from where she was perched on her rock. 'I know who you are,' she said.

Everyone, including the Doctor, looked at her expectantly.

'You have many faces,' she said quietly.

The Doctor raised his eyebrows. 'Yes,' he said almost to himself. 'Most, it has to be said, a bit more straightforward than this one.'

Freydis glanced at Corc, who was deep in conversation with a small tight group of suspicious-looking menfolk.

'You talk to him, you talk to us, you talk to the fishes as far as I can tell,' she said. 'But you take no one's side. I know who you are.'

Everyone stared at her.

'You are Loki. You're a God.'

The Doctor looked slightly embarrassed. 'Now, don't talk nonsense,' he said. 'You've had a dowsing.'

'You are the trickster. The shape shifter,' said Freydis. 'The joker.'

'I… uh, well…'

'What Siegfried has done to protect me, you will seek to undo.'

The Doctor scratched his head. 'What Siegfried… Oh!' he said. 'Of course. The ring of fire to protect his maiden. And you're Brynhild requiring rescue, is that it?'

Freydis stared hard out to sea. 'I am nothing but traded goods,' she said.

The Doctor moved closer.

'Stay away, trickster,' said Freydis, turning to look at him.

'You're cargo?' he asked gently.

'I was bought and paid for in Trondheim.'

'But no one will know where you are now.'

Freydis ran her fingers through her heavy hair.

'They'll find us,' the Captain Ragnor said heavily.

The other Vikings were muttering round the fire. 'She's too precious a cargo to run without an escort.'

'But how?' said Henrik. He glanced at the men of the settlement, who were still staring at them with hostility. 'And when?'

'Hello,' said the Doctor, bending down to talk to the small boy who had been the first to help the visitors. 'What's your name?'

'Luag,' said the child. 'What are you wearing?' He was eyeing the glint of the Doctor's buttons in the firelight.

Solemnly the Doctor looked down at his shirt and pulled off the very bottom button. 'They're buttons,' he said. 'Would you like one?'

The boy, who seemed to be around six or seven, nodded eagerly. 'I won't show Eoric,' he said decisively. 'He's too rough faced today.'

'Is that your brother?' asked the Doctor.

Luag nodded. 'He's *amazing* at fighting,' he said confidingly. 'But a bit grumpy.'

The Doctor nodded. 'He's a teenager. That's not a concept that's due to become fashionable for about twelve hundred years, but it really just means grumpy. And reckless, without impulse control, occasionally aggressive...'

He shot a quick anxious look into the woods where Eoric had retired with his friends. 'But mostly delightful,' he added, hastily. 'And what about you? You were very good at helping those people.'

'That water gets bad cold,' said Luag. 'Even the *seals* get cold.'

'Oh I *love* seals,' said the Doctor. 'They're *brilliant*. With the clapping and the little balls and everything.'

Luag nodded. 'Yes, delicious,' he said.

'Oh, yes,' said the Doctor. 'Now, I think we should get the Viking captain and your dad to talk, do you think?'

'What about?' said Luag.

'What do you talk about with your friends?' said the Doctor. He looked at the two groups of men; one huddling, looking defeated and anxious, but still defiant; still Vikings. And the other, curious; angry with remembered humiliations of the past; a desperation not to lose face or be invaded by strangers. Of extending hospitality to those who had killed; burned; taken. He was not sure he could hold the two sides apart for long.

'Bladderball!' said Luag, his face lighting up.

'What?' said the Doctor. Then he realised what he meant. 'The game?'

'I can get the bladder!' said Luag. 'It makes you nice and warm too.'

'You know' said the Doctor. 'I think you might have cracked it, my friend.'

The Doctor watched from the sidelines. He was torn – there was a mystery here, something needed sorting out. But the most urgent thing right now was to make sure the locals and the Vikings played nicely together.

Literally. However much it irked him, the fire would have to wait.

At first the two sides looked at each other nervously. It had taken all of the Doctor's persuading and geeing-up to get them to even consider it. But as soon as the ball – a sheep's bladder welked with tar – was thrown in the air, neither side could help itself.

Henrik charged first. It had already been the strangest of days, but he too had felt the awkward atmosphere with the islanders – had heard, too, from older men back in Trondheim of victories won and women kidnapped from the many settlements dotted over the bony head of the Celtic isles over the years – and anything that might dispel the tension without spilling blood on either side seemed a good thing to do.

Ragnor too had jumped up, keen as mustard. Luag had acted as throw-in then played exuberantly for whichever side seemed to be winning, as did his little friends who spilled out of the low homesteads as soon as their mothers realised the strangers were not here for the usual reasons.

The Lowith men, at first grudging, were pretty soon very keen to show their strength, and the game – a fairly free-running mixture of football, rugby and punching – went overwhelmingly in their favour, till the Doctor joined in on the Viking side to even it up a bit. He didn't mean to show off – well, only in as far as showing off was entirely essential under the circumstances, he rationalised. Probably doing that finger-spinny thing the Harlem Globetrotters had taught him in 1978 was overegging the pudding, but the little ones had enjoyed it, and the adults had been mostly admiring.

Freydis ignored it all, staring out to sea. Her certainty that she was being saved by the Gods – where were they? Apart from this… her gaze passed over the Doctor with something like disdain. If he was here to take her to Valhalla, she wished he'd get a move on. And if he was going to take her as a bride, well, he was better than Gissar that was for sure, though not what she'd have chosen…

Anyway, the stranger showed absolutely no inclination in that direction either, judging by the exuberance with which he'd just hit a sheep's bladder towards a tor of rocks whilst whooping and throwing his hands in the air. She sighed, feeling very lonely, even as a young woman from the village came up and, smiling, and with a few words, indicated that she was welcome to stay with them.

The game was evening up, but night was falling fast; the pitch ball was getting harder and harder to see. 'Last run!' shouted someone, and Henrik, his limbs tired but strong after weeks of rowing, found it hurtling in his direction. He leapt up, gracefully, his blond hair rippling down his back, and found it, just in time, sending it thudding straight into the winning tor, where it bounced off and found itself on Freydis's lap. Amidst great cheers from the Vikings, he advanced forward to retrieve it, bowing low before her.

'My lady,' he said.

Freydis tried to pretend she had not been watching, had not caught sight of his tall, strong body leaping in the air. His face was pink from exertion and blushing, his hair rippling from his head in a long mane. He grinned at her, showing very white teeth, then remembered her status and dropped his head and his knees. It felt strange here, in the middle of nowhere, miles from everything they knew, after facing almost certain death, to be observing the courtesies of a faraway court. But they did. And both sides, suddenly, started to applaud.

Corc hailed his guests to the great hall. It was nothing on the large, brightly coloured wooden buildings, many of more than one storey, that populated their home town of Trondheim, but they were polite and grateful enough not to mention it. The long low building was thatched with gorse and made of peat, and had as few window openings as possible to keep out the harsh westerly wind. A large fire in the centre made the space smoky, lit as it was by seal-rendered candles; but there was the hearty smell of fish and a huge cauldron of rabbit stew which made the men as hungry as only those saved from certain death, taking a long swim then hurled into a ball game can be. They advanced with merry hearts.

Corc had to first find Eoric. He excused himself

by saying he was going to the privy then headed off to their low homestead. Eoric was mooching around talking to his friends, but one glance from Corc and they shuffled off, heads bent low.

'My son,' said Corc. 'It did not... I did not like the way you defied me today.'

Eoric looked sullen. 'Well, I didn't like the way you welcomed in those killers,' he spat.

'They are human beings,' said Corc. 'There was a lady aboard. It seemed the right thing to do.'

'So they can eat our food and drink our mead then when it's done burn us all to the ground for a jape? Like they usually do? Because you're too scared to fight?'

'I am scared of no man,' said Corc, thinking to himself that whilst that was true, he had been terribly afraid of the flames he had seen on the water. 'But I do believe in mercy. I hope you can understand one day.'

Eoric had taken the loss of his mother hard, which Corc had found difficult. He was hardly the first babe-in-arms to lose a parent. Luag was bad enough, baaing around the place, but Eoric was five, and should have borne it better. At least his mother had died in the normal way, childbirth, rather than being carted off kicking and screaming... Corc put the memory away. The men in his village now were not those men. They were their guests. Therefore they would not behave like those men.

He had to tell himself that.

Eoric's posturing and fighting poses had only ever

been an attempt to cover up his sadness. Corc loved the boy, in his rough way. He remembered his father too. How, when he was that age, he thought everything his father said was foolish. But he would never have dared to mention it; his father would have whipped him spare. Maybe that was the problem. He'd been too soft on him, and little Luag. But he knew what it was to grow up without a mother; when the other boys had someone to soothe their hurts and listen to their childish prattling, the three males together had just had work to be getting on with. It was what it was.

'Son,' he commanded. 'You will obey me. And you will show a good face to our visitors.'

'Never,' said Eoric. He looked at his father with a burning loathing in his eyes. 'Never.'

'Fine,' said Corc, in a voice that had gone dangerously quiet. 'You still need to light the braziers.'

The two braziers on the easterly side of the island were a sign to the other islands further inland, Harris and Skye, which in turn could pass on to the mainland a warning: do not come. Things are dangerous. One brazier lit meant send help; two, a simple admonishment – we have disease, or war: stay away.

Corc saw no reason to invite his neighbours; if there was a monster haunting the waves, it could be a slaughter. And he couldn't imagine the other island folk would be able to help; he had never heard tell of anything like this. The strange man called Doctor was the only one who seemed confident that everything would be all right.

'I will not,' said Eoric. 'I'm going to drink mead at Gren's.'

'You are *not*,' said Corc, suddenly incandescent with rage. 'You will take your work seriously for once and do as I say, or you will feel the flat of my sword, and don't think for a moment that you're too large or that I won't do it. I assure you I will.'

Eoric saw in his father's eyes that he had pushed it too far. He exhaled loudly. 'I'm not breaking bread with those murderers,' he grunted.

'Very well,' said Corc. 'You're barred anyway. I don't want you sitting there huffing and ruining it all. Just light the damned brazier then you can do what you like. I wash my hands of you.'

Eoric, furious and embarrassed all at once, stormed out of the homestead, stopping only to give his dad one final glare.

It was rather a jolly feast, once you were used to the choking smell of the seal-fat candles and the smoke everywhere and the fact that there was one communal spoon used by everyone to ladle stew and soup onto large pieces of bread that acted like plates, which meant that it was a little bit messy and there was quite a lot of slobbering and some rather exuberant belching. There was one great horn of mead that got passed around for sharing, too – everyone laughed at the Doctor for attempting to wipe the edge on his sleeve. The Vikings passed on some of the more recent bawdy stories from court, particularly involving King

Gissar and his bride-to-be. It was probably just as well that Freydis had gone off with one of the women.

The women of the village – very honourably, possibly out of gratitude for the marked unwillingness of the Vikings to haul them off for brides, even though, as saucy Aelfret had remarked, they weren't the ugliest men on the island by a long shot – had done their best to render a meal fit for visitors, and the fire roared in the meeting hut. As night fell, a cask of the best of the summer mead was brought in and passed around; two whole sheep were roasted on a spit over the flames, turned slowly, their grease caught beneath them on iron pans, and poured over the top of them again; flavoured with the sweet bracken of the islands.

Henrik, slightly buoyed up on mead, leapt to his feet and announced that Annar had died a hero, and that they must toast him, which everybody did, despite the fact that Annar had actually tripped over his own enormous feet. All the men were remembered one by one, and somebody started a song that everyone else knew. The rabbit stew was good and hot; the turtle more of an acquired taste, but there was plenty of it. Corc stopped brooding on his wayward son and actually found himself enjoying the novelty of getting to know new people, even if they were their sworn enemies.

They turned on the newcomer, too.

'We owe you our thanks,' said Ragnor. The Doctor tried to look bashful, failing as usual. 'Are you of these isles?'

Corc shook his head. 'You are a stranger to us. I thought you must come for an advance Viking party.'

Ragnor translated back and the Vikings laughed.

'He's not one of ours,' said Dorcnor. 'Look at his hair.'

'Well, he's not one of ours,' said one of the villagers. 'Look at his clothes.'

The Doctor felt rather disgruntled that he had gone from being feted to teased so quickly. 'I'm a voyager,' he said. 'I was passing, that's all.'

They looked at him dubiously.

'Where's your ship?' said Corc.

'It ran aground.'

'Not much of a ship, then.'

'Actually, she's fantastic,' said the Doctor snippily.

Corc raised his eyebrows.

'So where are you from?' said Ragnor. 'Are you... are you an Angle?'

At this, the hands of many of the men in the room went instinctively to their swords.

'Nooo,' said the Doctor. 'Nothing like that.'

There were sighs of relief. The Doctor grasped for the only thing that always worked if he was standing out – he'd say he was from America.

'I'm from Vinland,' he said.

They looked at him and nodded.

'That'll explain the longshanks,' said Corc. 'Everything's bigger over there.'

'Tell me about Vinland,' said Henrik, eagerly. 'I've always wanted to go there.'

'Oh it's wonderful,' said the Doctor. 'Huge, and empty and full of amazing wildlife and clear water and…'

Henrik's attention strayed. 'Oh, like the rest of the world, then.'

'Well, yes,' said the Doctor. 'I suppose so.'

Corc leaned over. 'So the… the sea monster,' he said.

'Oh, it's not a sea monster,' said the Doctor. 'I've met a few. I can tell you, they're nothing like as elegant as this.'

'Whatever it is…' continued Corc.

'Yes. Whatever it is. I thought I'd go over, take a look as soon as the sun's up.'

For a moment all the men, particularly the Vikings, thought over the events of that afternoon. Then as one they all raised their swords and shouted 'Aye!'

'Well, no point in us all going,' said the Doctor. 'If a mighty all-consuming fire is going to shoot up…'

'Aye!' shouted the men again. The mead had been round a few times.

'Perhaps just a volunteer?' said the Doctor, pointing at Henrik.

'Me?' said Henrik. 'I didn't even say aye the first time.'

'Fine fine fine,' said the Doctor. 'I'll do everything myself, as always.'

A young woman with long red hair popped in to the great hall. Weaving skilfully through the men and the other women serving them, she finally caught sight of what she was looking for: little Luag, who had dropped off behind Corc's great seat.

'Just leave him,' grunted Corc.

Brogan shrugged. 'Oh, it's no trouble,' she said, picking up the sleeping child with some difficulty.

The Doctor immediately leapt up to help, lifting the figure out with ease.

'Thank you,' said Brogan. 'I know Corc doesn't care, but I don't think it's a good environment for a boy. There'll be a fight later, as likely as not, and he's... he's only little.'

'You're not his mother?' said the Doctor.

'Oh no, no. She didn't get past the bearing of him,' said Brogan, without emotion. 'You know the way of it.'

The Doctor nodded sadly. 'I do,' he said.

'Here we are,' she said, outside one of the little homesteads along the way. She turned her clear gaze on the Doctor, tenderly holding the child in his arms. 'I've never seen Corc so worried. Or Braan... that's my man.'

The Doctor faintly recalled a handsome, bright red-haired, sturdy-looking man with a beard, and a bow and arrow rather than a sword.

'We all knew something wasn't quite right with the dead animals...' she said. 'Is it really bad? Is it vengeance from the Gods for our behaviour? Freydis says so. She's staying here.' Brogan's voice tailed off. 'I can understand her sometimes,' she said, sounding surprised at herself.

'Well, don't mention this to Freydis,' said the Doctor, 'because she seems to be extremely well informed about these things. But I would say it's unlikely. We'll have a look in the morning, all right?' He handed over the boy. 'Corc must be so grateful for your help.'

Brogan snorted. 'If he notices that boy, it's to kick him away.' She looked straight at the Doctor. 'He's a good chief,' she said. 'But he's a terrible father.'

Eoric walked confidently through the dark night. He knew every inch of the island like the back of his hand; had wandered across it, learning all its caves and secrets since he was a tiny child. The glowing fierce cold light of the moon was enough, now the clouds had cleared a little, and he was as deft-footed as the rabbits that sprang out of his way at his approach.

Inside, his stomach was churning. Part of him was furious, still; how dare Corc forbid him from the feasting, send him off to do some stupid chore whilst everyone else was having a brilliant time, and, hopefully, gearing up to show those Vikings who was boss. The other half of him was upset. He wanted so much to belong sometimes; to make his dad proud of him; proud and pleased of the man he was growing into. If his father noticed him at all, it was to tell him off for being slow or not doing enough work or not standing up straight or some other absolute nonsense that didn't even matter. Even surrounded by all his friends, he could still feel alone. It was all right for Luag – half the women in the village doted on his silly little sheep face. Luag tried to follow him about, too, but he usually just told him to get lost, he was annoying. And Eoric was jealous of all the attention little Luag got. He wasn't the only motherless child. And if it hadn't been for him, Eoric would still have a mother. Eoric kicked a stone on the ground, as he approached the empty braziers.

Chapter
Six

Brogan's little homestead was low-roofed, and sturdy rushes covered the earthen floor. In the middle was the hearth, with a hole through the straw roof to let out the smoke from the cooking pot. On one side of the fire was their living area; they had a bowl each, and a raised platform for sleeping under rough woven blankets. On the far side, their goat was already asleep, where one side of their home was open to the elements, but on the most sheltered side. It was still not terribly sheltered, but the cosiness of the fire and the warmth of the animals was enough to make it snug. Freydis looked around, trying not to wrinkle her nose. The woman from the beach, the one who had gone forward to help Luag, smiled hopefully.

Stepping inside again, Brogan was nervous. She had never met a foreigner before, especially not one so beautiful. Even though Freydis's clothes had been soaked through, Brogan had never seen anything like them, not even on trading ships. The heavy heft of the brocade; the tiny stitches of the corsetry. She longed to touch them. The radiant gold of Freydis's hair, and her imperious carriage... Brogan glanced around the cottage again. It was neat, wasn't it? And warm? She prided herself on having a nice homestead for when Braan came home at night. And for Luag too, that poor little motherless chick. She popped him up on one end of the low sleeping shelf and covered him with a rough sacking blanket. He didn't stir.

Freydis was wishing with all her might for a hot bath. In the depths of winter, she and her ladies-in-waiting would go for a snow scrub in the orchard, and roll themselves in the freezing snow to get clean then, tingling and giggling and red-faced, would rush into the steaming great baths set over the crackling fires and jump in through the steam, till it was too hot to bear and they would do it all again. This is what she felt like doing right now, but it wasn't possible, she supposed.

'Eat?' Brogan indicated the soup tureen held over the flames, and Freydis nodded gratefully. She was starving, she realised; the combination of a dip in the ocean and living off whatever the Vikings had cared to throw at her over the last few weeks, little of it palatable

Inside the rough pot was a deeply flavoured, heavily scented turtle stew, well salted, with root vegetables.

'Fish... fish die,' said Brogan.

Freydis nodded. She thought Brogan was telling her that the meal was fresh; not that it had come as

62

a bounty. If she had looked closer in the bowl, she would have noticed some tell-tale markings; a zigzag black mark across the flesh that showed that someone, or something had shot a line of fire through them. But Brogan ordered her to eat; gave her the communal spoon. Accustomed once upon a time to her own cutlery, Freydis nonetheless gave in to her appetite, wrapped in another rough-hewn blanket over her undergown, as her dress dried off by the fire. Brogan stroked it in passing, lovingly, and Freydis smiled up at her.

'You want?' she said, trying to indicate in the few words they shared. 'Want try it on?'

Brogan giggled and blushed and shook her head, and Freydis smiled – she had many fine robes, although now, she thought, they were all at the bottom of the ocean, or burnt up – and she detested wearing them. The buttons, the lacings, the intricate arrangements were tedious, impossible to do yourself, hard to move in and, as she had certainly found at sea, ludicrously uncomfortable for sleeping in.

Freydis finished her spoonful of soup, soaked a piece of flat bread and ran it round the rim of the pot, then stood up, urging the younger woman over. They were about the same size; Brogan's broader shoulders and brawny arms, from a lifetime of manual labour, were offset by her tiny waist and narrow hips; a reminder that however hard she worked, the balance of calories in and calories out was always precarious.

Freydis helped her clamber into the nearly dry

kirtle, followed by the stiff petticoat. Then she took hold of the laces at the back and pulled them tight. Brogan giggled and wriggled, and Freydis laughed too. Then she sat Brogan down and untied the stiff tight plaits in her hair – that were undone only very rarely, for feast days and special occasions – and plaited up her red hair in the softer, more looping style of her homeland, so that it framed her face.

'I wish I had my comb,' said Freydis, though she knew that Brogan couldn't understand. 'You look very pretty.'

Brogan understood enough of her tone of voice to blush.

'In my father's house…' said Freydis. She had wanted to talk about the glass – they had a mirror, an astonishing tribute one of the raiding parties had brought back one time all the way from Gaul. But as she said the words, she felt them die in her throat. She had thought she hated her father for sending her away to be married. But suddenly, the idea that she would never see her home town again, nor her friends, nor her family overcame her.

It was, suddenly, almost overwhelming. All the weeks on the boat she had fuelled herself with anger and rage; now, here, it was as if all that righteous fury had gone; to be replaced simply with wistfulness and homesickness. The God, she quickly told herself again. The God would save her, wouldn't he?

Brogan did not have to know the ways of princesses to understand. 'You miss home,' she said, carefully.

Freydis nodded, just as the low stable door to the home was pushed open.

Brogan jumped back and straightened up. Freydis smiled to see her look so proud and haughty all of a sudden, as the small but handsome, muscular young man marched in. His face was downcast, but it lit up when he saw Brogan.

'What *have* you done?' he asked, shaking his head in disbelief.

Freydis pulled the rough blanket round herself tighter and smiled, and then he noticed her.

'My lady.'

'She lent me her dress,' Brogan said to Braan excitedly. She couldn't stop stroking the fabric under her fingers, in a way that made Braan smile, but also worry a little; they were not travelling people, or traders. He hoped she did not get a taste for fine things. The strangers arriving troubled him gravely; almost as much as the fire at sea. He was a hunter, a killer. He would not expect a stag to invite him to his herd.

But here at home all, for the moment, seemed safe and cosy.

'You are my princess,' he said simply. 'With your fancy dress or without.'

Brogan's smile was radiant and she kissed him full on the lips. 'With,' she said, then cast a quick glance at Freydis. 'Oh, no, I shall take it off.'

Braan smiled roguishly. 'I shall take it off,' he said.

'Ssh,' said Brogan, who had caught Freydis's half-smile and realised she understood more of the language than she let on.

Braan put his hand through her hair, then left her to go to the cooking pot. He frowned.

'There were no more gift creatures today,' he said. 'And of course no fishing.'

Brogan looked concerned. 'You think...'

Braan shrugged. 'After what I saw, I no longer know what to think.'

'Do you think the God of the sea has taken his sacrifice?'

'I hope so,' said Braan. 'I hope he has finished with us altogether. For it will make our life perilous hard if we cannot fish.'

Brogan and Braan looked hard at each other and Brogan, suddenly feeling oddly ashamed to be so carefree when their situation was so precarious, began to take off Freydis's lovely dress.

Now dry, Freydis redressed herself. She felt she should be tired, but she was not; she was anxious and wound up and enervated and, watching Brogan affectionately take off Braan's leather sandals and rub his feet warm in front of the fire, a pang for something – she did not know what – went through her, and she felt as if she was intruding.

'Stay!' said Brogan as she got up, but Freydis shook her head.

'I will come back in a little while,' she said, donning her fine heavy cloak, now nearly dry, and leaving the comforting scene.

*

Under the water, it sparkled and moved. Today, everything had changed. It stretched out its tentacles. Now it had made contact. And its collective consciousness was screaming, begging for more; the hunger, the urge to connect; to find a power source was there, sharp as a knife. Although it was legion, although it was many, it had only one thought, one will: continue the line.

Eoric took out his flints from the small leather bag he wore over his shoulder. He gathered dry dead bracken and piled the brazier high. There were two. Only the older men on the island like Corc could remember the second being lit, at the height of a terrible bloodied raid. But now it needed to be lit again. Stay away, until we are safe again.

The islands traded with each other, occasionally fought and sometimes married amongst themselves. There would be many worried in Harris tonight.

Eoric struck the flint until the dry leaves caught with a crackle, then the twigs, then, eventually, the dull, smouldering peat.

The feasting continued: seaweed was roasted crisp in pans and served crunchy and covered in fresh sea salt; neeps boiled sweet and served with honey and small seeded buns. The noise levels in the meeting hut grew louder as the feast went on; the differences in their tongues diminished; stories of their exploits were passed around by the captain and took on higher magnitudes of bravery every time. Dorcnor turned out to be a passable musician and took to the crude island harp with a will and, with a local boy on the bladder pipes, some dancing began and grew steadily wilder. The captain and Corc arm-wrestled, to the delight of the onlookers, and were both coming out even, although, as the captain pointed out, only one of them had nearly died that day.

After it finally became clear that there wasn't going to be an enormous fight, the Doctor moved slowly through the happy throng and walked out under the pitch-black sky towards the sea.

'Well. That's the immediate danger muted,' he thought to himself. 'Priorities, priorities. Stop them ripping themselves to bits first. Now… Now for *you*, whatever you are.'

He stood on the edge of the sea, the incoming waves soaking his boots. He didn't notice. He looked around. The stars were bright and cold and seemed, from here, almost impossibly distant. The moon was a sliver. And there was nothing else to be seen. Not a light, not the passing blink of an aeroplane or a starship; a satellite or a motorway or a lighthouse. Nothing but the glow of a fire and those foul-smelling rendered seal-fat candles.

It took a lot to make the Doctor feel small. Normally he felt like he danced across the universe on the tips of his toes like Fred Astaire. But this, somehow, seemed like a world that was not quite yet his to play in.

'A world lit only by fire,' the Doctor said softly aloud to himself.

He stared out at the sea, the tips of the waves intermittently lit by the moonlight.

'So, what are you? Underwater gas? But you were thinking. You had a plan. I'm sure of it. Marine mammals... then men. And who lit you? Hmm? Are you there?'

He waited. Nothing.

He raised his voice. 'Hello! Big firey hose snake thing? You remember? Killed all those folk? I just... I just... well, you know. Killing all those folk. Not cool. And I'd like it if we could talk about that. Because if you can direct a gigantic fire hose from under the sea, I bet you can hear me. I just bet you can.'

Nothing.

Sighing, the Doctor took out his sonic screwdriver. 'This is such an unsullied world,' he went on. 'So pure. I mean, a *bit* horrible, with the scrofula and pillaging and everything, but it's doing its own thing. Clean air. Clean water.' He took a deep breath. 'So many fish you could cross the ocean walking on their backs. Really really really long poems. I like really really really long poems.'

He switched on the sonic screwdriver. The small device glowed an artificial, luminous green in the darkness; a tiny point of artificial light in a dark universe. It felt wrong, somehow. To contaminate this pure world. On the other hand, he reflected, they started it.

'Come out, come out, wherever you are,' he said softly, holding it aloft. 'Come and find me now.'

He glanced worriedly up at the stars, hoping some passing megacruiser didn't have its antennae out, then addressed them. 'Just the thing in the ocean please. This planet is very much not open for business to the rest of you, thank you.'

'*Eoric.*'

The voice was so soft and gentle that for a moment – a ridiculous moment, and he cursed his weakness in seconds – Eoric thought it might be his mother. She had a soft voice, and the way she always said his name had made him feel like he was the most important boy on the island. He loved to hear her say his name. But it was not her, it couldn't be. She was gone, and all he had left was an idiot for a father and a bleating sheep of a brother who picked flowers, drew pictures and romped around accepting affection from any woman in the village (of which there was much) like a little lost lamb till he was soft and spoiled and daft and he hadn't even known their mother…

'*… Eoric.*'

He looked around. 'Who is it?'

This was tiresome. Ever since he'd started growing his little beard, the girls of the village had turned into total idiots who were always teasing him and going all pink and laughing whenever he walked by and making him embarrassed.

Silence. He couldn't hear a footfall or a rustle of the rushes.

'Who's there?'

He made his voice sound as strong as he were able.

He certainly wasn't going to be scared of a girl's voice.

'*EO… RIC.*'

It couldn't be. But it seemed as if the voice was coming from… the flames?

Most people wouldn't have heard the gentle footstep on the soft sand. The Doctor was not most people. He whirled around.

Freydis stood there, gaping at him and the sonic screwdriver. 'Godlight,' she said. 'Sacred fire.'

The Doctor gulped and uselessly tried to hide the sonic screwdriver behind his back.

'Well, I could see why you would think that, but I can assure you there's a perfectly innocent expla—'

'Are you signalling Odin?' said Freydis fiercely. 'Is he coming to rescue me and take me to Valhalla?'

'Um…' said the Doctor, still desperately scanning the horizon. 'Um, well. If there is one thing I hate to do, it's disrespect people's beliefs.'

'Loki speaks in riddles,' said Freydis.

'Aren't you cold?' asked the Doctor.

'I am a princess of the North,' said Freydis. 'Cold is my birthright. Now you must tell me your plans for me.'

'Must I?' said the Doctor confused.

'Loki speaks in *riddles*. You have saved me from my fate of marrying the old King. Now, what would the Gods do with me?'

The Doctor blinked quickly. 'Oh, was it all about you? I'm sorry, I hadn't realised.'

'There is a plan for me,' said Freydis smugly.

Just as the Doctor was considering correcting her, a figure appeared silhouetted on the other end of the beach.

'Oh, look,' said the Doctor. 'Maybe it's that destiny thing.'

Freydis glanced at the rapidly approaching figure of Henrik.

'My enemy, my jailer, a farm boy?' she said.

Henrik arrived, panting, in front of them. 'Oh, there you are. I... I was worried.'

'Well, thank you so much,' said the Doctor. 'Oh. Sorry. I thought you meant me.'

Freydis looked at Henrik, his bright grey eyes and yellow hair glinting in the moonlight. She couldn't deny that he was well-favoured. But he looked unkempt and a little confused. Still a farmer's boy, she thought. Still the farmer's boy who had kept her captive. Then rescued her, she thought. Her hand fluttered in front of her mouth, as it did when she was nervous, then she regained her composure.

'Worried your prize might have escaped?'

Henrik looked at her shyly. He took a deep breath. 'I was hoping... my lady... I will no longer try to take you anywhere you do not wish to go. But I will be in your service...'

Freydis smiled. 'And when they come and drag me away again?'

Henrik shrugged. 'Who knows where we will be?'

'We will be sailors' tales,' sniffed Freydis. 'Or

must we live out our lives here on this forsaken rock then? Perhaps I will learn to feed chickens and tend livestock.'

'I can imagine worse fates,' interjected the Doctor.

Henrik looked at Freydis for a moment. 'We do not know what the Gods decree, my lady.'

Freydis eyed the Doctor coldly. 'Some of us do, some of us do not.'

The Doctor looked up again from where he was fiddling with his screwdriver. The settings now glowed blue, and Henrik gazed on it, astonished.

'What fresh witchery...'

The Doctor raised the screwdriver high, pointing it towards the sea. But just as he did so, they all heard a loud barking shout.

All three charged back in the direction of the sound, which had come from somewhere to the north of the settlement. The noise had not permeated the meeting hall, which still echoed to skirling pipes and the thud of feet dancing and cups of mead bouncing on table tops. Henrik rushed in to tell his fellows as the Doctor and Freydis ran in amongst the low dwellings.

At the very edge of the village now stood a teenage boy – the Doctor recognised him as Corc's son, the one who had stormed off to set off the braziers.

'Eoric,' he said.

Eoric turned his head. His face was still full of sullen defiance. And something else; a look too old for him. The Doctor could not quite ascertain what.

'Did you hear that noise?'

'Yes,' said Eoric. 'It was me. I accidentally fell asleep in front of the fire, and my foot fell in it. Look.' He showed the Doctor his burned toe.

'You should get that bathed,' said Freydis. 'In the sea, if you can bear it. Cleaner is better. Quickly! Or it will continue to cook, all the way down.'

'It doesn't hurt,' said Eoric.

'Are you *sure*?' said the Doctor. The skin was blistered and raw-looking in the light of the fire.

'I'm sure, stranger,' said Eoric, giving him a cold look. And without another word, he turned and went back into his home.

'I don't like this,' said the Doctor. 'I don't like this at all.'

'Are Loki's plans going awry?' asked Freydis.

'If I *had* a plan,' said the Doctor, 'it might be going awry. As it is… there is something afoot. And not just a burn that does not burn.'

Chapter
Seven

The Doctor was lying down, feeling extremely uncomfortable, waiting for the first whisper of a dawn. It had been a long time coming. His every instinct had been to continue trying to track down the thing under the water. But he needed to think, he needed to see what he was doing, and he needed help – and help was best when rested and properly awake.

So instead the Doctor was on top of some straw on the floor in the corner of the main hall, amidst a pile of grunting Vikings. There were two helmet horns sticking in his face. The fire was burning low, but the warmth of the bodies meant the air was at least comfortable, if not particularly fragrant.

One Viking snorted loudly and scratched himself under his leathers. The Doctor's eyebrows arched and he sprang briskly to his feet.

It had simply not been possible, the previous evening, after Eoric had turned for home, to make enough polite excuses that would allow the villagers to let him disappear into the howling rain and pitch dark for the night. He was aware, too, that their deep-seated hospitality would be offended if he did not take up their offer to stay at the feast, and he had to make sure they were chatting and singing, not fighting. But it had made for an unpleasant few hours.

Managing not to wake anyone, he crept stealthily out of the hall and into the early morning. The sky and the sea and the land were all layered colours of softest grey, worn pebbles and flints on the beach; tranquil and beautiful. It was almost impossible to imagine anything bad ever happening here. He moved down to the water. Nothing, not a thing. Now it was light, he was ready. He looked around. Henrik was crunching down to the water's edge.

'Well met,' said the Doctor, pleased for some company. Henrik bent down and washed his face and his hair, rinsing the freezing water all over his body.

'Good man,' said the Doctor. 'Look at you, not in the least fazed by the cold water... Of course, you've probably only ever known cold water... You really should have listened to *some* of those Romans.'

Henrik brought up his head. 'What's that?'

'Oh, nothing, never mind. So, today's the day, then.'

Henrik looked confused. 'What day?'

'Why, the day we find out what burnt up your ship, of course.'

Henrik eyed the Doctor up. 'Oh yes? Um, how?'

'Oh, I don't know,' said the Doctor airily. 'Thought we'd borrow a little coracle, take a paddle out, try and catch us some fish… or a gigantic fire.'

'I don't want to come,' said Henrik. 'You're mad.'

'People don't usually say that till they've got to know me better,' complained the Doctor. 'Shall we see if there's any tea?'

By the time they'd tramped back, the settlement was waking and cooking smoke could be seen in the air.

'Excellent,' said the Doctor approvingly. 'Let's see who'll lend me a kayak.'

As he explained his intentions round the main campfire, Vikings and islanders alike regarded him with astonishment.

Corc alone stepped up to him. 'You're going to go straight to the fire?' he said.

The Doctor squinted at him. 'Did you really not notice anything before?' he asked, carefully.

Corc looked away.

'Please tell me' said the Doctor gently. 'It might help.'

'No, Doctor,' said Corc. 'I have not seen it before. But from where we received the gifting creatures, I would say it does not move. They came from the same place we saw the ship attacked; just rounding the headland. The Viking ship washed up in the same spot.'

'That's very useful. Thank you.'

'I should have… I should have investigated it before,' said Corc, shaking his head. 'Saved us from all this.'

The Doctor looked at him. 'Please don't think this is a natural phenomenon,' he said gently, 'or witchcraft, or anything you could get rid of by sacrificing a goat. My guess is, this is something that comes from very far away indeed. Like I do. So I'm the person best-placed to deal with it, all right?'

Suddenly the Doctor felt a small hand slip into his. He looked down. It was little Luag, who beamed up at him.

'Hallo.'

'Hallo!'

'Are you going in the water? You can have my boat. But I don't have a boat. One day I will have a boat.'

'That is very kind of you,' said the Doctor. 'Thank you for the promise of your future boat.'

'Are you going to find the fire thing?'

The Doctor nodded. 'And I might do some fishing' he added.

Luag grinned. 'Yay!'

'And who knows, if the two things meet – well, we can cook them there. Do you like fish fingers, Luag?'

Luag looked uncomprehending.

'Of course not. Such a shame. You would *love* them. OK. Corc?'

Corc looked worried. 'You know, we don't have many boats…'

'It doesn't matter if you have a fleet if you can't outrun the fire,' said the Doctor. 'I will be careful.'

The Viking men had gone very quiet. They remembered what it was like out there.

Two men brought forward Corc's boat. It was incredibly small, made of tightly stitched animal skins stretched taut over a frame of bowed wood, with two light paddles. It didn't look seaworthy for a Sunday duck pond, never mind the wild North Atlantic.

The Doctor coughed politely. 'Well! Isn't she just lovely! Great!'

He took the boat from the men with thanks. It hardly weighed anything.

'OK, let me just go… with this boat… and sort everything out… Who needs a TARDIS, I am perfectly happy not bothering the local ecosystem and causing mass panic… perfectly.'

He reached the water's edge, took off his shoes and dipped in a toe.

'It *is* rather parky, isn't it? I remember this from yesterday.'

He put the boat down on the bobbing waves. It immediately capsized.

'Ha! So funny when they do that, isn't it.'

The audience watching him on the shore remained completely silent.

'Well, here goes!' said the Doctor. 'I will say, I do feel I am slightly better at the infinite empty voids of time and space than I am with…' he touched the water, 'you know. This stuff.'

There was a pause.

Then, suddenly, a figure was running down the beach.

'Wait! Wait!'

The Doctor squinted. It was Henrik.

'What is it?' said the Doctor. 'You can't talk me out of it, you know. You can't talk me out of this obviously suicidal, not to mention dreadfully uncomfortable outing, even with three or four randomly chosen words. Absolutely definitely not… I mean, you could have a shot…'

'No,' said Henrik, his handsome face stoic. 'It was our ship. It was the will of the Gods. I will come.'

Freydis watched with unavoidable interest as he strode towards the coracle and took off his boots, and fixed his sword high above his muscular back.

'Gods be with you,' she said, but Henrik was already striding into the freezing water.

'Now, remember…' The Doctor was much brisker now he had someone to give instructions to. 'One hint of a spark – one hint – and we get straight under the water, no excuses, right?'

They were paddling out to the exact spot the boat had gone down, keenly watched by Corc and his men from the shore. The gulls keened overheard, and a huge osprey swooped down right in front of them to take one of the huge fish that thronged in the water. It was a beautiful sight.

'There are worse places to be shipwrecked,' said the Doctor.

Henrik had in fact been thinking the exact same thing but for a different reason. Freydis had looked very lovely that morning, her long hair free from its nets and tumbling down her back. She had slept late and emerged from the hut with a dazed dreamy look on her face. When she wasn't angry and superior and grand and shouting at people about Gods, Henrik had reflected, she really was most terribly pretty. And a princess, yes, but that was in the Norse country. Here, on this tiny island in the middle of nowhere, a place without coin or horses or a theatre any of the trappings of civilisation… here, she was just a girl.

Henrik rowed a little faster than the Doctor, but even so, going against the tide it took them a little while to get to the spot, or as near as possible. Once there they stopped and bobbed about. Henrik looked at him.

'Are you going to use that… thing?'

The Doctor took his sonic screwdriver from his inside pocket. 'Well, I *think* so. That, and…' He brought out the fishing line, with a tiny iron hook on the end.

'We're fishing?'

'In a manner of speaking. Now the fire came from underneath, yes? But it could only detect us moving in air?'

Henrik nodded.

The Doctor tied the screwdriver securely to the fishing line.

'OK, let's make a little bit of noise.'

He stood up, very awkwardly, in the tiny boat, then extended the line to its full extent, and started to swing it round his head, like a very long lasso.

Henrik was hypnotised by the way the light blinked

round and round. 'I saw, once… in a theatre house in Trondheim… a sorcerer…'

'Yes,' said the Doctor quickly. 'It's just like that.'

They both watched the light flicker round and round the grey sky. Then, suddenly –

'*Look!*' shouted Henrik, pointing.

Chapter
Eight

It was on the horizon, gradually taking shape. At first it was hard to make it out exactly. Henrik was the first to realise exactly what it was.

'Odin's teeth,' he said, ashen-faced.

'What is it?' said the Doctor. He could see now as the shape resolved itself into another Viking boat, the cruel prow stretched out ahead, the striped sail making itself visible. 'Who?'

'It's one of our sister ships,' said Henrik, shaking his head. 'But how… how can they be here so quickly? It's just not… it's not possible. Unless…'

The Doctor waited.

'Unless they were following us all along. Spying on us.'

'Making sure you got your very important package to its destination.'

'We were carrying her dowry, too,' said Henrik. 'I didn't even think of it till now. There was a lot of gold on that ship.'

'Enough to make a team of sailors turn tail and

mysteriously disappear?' said the Doctor.

'We wouldn't have,' said Henrik, crossly. Then he sighed. 'But it's possible, I suppose.'

The Doctor sat back down and grabbed the oars. 'Well, quick then. We have to steer them away.'

Henrik looked unhappy and didn't pick up the oars straightaway.

'What?' asked the Doctor.

'Nothing,' said Henrik. 'I suppose it's for the best.'

'Would you prefer it if they just went straight past?' said the Doctor, with an amused look on his face. 'Leave you shipwrecked? Never see your friends or family again? Have to live on a rock in the middle of the ocean?'

Henrik shrugged. 'No,' he said. 'I suppose.'

'There's no supposing about it, we have to at least warn them,' said the Doctor, starting to row.

'I know,' said Henrik, joining in. Then, after a pause, 'But Doctor… you know, between the islanders and us… I mean, it seems to be calm at the moment, but…'

The Doctor looked thoughtful. 'But this lot might not be quite so accommodating?'

'Well, it's just not what we're meant to do. You know. We're all Norsemen. They might not realise how much in the islanders' debt we are, as guests.'

The boat was growing closer now, and a tiny figure could be spied in the crow's nest, waving furiously.

'Ah,' said the Doctor. 'Yes. I see.'

'I mean, they're capable of… we're capable of…'

'Yes,' said the Doctor. 'Well, we'll just have to ask nicely.'

They both looked towards the advancing ship, the dragon prow fierce and proud coming out of the water, the oars beating a steady rhythm against the waves. No one on board appeared to have noticed them, and suddenly it became very clear why.

'Well,' said the Doctor quietly. 'It's a little too late to worry about the social niceties.'

Because, just round the back of the ship, suddenly, quick as lightning, a line of shuddering flames could be seen, dancing over the water as if it were burning through a fuse.

The Doctor tapped his sonic screwdriver several times against the side of the coracle.

'What are you doing?' said Henrik, out of breath on the oars as they struggled to reach the ship. Already they could hear the cries of fear and horror, before the fire had even reached the ship's timbers, and one man had dived in, with the same horrible consequences that had greeted poor Annar.

'Well, this thing here...' said the Doctor, adjusting the settings one final time. 'The thing about it is that it's sonic. That means it works with sound... HELLO! HELLO! IS THIS THING ON?'

Over the noise of the sea and the winds and the beating of the oars and the terrified cries of the men aboard, the Doctor's voice, amplified by the sonic screwdriver, boomed out like it came from the heavens

85

themselves. The men, terrified, stopped and ran over to the other side of the boat.

'GREAT. LOVELY. NOW, HELLO THERE, I'M THE DOCTOR, AND THIS IS HENRIK, VERY NICE TO MEET YOU. NOW I DON'T WAN'T ANYONE TO PANIC, BUT THAT IS A BIT OF A KIND OF KILLER FIRE THING COMING AFTER YOU. TO KILL YOU. BUT DON'T PANIC.'

He lowered the sonic screwdriver.

'How do you think I'm coming across?'

Henrik stared at him, cowering.

'Oh Henrik, it's just a clever… don't worry about it now…'

He lifted it back to his mouth.

'SO. IF YOU COULD ALL JUST GET DOWN TO THE BOTTOM OF THE BOAT… YOU'LL NEED TO CLIMB DOWN THROUGH THE CARGO HOLD AND OUT THE ANCHOR HOLE, THEN SWIM UNDERWATER TO THE SHORE. HAVE YOU GOT THAT? DOWN TO THE BOTTOM AND KEEP YOUR HEADS ABOVE WATER AT ALL TIMES. DO NOT DIVE IN. I REPEAT…'

At the front of the crowd of men on the poop deck stood one, with a fearsome red beard and a huge helmet. He stared at the Doctor for a second, then turned round to his men.

'Down below, men,' he hollered, in a voice not much quieter than that of the Doctor through the amplifier.

'Ah, good,' said the Doctor. 'That's right. What

Redbeard says. Down below. And through—'

'And *row*!'

'No!' shouted the Doctor, then remembered to lift his screwdriver up. 'NO! DON'T ROW! IT CAN GO FASTER THAN YOU! YOU HAVE TO GET UNDER THE WATER.'

But from inside the boat, with the men disappearing, and the flames licking at the prow, came an ominously fast drumbeat as the men started to row for their lives.

'It won't work,' agonised the Doctor. 'They can't move faster than the flames.'

But as the boat started to move, hell-bent for shore, its prow on fire but its men safely below, the Doctor gradually realised the real danger.

The dragon prow passed their little coracle by on their starboard side, picking up speed now – if the men could get to shore, they might indeed outrun the flames. Not through speed alone. But if they exposed something else in the direct path of the fire…

As the boat passed by, the coracle was now closer to the source of the flames and completely exposed. And sure enough, the line of fire moved: it focused in on them, the flames rising.

'Oh, fantastic,' said the Doctor, gloomily. He didn't know when he was going to get a chess game at this rate.

'*Doctor!*' screeched Henrik, grabbing the oars. But the Doctor was leaning dangerously far out of the boat, forward, towards the danger.

'Hello,' he said, encouragingly. Nothing happened, except that the flames took hold of the furthest oar with a hissing, spitting crackle.

'*Doctor!*'

'Now. You have to tell me,' said the Doctor. 'What's up? Where have you come from? No fighting, hmm?'

The flames leapt and danced on the water.

'*DOCTOR!*'

It was too late to capsize the little coracle; too late to paddle to escape. Henrik cursed his luck and prepared for certain death. The Doctor turned to the back of the boat and pressed a setting on his screwdriver.

Suddenly, from out of nowhere it seemed, an enormous wave appeared behind them, sucking the water before it as it built up, higher than a wall, higher than a house.

'OK, quick,' shouted the Doctor. 'Crouch. We only get one shot at this.'

'What?' shouted Henrik but he did as the Doctor said.

'Try and keep your weight on the back foot...'

The roaring of the wave was everywhere; it was enormous, a huge mountain of water, filling ears and eyes.

'And when I say UP, get UP! Fast as you can.'

Henrik didn't understand anything but the wave now was bearing down on them, the first line of froth just visible on the very top, far above.

'Don't look back! Now 1, 2, 3...'

It all happened very quickly. The Doctor and Henrik

jumped up on the back of the coracle just as the huge wave picked them up and pushed them poundingly fast, throwing them to shore as they held on – just – and surfed the top of the crest, like going downhill on the fastest sledge Henrik had ever known.

The line of flame shot harmlessly into the wall of water and instantly halted as they flew through the wave and were deposited, shouting, and exhilarated, just behind the Viking ship, onto the pebbled shore.

Chapter
Nine

The Doctor leapt up first, coughing up sea water on the pebbled beach. He glanced up to assess the situation. Henrik was lying on the sand laughing and occasionally saying 'woo hoo'.

But it wasn't a laughing matter, the Doctor realised immediately.

The longboat looked much larger here, resting on the sands it had been pushed onto by the great wave.

The big red-bearded sailor had jumped down, and was now standing in front of Corc, hollering at him. The two men were squaring up to one another; the other Vikings behind their captain holding axes and spears and looking menacing. The Doctor glanced around. All the women had disappeared with the children. This rarely boded well. Some of the rescued Vikings, he noticed, were with their captain, Ragnor, but standing on Corc's side. This was definitely a better sign.

The Doctor leapt up. 'Hello, everyone!' he announced. 'Welcome to Party Island.' He shook hands with the Viking captain, Corc and Ragnok, beaming happily. 'And you are?'

'Erik,' growled the Viking captain.

'Erik! Fabulous! All the Eriks are great, did you know? Especially ones with red beards. They sing songs about you, you know.'

'Their widows do,' grunted Erik, fingering his axe.

'So, my understanding,' said the Doctor, 'is that you're very keen to be on your way, is that right? So we have a *minor delay* whilst I try and sort out what's going on out there – it doesn't seem to respond well to friendly chit-chat, which is disappointing, as friendly chit-chat is generally my preferred negotiation tactic of choice, but hey ho. Now. Whilst these kind people extend their hospitality towards you…'

Behind him, the Doctor could feel Corc stiffen.

'… can you give them your word you'll be duly appreciative guests?'

There was a moment's pause. Then the entire crew of the second Viking ship burst out laughing.

'We'll be *appreciative*,' said Erik. 'Appreciative of their plate, their women, their goats, their grain, their gold, their ale and anything else we can rip out of this forsaken hole.'

The men roared. Corc and his men put their hands on their swords. They may not have understood the words, but the sentiment was clear. Then Ragnor stepped forwards.

'Erik,' he said.

'Ragnor!' bellowed Erik. 'You have changed into a

woman, I see.'

'These people… these people have been kind to us.'

'Kind? Or is this a hiding place for your gold? Hmm? I see no sign of your ship. Have you hidden that here too? With your cheap flame tricks to scare us?'

'That was no trick, Erik, I swear to you. It's dangerous. It killed thirty of my men.'

'Oh yes? Or did you drown them, trying to get the gold off? Did you kill the lady?'

'No!'

'Oh good,' said Erik. 'Good. Because she has somewhere she needs to be.'

'Erik. Please.'

The Doctor could see how much it cost Ragnor to say this.

'Why do you think we were sent after you, Ragnor? Hmm? Because they know you are losing your *stomach* for being a Norseman, hmm? Too old? Too soft?'

'Never.'

'Well then, why are we parleying? When there is raiding to be done.'

'No!' said the Doctor loudly, stepping between them. 'You will spill no blood here.'

Erik gave the Doctor a long look. 'And you are going to stop me… how?'

The two lines squared up to one another. Ragnor looked from one line – his brethren – to the other – his saviours – unclear what to do.

'You will be on the end of my sword soon enough,'

said Erik, lifting it high in the air above his head, and fingering his axe with his other hand. 'Come on, men.'

'There is everything to lose and nothing to gain,' said the Doctor. 'Let me fix this and you can be on your way.'

'I will,' said Erik. 'Just as soon as we've got what we want.'

The line of men advanced, their faces full of viciousness. The Doctor looked from one to another. Mob rule. So difficult to influence. The first ship, their friends had died, were scattered. They were free to follow their own consciences. But Erik's men had no such qualms.

Down by the water's edge, Henrik wished his sword were not so wet, but it would do the job. He unsheathed it, his hands shaking. He told himself it was from the cold. The attacking party looked terrifying. Was this really what he had looked like? Been like? He always thought of raids as fun; as a skirmish, something everybody did. But perhaps it was not.

'*My wolves!*' howled Erik. '*Attack!* And leave not a single one standing; savages and turncoats who are not fit to call themselves Norse when they protect neither their gold nor their blood. And we will feast well tonight.'

The men set up a hullabaloo, a terrifying war cry. The Doctor thought of Luag, sheltering indoors. Could he hold back Erik? The Doctor rushed for Erik; bring down the head and the rest would scatter. But just as he reached him, jumping for his back, there was another shout from one of the advancing party, pointing over his shoulder.

Behind, in the settlements, where normally there was the smoke from the cooking fires and burning peat, there was a lot more smoke than usual. Small fires had suddenly appeared everywhere; gorse and bracken were on fire, sending thick, choking black smoke funnelled into the sky.

'The Gods,' breathed one.

'They are doing our work for us!' shouted another. The Doctor desperately wrestled the huge Erik to the ground, but his thin frame was no match for the heavily armoured Viking; with a dunt of his huge wooden shield, the Doctor was knocked sideways, only for Erik to roll on top of him, holding up his axe for the final blow.

'You don't understand,' coughed the Doctor. 'This wasn't us. It's *them*.'

But suddenly, Erik had frozen, his attention caught elsewhere. His mouth dropped open, giving the Doctor the tiniest fraction of a second just in time to wrest his left arm free and push him off and over. Erik hardly noticed. His eyes were caught on the figure emerging amongst all of them, registering none. All the men dropped arms.

'What fresh sorcery is this?' said Erik.

Eoric had felt his power of the fire grow within him throughout the night. He had not slept, but instead taken himself out; to better feel the glow within him.

It was warm, hot, feverish, delicious, all at the same time. It was pure power; he had the power to light up the world. He could flicker flames from his fingertips; spark grass with his footsteps.

This was the best he had ever felt, since before his mother had died; full of jumping, pulsating energy. Who would ignore a boy who could talk to the flames? Not a boy, he thought. Not a simple boy. A man. Maybe even… perhaps I am a God, he had thought. It must happen like this. The Gods came down and filled you with their power. And now, how he felt that power.

He had crept secretly down to witness the commotion on the shore. It had been just as he had predicted, he thought, his lip curling. There they were. Of course his father had been far too soft on the invaders, so what did they get but more invaders? It stood to reason. Nobody ever listened to him.

But the fire had. It had called his name and flattered him and told him he was special amongst his kind and that he had a special message to deliver from the stars. Oh yes, it had hurt at first, to give himself up to the flames. But now it felt so, so good.

Within him, the power raged. '*Hold the line. Continue the line*' pounded in his head. He felt compelled to touch someone; join with them. The voices in his head kept him moving forwards. Now, as he walked down, he saw the men bow before him in fear, which pleased him beyond measure. He did not know that his eyes glowed orange; that sparks popped and fizzed from his fingers; that his footprints scorched the heather beneath his feet. But he saw the big brave Norsemen – not so brave now – flinch and jump as he sent out flames. Whoosh, and a wooden shield was now nothing but black ash. Whoosh, and a cape left on the floor evaporated.

It wasn't just the invaders who were horrified. The local people too – the ones who had grown up with him, seen him as the awkward, motherless boy, defiant son of the chieftain – why weren't they lauding him? Falling in front of him in gratitude as, whoosh, he set a high ring of flames dancing around one of the invaders' feet, causing him to dance and scream in terror. And whoosh, there now, a stream of flame knocked off the captain's helmet, singed the top of his head, turned them all into screaming, wobbling ninnies. He laughed, a strange, empty sound, and now his mouth drew back in a tight mirthless grin as he sought his first partner.

All the bluster had gone out of Erik. His swagger and his violence and his guts were dribbling away confronted with this monstrosity.

'*Men – turn!*' he commanded, but the men needed no prompting. Four were already in the sea, pulling the great weighed-down ropes of their ship, pushing her back out to the water.

'They're going,' said Corc, in disbelief, barely able

to tear his eyes from his son. Ragnor too was staring, open-mouthed. One of his men, the young one called Dorcnor, also dashed into the splashing water, jumping in with his old fellows.

'Stop!' yelled Ragnor. 'You know what's out there on the water!'

'But it's everywhere!' shouted back Dorcnor. 'I'll take my chances with my brethren!'

At that, two more of the rescued turned tail and went with their fellows. Eoric stood, orange flame flickering in his eyes, watching the scene. Everyone made a wide circle around him, as far away as they could possibly be.

The boat was pushing off now, more and more of the Vikings shinning up the side, as Eoric continued making that high-pitched noise that may have been a laugh.

The Doctor shook his head. 'It's out there too,' he said. 'It's out there too! Don't leave!'

But there was not a chance that they would listen to him. He ran towards Eoric, but felt, and smelled, the strange, fiery crackle that surrounded him.

There was no doubt. There was a connection. And to his eyes, it was quite clearly alien.

'Who are you?' he asked, keeping his distance. 'I mean you no harm. Please, just tell me who you are.'

Eoric's head was pounding. He was the line, he had to continue the line. Yes. That was it.

The voices in his head did not care who were his own people and who were not. *Join them*, they said.

Let them join the line. Let them feel the power and the light.

But Eoric's head was burning. He was beginning to feel a terrible pressure bear down on him. A smouldering inside, that hurt like nothing he had ever known. A pain he could not contain.

'I'm…' Eoric looked confused suddenly, as if he couldn't quite remember. 'I'm… I am the fire. I am the sea. I am…'

'Please,' said the Doctor urgently. 'Please tell me all you can.'

The sail had been turned around to catch the offshore winds; the oars were being roughly fumbled into position. Suddenly, there was a loud shrieking. Just as the ship began to take off, two of the final Vikings ran charging out of Braan and Brogan's house. Over the shoulder of one of them, kicking and screaming for all her worth, was Freydis.

Henrik was the first to react, but he was too far up the beach, readying himself for a fight. The men splashed through the water and eager hands came down from the boat to help them scramble on, pulling up Freydis with rough hands as she screeched and hit out at anything and anyone she could reach, as the oars started to beat in a steady rhythm, and the ship started to pull away from shore.

'*No!*' cried Henrik desperately, and threw himself into the water, uselessly hurling himself through the pounding waves in an attempt to reach the ship. It was pointless.

With an ominous slowness, still cackling to himself,

Eoric turned himself around to face the departing ship. He gradually raised his hand.

'*No!*' screamed the Doctor this time. 'Whatever you are, inside Eoric. Do not do this! There is no purpose to it.'

Eoric's skin now looked as if it was on fire; his entire body was aglow, as if it was being consumed from the inside. His voice had taken on a terrible, choking timbre.

'I am the fire. I am the sea. I am the line. Continue the line.'

'The line?' said the Doctor. 'What do you mean, the line?'

Ragnor was still staring out to sea. 'It'll get them out there,' he said, trembling. 'The fire. It'll get them all. Henrik!'

But the young man was already striding up the shore towards Corc. 'Give me the coracle,' he demanded. 'I must chase them.'

Corc could not answer. He was staring in horror at his son, whose arm was still raised to point to the boat, fire jetting from his fingers.

'The line, the line, the line,' pondered the Doctor. 'An ancient line? A royal line? Argh, *think*!'

Suddenly, the thing that had been Eoric turned again, its attention caught. It looked down.

The voice, when it came, was very little, but very brave.

'Please can I have my brother back?' it said. 'I want my brother back. He's not always very nice to me, but he is my brother and I do like him and I would like him back.'

There was a tiny fractional pause, then the Doctor leapt just in time in front of the boys, pushing Luag to the ground, just as the fire jutted out of Eoric's fingers as he reached out to grab his little brother, and missed by inches.

A hissing noise came from Eoric's mouth, now blackening and curling at the edges in a hideous rictus. He turned. There stood an unfortunate Viking from the second boat who had gone hunting for Freydis and arrived back too late. Eoric moved quickly as a snake, grabbing his wrist. The Viking's mouth opened in an 'o' of horror as his entire body lit up bright orange from the inside. His eyes went, his entire skin seemed to glow. Then, as the villagers backed away in horror, he turned towards them, flames at his fingertips.

'*I am the line.*'

And then screams came from the sea, as they had all known they would. The boat was at the headland, ready to turn round from the island and disappear for ever into the great stretches of cold ocean between here and the land of ice, where Erik no doubt intended to complete the mission, dowry or no dowry. It was almost – almost – out of sight. Safe; as safe as an open boat could be in the Atlantic in September with no navigation tools; without a compass or a sextant or charts, or communication devices, or anything except stout hearts, some barrels of salt venison three barrels of mead and the bright stars above.

The islanders watched, frozen between the burning men on the shore and the imperilled boat with a mixture of trepidation and horror. The women had vanished, hauling the children with them; the men were unsure whether to fight or flee. These were their enemies, yes. But even so, part of them couldn't help wishing for the threat, for whatever it was simply to go away and never return; that longed for the dragon prow of the large wooden boat to sail on, past their island and their homes and families, and never return; wash up on a different shore, or sink, quietly, out of sight and mind of them.

Of course, it was not so simple. The line of fire shot across the entire bay, even as the Vikings were clearly rowing for their lives. Then, just as suddenly, it stopped, and paused in mid air, quivering; as if it had discovered something else.

Then it turned towards the shore.

Eoric didn't know where he was any more. He couldn't remember if he was happy, or sad, or anything except the fire, and the burning, the burning inside him. He couldn't remember what he was trying to do or where he was, and could focus on nothing, except that down by his feet was something... someone... he couldn't recall; could see nothing in front of his eyes except dancing flames and crackling heat. But something was tugging at him inside; at Eoric, at the essence of Eoric he had once been. He crouched down, a hideous black shape now almost entirely consumed in flames.

'Don't touch him,' shouted the Doctor, still holding Luag. 'Don't touch him, Luag.'

Luag looked at the Doctor steadily. 'But he's my brother.'

'I'm so sorry,' said the Doctor. 'I'm so sorry. But he's not.'

Eoric's voice was nothing more than a charred wisp; a gasp through blackened vocal cords.

'My... my...' he husked.

'Your brother,' prompted Luag.

'br... other...' came Eoric's dreadful voice. Behind him, the Viking on fire was staggering slowly towards the villagers, who were backing away.

'Continue the line.'

Eoric and Luag had put their arms out towards one another. Out at sea, the flames were ripping across the tide as if forced from a gun towards the beach, desperately searching for its connection.

'Get back!' cried the Doctor, but it was unnecessary; both he and Luag were flung by the force of the blast. And by the time they got up again, there was nothing left of Eoric and the Viking behind but blackened figures, blasted onto the stones.

And the great Viking longboat carrying Freydis had rounded the headland and disappeared from view; and all the small fires had gone out, leaving only the heavy grey clouds and the unfailing waves.

Chapter
Ten

The islanders had all withdrawn. It was not seemly to surround the dead, to witness their leader collapsing into this terrible, keening grief. The Doctor had taken Luag to one side, the boy's pale grey eyes beneath his red hair wide with grief and horror.

'Did I do it?' he asked. 'Was it me? Did I do it? I'm sorry. Tell him I'm sorry. Tell my dad I'm sorry. I didn't mean it.'

The Doctor held him tightly. 'No, Luag,' he said. 'You didn't do it. You didn't do it. Something else was trying to use your brother and failed. And I will find whatever it was, and I promise you, *we will work it out*. I promise. But you are going to have to be so very, very brave.'

Luag looked up at him, the tears making lines of white down his filthy cheeks. 'Can you make it all right?' he choked. 'Can you?'

'No,' said the Doctor gently. 'No, I can't. But I will do my best to stop it happening ever again to anyone else. I promise you that.'

He let one of the other villagers lead the boy away, and went to stand next to Corc, who rose in a fury.

'You!' he said. 'This happened when you came here. You stood by and let it happen.'

The Doctor said nothing. If it helped Corc to release some of his rage, then he would let him. That was mostly it. But Corc was right. He'd known that was no ordinary burn. What kind of burn showed on the skin but did not hurt? Why hadn't he pursued the matter? Insisted on the teenager explaining himself? He had lain all night trying to fit the puzzle together of the fire on the water; why hadn't he been talking to Eoric? The line, the line; the fire and the line.

'Something is trying to make contact,' he said. 'Something is trying to make contact and making a very clumsy job of it. We should probably have figured that out from the turtles. I wish they'd just send us a text.'

But he didn't feel flippant. For here was a boy with his life ahead of him, reduced to a ghastly outline on the shore; and the proud man who loved him howling in pain.

'I'm going to figure it out,' he said, and turned away.

'*All of this*,' shouted Corc at his departing back. 'All of this started when you came along. You don't know what it's like! You don't know what it's like to lose a child.'

The Doctor's back stiffened, and his long stride broke momentarily. But he did not turn around.

*

'Come on!' the Doctor barked to Henrik. 'I need you.'

'What for?' said Henrik.

The Viking ship had disappeared now; had safely made it to the open sea. The Doctor reflected for a moment that Eoric's terrible fate had saved it. Henrik just wanted to get in the coracle.

'I have to go,' said Henrik. 'I have to rescue her.'

'We'll take my ship,' said the Doctor.

His determination came back as they strode out across the heaths of the island, rabbits scattering playfully as they went.

'I will say, first off, it's not the most seaworthy of vessels,' he announced.

'Worse than the coracle?' asked Henrik, surprised.

'Different,' said the Doctor. 'A little different.'

Henrik kicked out at a stray rock. 'It doesn't matter,' he said sullenly. 'With just us, we're going to be too late now, anyway.'

'I wouldn't be too sure about that,' said the Doctor. 'She can move.'

'What, faster than thirty men can row?' said Henrik, with heavy sarcasm. 'All right. You know the Norsemen have the fastest ships in the world,' he added, with some pride.

'They do,' said the Doctor. 'Although, I will say, you wouldn't believe what the Chinese are up to round about now.'

Henrik looked confused.

'But never mind about that. Um. Now.'

They crested the brow of a low rise. Beyond it was the TARDIS. Henrik made a sharp intake of breath.

'I know,' said the Doctor. 'Isn't she beautiful?'

Henrik descended the ridge and walked towards the TARDIS, awestruck. He toured round her and returned, his mouth open, staring at the Doctor.

'It's the… the colour.'

The Doctor squinted. 'The what?'

'Where did… where did you… I have never seen the like of it…'

'Yes, well, you see, it's a very fine…'

The Doctor paused and ran his tongue round the inside of his mouth.

'Well that's odd,' he said. 'Your language doesn't seem to have a word for the colour of my ship.'

Henrik was gazing open-mouthed in awe.

'I forget how young your world is,' said the Doctor, shaking his head. 'I have, now let me see… I have a kind of bluey-grey-black word and a light-y-watery-summery sky kind of a word, but for such a fine, strong, pure pigment…'

'It's the most beautiful thing I've ever seen,' Henrik said.

The Doctor took out his key.

'Come aboard, fellow traveller,' he said.

'Freydis was right,' said Henrik, safely inside. Oddly, the inside of the TARDIS had impressed him much less than the outside, which was something of a first, to the point where he had actually asked the Doctor why he hadn't made it all that colour.

'Was she?' said the Doctor, twiddling with some dials and, as usual when he had guests aboard, trying to modestly play down the TARDIS and pretend she wasn't really that big a deal and he could take or leave her really, whilst waiting for the compliments and gasps of how amazing she was.

Henrik, however, just automatically assumed the Doctor hadn't been able to afford the best wood and was feeling rather sorry for him.

The Doctor drummed his fingers on the console.

'I realise you haven't really invented perspective yet,' he said finally. 'But everything in here is actually bigger, you know, not just closer.'

'Yes, yes, you're a God, Freydis said,' said Henrik, dismissing the TARDIS with a wave of his hand. 'Now, where are the oars?'

The Doctor looked up from the dial panel.

'Would a God let a young man burn himself to death?' he asked quietly.

'Some would,' said Henrik. 'If it served their purposes. If they had two faces and looked two ways and tried to cause mischief.'

He paused.

'Are you going to harm me for saying that?'

'No,' said the Doctor. 'I'm not going to harm you. I'm not in the business of harming anyone, if I can possibly help it. I'm in the opposite business to that. And a lonely old business it is too. I have – and I can't tell you how much I hate the sentence I'm about to utter – I have absolutely *no idea* what killed young Eoric. But whatever it is, we're going to stop it.'

Henrik looked around. 'With this?'

'Yes, "with this",' said the Doctor, incredulously rewinding a porthole lever that had been steadfastly refusing to move.

'This ship is… I mean, she's amazing, can jump galaxies in a heartbeat; can throw herself headlong into hundreds and thousands of years; once we bounced along the very edge of the universe; the very line of existence, the knife edge of being and nothingness… just for fun, just because it was her birthday.'

He finally got the lever to turn.

'But I must say, she really, really, really doesn't like the water very much.'

Henrik raised his eyebrows.

Chapter
Eleven

The cold. It was the terrible, terrible cold. Brogan's home, where Freydis had returned the previous evening, was surprisingly cosy; the animals helped add heat to the room, and the fire burned low but steadily. There were furs and skins piled up on the raised bed area, and she and Brogan had curled up close, whilst Braan slept by the fire. She had been dragged out, still fast asleep, completely unaware of the drama outside as she recovered from the peril of the last few days. She realised she was being grabbed by the men of her homeland – grabbed, so that the last few days would turn out to be nothing but an illusion of rescue; a dream image of a life where she would not be the bought wife of fat, dribbling Gissar, in an ice prison where she knew no one and no one would care for her.

She had screamed, she had raged, and in her fury had not felt the sting of the rain and the salt spray on her face; her wrath had kept her warm, until they had slung her below, once again, behind the rowers, in a cage that fastened above her with a man standing full square on top.

The men had all cheered when they rounded the headland and escaped the cursed fire island and, after that, the more she pounded her fists against it and screamed out the curses of the Gods on him, the more her guard had laughed and said what a funny little thing she was, and she knew that of course – of course – this was no Henrik, who cared, who cared about her. This was a man who simply wanted to get paid, and knew without the dowry it was going to be a lot harder, and there was nothing she could say or do that would change that. In despair she went and sat down between two barrels of salted pork, and started to shiver.

Somehow, even though on the surface she was in the same situation, somehow now, it was so much worse. Because just for a moment, just for an instant, she had seen something else that could be. Two people she'd met that had made her think that there might, after all, be something else in her life. Loki, the stranger, with his strange lights and clothes and ways, whom she knew she should not trust, but somehow did.

And Henrik. Her captor, her imprisoner, who had turned into her guard, her saviour.

Lowith was nothing like Trondheim. There were no grand nobles, or fine dresses, or ordered gardens. There were no bustling markets filled with fascinating curios; no jewelled combs or coronets or minstrels or storytellers or high-talking merchants. Nothing but grey sky and grey sea and hard unending graft to hack a life from the earth and fire and water.

But in such a short time she'd been shown so many kindnesses – Brogan had sat down with her the previous evening when she'd arrived back and combed out her hair, which she had not done in so long; gently smoothing through the tangles with seal oil, until it shone once more by the light of the fire and Brogan had found a word they both knew to describe it: river.

Little Luag had woken up to join in the fun and instantly been welcomed in and fussed over. Freydis, raised to be stiff and a little imperious with people, had taken her cue from them, and had allowed the little boy to stroke and play with her hair, whilst Brogan plaited it tightly by the sides. Then Braan had brought them all hot tea and somehow, over a few words, Brogan had indicated that she loved him, but that they didn't have any babies yet and that she was worried, and Freydis had found herself in a conversation – a proper conversation – with a girl her own age, who wasn't a servant or a cook or a dancing master. And Henrik had accompanied her home, so polite and solicitous; nothing like the monster she had feared him to be. Brogan had pointed out how handsome he was, and Freydis had found it hard to disagree, and they had giggled together. Like real friends might.

It had been nothing but a chimera, a glimpse into another life; a joke of the Gods.

Freydis wrapped her arms tightly around her thin shift. She found, to her surprise, that she was thinking about Henrik, his soft eyes and the fact that she was never going to see him again. And to her further surprise she realised that of all the fates that might await her – she might freeze to death; the fire may strike the boat down at any time; the Vikings might kill her; the boat might sink and she would drown; or the voyage may prove successful and she would be handed over without dowry and would be killed for that; or she may be married to a fat old drooling man and live out the rest of her life surrounded by ladies in waiting, and furs, and handsome sleighs and awful, unutterable tedium – the worst of all of these fates she could imagine was that she might not see him again. Whatever happened now it barely mattered whether she lived or died, because, she realised, a life without ever seeing his face again… This was very new to Freydis. Heart pounding, she pushed her hair away from her face. She couldn't think about that now. And she couldn't sit here either. Waiting for a fate she could not control was unbearable. And if she didn't move around, she would freeze.

Flexing her fingers and toes, Freydis stood up in her cage, still bent over. Above, the soles of the Viking – Snor was his name – were standing casually on the top of the grate, one foot bent over another, chatting to someone Freydis could not hear. He was paying her no attention at all, apart from occasionally laughing down at her and calling her a hellcat, and making sharp remarks on how the Icelandic king would sort her out sooner rather than later. The more Freydis heard about Gissar, the less she liked him. It took a lot to make a Viking complain about cruelty.

Trying to hop up and down a little on the spot to warm up without losing her balance as the boat pitched up and down over the waves, Freydis looked around the gloomy interior. It was like a small cupboard or storeroom, holding the rain casks, salted meat, hard tack and mead designed to see the men through their arduous journey. Chickens lived up on board in the daylight, though the heavy seas often prevented them laying. Their corn was there too. The swords and spears were tied high on the mast to keep them dry; there was nothing there for Freydis to use. Or was there? And even if there was, where on earth would she go when she got up top?

One problem at a time, thought Freydis. One problem at a time.

Slowly, methodically, she started to scan every bit of the walls and floor, over and over again. Until, finally, she saw it.

The TARDIS materialised on the surface of the water with a *vworp*. It bobbed unsteadily, only its topmost blue light visible above the waves. Then it would submerge, then pop up again, like it was uncomfortably treading water.

Inside, things weren't much better. The interior was shifting in a most alarming, unsettling way; the

TARDIS was wheezing and changing direction almost continuously just to hold herself in and out of the medium at all, and the screens showing the outside world were running ever so slightly slowly, meaning the view they were getting of the empty sea and waves bobbing up and down was a tiny bit out of sync with what they were feeling at the time, which managed to make the entire effect markedly worse. The Doctor and Henrik were both looking extraordinarily pale, breathing deeply and holding heavily onto the console balustrades.

'Of course, I've travelled through many meteor storms and any number of wormholes,' gasped the Doctor. 'I'm completely fine. Just give me a second.'

'My father put me in my first kayak alone at the cracking of the ice in my third year,' said Henrik, trying not to look at the screens. 'This is nothing to me.'

Two beads of sweat popped out on his forehead.

The TARDIS made an unfortunate noise and lurched onto its side, only to be bounced back upright from the waves.

'And now for the daring rescue,' said the Doctor, swallowing, as he sighted the Viking ship on the screen, some way ahead.

Henrik, head almost to his knees, nodded. 'We shall go forth with all our might and…'

The Doctor lurched over, arms and legs flailing everywhere, and pressed the plunger to get the TARDIS to move closer. With a sickening, jarring lurch, she dematerialised, then, instantly, rematerialised at the same height, but closer to the ship. The Viking ship in full glory, the wind billowing taut through her striped sails, the dragon prow advancing, and the men rowing in unison, was a fearsome and glorious sight. The TARDIS was barely visible on the surface at all – not for fear of the flames, the Doctor truly believed they would mean nothing to her – but to stay out of sight of the Vikings (to avoid giving away their whereabouts) and the islanders (the Doctor felt they'd already been through quite enough without seeing something new to be terrified of).

Now they were nearly at the bow of the ship.

'In your considerable experience,' said the Doctor carefully. 'What would you say is the best way to board a Viking ship from a moving vehicle?'

'Crossbow with a rope attached,' said Henrik promptly. 'There's always some idiots who'll come up on deck to take a look. Though hard to... hard to aim when it's.... is the sea always so rough?'

'No,' said the Doctor, although the sea was utterly normal for the North Atlantic in autumn. 'It's unusually rough today.'

'Yes, I thought so,' said Henrik. 'You know, if your boat was flatter we'd manoeuvre a lot better.'

'Thanks,' said the Doctor. 'I'll bear that in mind.'

'Also, better than crossbows would be... if you had arrows dipped in pitch you could light?'

'Oh, Henrik,' said the Doctor. 'At some point, do you think you'll have had enough of setting ships on fire?'

'You did ask,' said Henrik, who was beginning to think that being in a sinking ship wouldn't probably be quite as bad as this; at least everything would only move in one direction. He looked around. 'But you know how your boat can jump through the air?'

'I like how cheerily unimpressed by everything you are,' said the Doctor. 'It's cool.'

'Sir,' said Henrik, bracing himself against the rails and staring at the floor. Then he took a deep breath.

'When I set off on my first voyage, I was four and ten. All my life I had been told of the great wonders of the waters: of huge sea monsters that rose from the deep; of women who appeared to be great beauties but were just the shadows of a dream, there only to lure you to your death; of men who were by day men and by night seals; of hurtling cyclones that would lift your boat in the air and deposit it in another part of the ocean; of golden riches; of fruit that fell sweet and juicy from branches on islands straight into your arms; of honeyed milk that grew in gourds on trees and was better than that from the finest cow; and of the very end of the world, where all boats and fish and men drop into the eternal waterfall and fall, rushing and tumbling through the stars for ever.'

He swallowed hard.

'I have been travelling the shores of the known world for eight years and I have met none of these wonders, but endured boredom, and hardship, and poor rations, and discomfort, for less gold than had I stayed on my father's farm. Until now.'

He looked up and around him.

'This is all I was promised and more. I am impressed, sir.'

He paused.

'Although I will confess, it affects my innards more than I thought it might.'

'I think you're doing very well,' said the Doctor.

'Thank you,' said Henrik.

'Adventure is the prerogative of a young man,' said the Doctor. 'I... I am not a young man. But I've never quite got out of the habit.'

They grinned at each other across the console in mutual understanding.

'Although I think you have a point. Next time, flatter.'

'Well,' continued Henrik. 'Are you too big to jump onto the ship? Is there more of this? Is it heavy?'

The Doctor looked around them shrewdly.

'Well,' he said. 'That very much depends.'

Chapter
Twelve

Freydis had nearly missed it, it was so tiny and thin. But it was there. Underneath the barrel of mead she had moved out of frustration the fourth time she had crawled through across the planks and into dusty corners, scattering mice and weevils as she went. And underneath the large barrel, just tucked underneath the largest hoop, there it was. A tiny carved sliver of iron. It must have dripped off the hoop when it was being smelted, then formed solid and stuck to the underside even when the barrel was being put together. The cooper almost certainly hadn't thought anything of it.

But to her, it was everything. Carefully she bent it where it had corroded and snapped it off. The top, squashed against the wood of the barrel, had formed a point almost as sharp as a needle, and the iron remained good and strong, even so close to the salt water.

Next she needed something to bind it to. There was nothing that would serve, nothing at all. Freydis sighed. This was going to hurt more than she had expected, given what she'd been through. Still. It had to be done. Painstakingly, and trying not to cry out, she set about plucking out long strands of her thick yellow hair, gradually plaiting them together.

The weapon had to be bound well, so she didn't lose her blade the first time she drew close to a Viking. If only her teachers had taught her knot work, and how to fight, rather than dancing and embroidery. Still, even though she was shaking, her hands were nimble and quick, and she patiently bound and rebound the sharp pointed blade to the long stout piece of wood, until it made as strong a weapon as she could manage.

She was not looking forward to using it. She could feel the blood beat in her veins. She told herself these men, her captors, were evil. But so was Henrik, once. She steeled herself. These men were nothing like Henrik.

And one thing she had seen were the jousts and fights held at high feast days at her ancestral home. Although she did not share the blood lust of some at court, she had watched enough to know that she could always tell which fighter was going to win. It was always the one who looked carefully and who, when they had made a decision, never dallied. They would find the weak spot and then attack without pause and without mercy, quickly and cleanly. That was what she must do too.

Balancing the spear in her arms she went to the furthest dark corner of the hold. Quickly, she centred her gaze and her arm flashed out as fast as she was able. And when she looked down, a rather large, grey and unpleasantly limp weevil was skewered on the very bottom of her blade.

The Doctor was trying to do sums on a piece of paper and complaining about it, as the TARDIS continued to bob up and down. At one point he tilted the TARDIS on its side and opened the door. Henrik got ready for an inrush of water, but there was none.

'Protective field,' said the Doctor. 'There's a couple of metres.'

He popped his head out into the open air to see if he could risk it on his own. The waves loomed ominously and he listened to the booming of the drums on the oars and hopped back in again.

'It's important to thoroughly investigate all the options,' he explained. 'Now, we could put our perception filter on – make us basically invisible, or at least blend-y-in-y. The problem with that is, you have to make yourself visible again when you want to rescue someone. So. Let's not do that.'

'You've done this before?' asked Henrik, hopefully.

'Rescued princesses from Viking longships? All the time,' said the Doctor. 'The trick is you need the element of surprise. But not too much surprise. If you suddenly appear in front of people they tend to yell, and other people tend to hear them and draw laser guns. Or broadswords, just whatever they have to hand, really.'

'So…'

'So, rather than us appear out of nowhere, we might as well just have the TARDIS appear along with us. Give us a bit of protection. I've worked out all the physics on this piece of paper here, and I am, you should probably know, a super-genius, and if we land the TARDIS just ahead of the stern, the wood will warp a little, but it will support us. Infinite mass, but standard g weight, you see?'

Henrik did not see, but suspected that if he admitted as much then the Doctor would try and explain it to him, so he nodded slowly, as if in a considering manner.

'Then,' said the Doctor, 'you just have to run out and snatch the girl.'

'Me?'

The Doctor rolled his eyes.

'If it's me, she'll say, "What weird God thing is this you're doing now?" Whereupon someone will chop off my ears and wear them as a necklace. If it's you, she'll say, "Oh, Henrik, my hero, you have saved me, mwah mwah mwah, and you can cart her on board and we'll be out of there in under four seconds. They'll never follow us back, not with those bad fire thingies.'

Henrik coloured and said nothing.

'So. Are you ready?'

Henrik nodded.

The Doctor smiled. 'I know women, you see.'

He thought about it.

'Well. I don't actually know women at all. I've

always wanted to try that sentence out on someone who might believe it. Why are you sniggering?'

'No reason.'

'What?'

'Nothing.'

'Primitive worlds,' sniffed the Doctor. 'No sophistication.'

'I know, it's awful the way we make our boats just glide along on top of the water,' said Henrik.

The mood on board the Viking ship had turned celebratory. They were congratulating themselves on their daring raid, although they had done nothing more than grab a defenceless girl then run away like rabbits. Olaf, largest of them all and slowest in the head, but tolerated because of his beautiful singing voice, started on a victory song, and Lars, youngest and most obnoxious was explaining to everyone who would listen how he had just been on the point of sticking some of those old men when they'd been forced to leave. A cask of mead had been opened and, although the clouds were dark, the wind was brisk. Erik, their captain, knew these routes like the back of his hand. He would wait till night to navigate further by the stars, but he could tell by the shape of Lowith, falling behind them, exactly which way to point their ship.

Freydis crept towards the hatch entrance. She had piled up the barrows to climb to the upper reaches; there was so much noise above deck with the drums and the oars that she could make as much commotion as she chose without being overheard. And she didn't know who was meant to be guarding her, but he was a lazy pig. When it was Henrik, he'd come and check on her every candle section. Now he was a good guard. She sniffed. This one hadn't even bothered to stoop down to ogle her.

She held the weapon tightly in her fist, until her knuckles turned purple, and concentrated on trying to slow her fiercely pounding heart. She told herself not to fuss; she was a daughter of a king with the Gods on her side, albeit in a roundabout fashion. She had something to fight for. She would turn this ship around, and if they all burned to death in the process… well. At least she would die free.

Steeling herself, she counted to three, then thrust sharply upwards with the weapon.

For what was, on reflection, just a jab on the foot, Freydis thought later, the Viking did make the most gigantic fuss, screeching and hopping around the deck.

Quick as a flash she pushed up the trapdoor and jumped through it, pushing the Viking down below as she went, then charged up to the back of the boat, where Erik sat with a tumbler of mead, one hand on the helm. In the blink of an eye she was beside him – she could smell his heavy, beery breath; the salty tang of his beard and the old leather of his jerkin. Undeterred, she put the point of the knife just behind his ear, on the big lifeline vein that ran there.

'You move, you die,' she hissed in his ear, and nearly broke his skin to make her point.

Erik was a brave Norseman, always had been. But even he had seen too much in the last few hours. There were things going on here he did not understand, and the fact that a princess had appeared from nowhere and was now holding a knife to his throat made him disinclined to fight with her. Anyway, it wasn't as if women didn't know how to fight, however high born they were. His mother had taught him that.

It took the men a short time to respond, but they put their oars down and stared, horrified, unable to act without their leader.

'Turn the boat around!' shouted Freydis, trying to make her voice heard above the noise of the water and the wind. 'We're going to turn this boat around.'

'We are not,' said Lars. 'There's monsters back there.'

'Then I'll kill him,' said Freydis, hoping, suddenly, that Erik wasn't fearsomely unpopular. She didn't want to kill anyone, especially not if it was only going to end up in her being thrown overboard with a rock tied to her skirts and the longship carrying on.

But Freydis got lucky. Erik had been a Viking captain a long time. He had water knowledge in his genes, in his very bones. Every man on board that ship knew that their lives depended on Erik's boundless, handed-down knowledge of the shorelines, the starlines, the period of the year and the moon. They could not get back alone, and every man aboard knew it.

'Do as she says,' grunted Erik.

'But it'll be suicide!' said one of the others. 'They've got fire monsters back there!'

Olaf started up a worried, tuneless humming.

'I know what to do,' said Freydis. 'Get me close enough to land round the headland, not even by the bay. Just get me close enough and I'll swim under the entire way. It's safe. I've done it before.'

There was general muttering. Freydis showed them the glint of her blade, and pushed it into Erik's neck until one, solitary tear of blood showed, the only colour for miles. There was a long pause as all the men watched it drip, deadly and viscous, down Erik's thick neck and onto his leather jerkin.

Then, gradually, complaining bitterly about lost jobs and bad dowries and wastes of everybody's time, the men switched their oars to the left-hand side and, slowly, started to beat the boat around, the dragon head pointing back towards the distant dot of the island.

'No one approaches!' barked Freydis.

'No fear,' said Lars, trying to show he wasn't afraid. The guard Viking was still howling and moaning about his sore foot down in the bows. Erik made a mental note to cuff him later when they were free of this hellcat.

'You're more trouble than you're worth,' he grunted, feeling the sting of her blade resting against his neck.

'I'm not "worth" anything,' said Freydis. 'I'm a free person.'

'I'm not,' sniffed Erik.

'Be quiet' hissed Freydis.

The great ship was nearly halfway turned around now when suddenly, out of nowhere, there was a strange wheezing noise. The men stopped what they were doing and stared. Gradually, a large oblong outline began to materialise in front of them. The TARDIS was square on to them.

Unfortunately, the boat was in the process of turning around, changing its load-bearing capacity completely, and throwing out the Doctor's calculations. The Vikings watched this scene unfold with their mouths open; all rowing ceased immediately. Freydis blinked several times. Was someone inside this thing? What was it? She kept the point of the blade very close to Erik's neck still, daring him to take advantage of the situation.

The big box gave a final *vworp* and materialised finally, solidly, placed diagonally on the deck. Nobody breathed. Then the door creaked open and the Doctor and Henrik popped their heads out; the Doctor to cause a distraction and Henrik to perform the rescue.

'Hello!' said the Doctor. 'Happy Thor's day… it is Thor's day, isn't it? I have some trouble keeping track. Maybe it's Wodin's day…'

After that, things happened very quickly. Henrik pushed past the Doctor with his sword. Freydis gasped to see him and dropped the weapon she was holding.

'Henrik,' she whispered, unable to believe he was here; he had come for her. His eyes were fierce and full of joy to see her.

Then there was an ominous crack. And then another. One of the sailors shouted out, and another stood up and pointed. A plank broke free of its caulking and pinged its way up in the air. Then, as Henrik tried to take a stride forward out of the TARDIS, with a huge bang, the entire box collapsed through, crashing through timbers and the heavy oak hull as if they were made of toast. The doors slammed shut automatically with the Doctor and Henrik back inside.

'HENNNNNRIKKK!' screamed Freydis. And without thinking a second more, she threw Erik to one side and hurled herself on top of the disappearing box, grasping the casing of the topmost light.

'Oh no you don't!' roared Erik, and hurled himself after her, his prize. He grabbed her ankle, as the TARDIS began a steady, inexorable descent below the icy waters, leaving the sailors clinging to a broken raft above their heads, the waves insistently beating them back to shore.

Chapter
Thirteen

The Doctor was working the dials on the console in a panic.

'Come on, come on, it's just a bit of water,' he said, pulling on a lever. 'You're worse than a kitten.'

But there was no denying it. After they'd crashed through the longship, the Doctor had planned to dematerialise at first. But the TARDIS simply would not do it. Neither could he stabilise her. She had become unresponsive to instruments; worse, she seemed to be slowly powering down, even as they continued to sink.

'I thought you'd worked out the weight…' said Henrik.

'Yes yes yes,' muttered the Doctor. 'Interdimensional planetary maths. I wouldn't expect you to understand.'

'But if it weighs the same as a normal box…'

'I'm *very busy* with a complicated manoeuvre involving twisting space stuff two different ways at the same time. So please be quiet!'

The Doctor had managed to slow but not halt their

descent – no more than that – when he called up the screens to look about him.

'Oh no,' he said. 'Oh no, oh no. Oh, thank goodness we didn't dematerialise.'

Henrik looked up from where he had been staring at the console, trying not to think about being trapped in a box at the bottom of the sea.

'By the heavens,' he cursed, as the screen plainly showed Freydis, her eyes tight shut, her hair streaming behind her, clinging to the outside of the TARDIS with all her might – and, behind her, the enraged Erik.

'Come on,' said the Doctor. 'Come *on.*' He banged his fist hard on the console and there was, finally, a faintly cheering *woop* noise as the air pocket appeared. On the screen, Freydis opened her eyes in surprise – and took a deep breath.

'Air field,' said the Doctor in some relief. 'But quick, we're still falling and the pressure is building all the time; I don't know how long I can hold it together… I don't know what's wrong with my ship.'

'It's not very good,' said Henrik.

The Doctor ignored him. 'Hang on, I'll go and get her. Stay here. And don't touch anything.'

The Doctor immediately opened the doors and beckoned Freydis inside, but she was frozen in terror. He stepped carefully out of the TARDIS, clinging to the side and gently inching his way upwards.

Freydis stared at him. 'I can breathe!' she said.

'Yes,' said the Doctor. 'Can you climb down?'

The TARDIS was sinking slowly, almost in a

leisurely fashion, so slowly you could hardly feel it moving at all. Above was the underside of the broken-up Viking boat; the legs of the men kicking it could be seen. The world beneath the waves when one could breathe was an extraordinary place.

Freydis looked beneath her. Beyond the air bubble and the light on the top of the TARDIS which cast eerie pale beams towards passing fish around her who had come to take a look, she could scramble over the roof of the box and down towards his outstretched hand.

'But…' she said. She indicated behind her. Erik was holding on to her ankle with all his might, his eyes wild and bulging. 'Can I shake this thing off so he can have his eyes eaten at the bottom of the briny deep?' she asked.

'Um, no,' said the Doctor apologetically. 'I try and maintain a strict eyes-having policy around the TARDIS.'

'Let go of me, you big oaf,' screamed Freydis looking behind her and kicking him hard in the chest.

'Where am I?' said Erik. His bluster was gone now; he was plainly terrified.

'It doesn't matter,' said the Doctor. 'Just hold on to the big square not-quite-the-colour-of-the-sky-in-spring-nor-the-look-of-a-lip-on-an-icy-day thing till I come and get you.'

Freydis jumped first and landed gently on the rim of the door. Henrik was there to help her and she spun down into his arms, laughing, amazed by how thrilled she was to see him.

'I never thought… I never thought…'

She went quiet as she entered the TARDIS, awestruck.

'It's his ship,' said Henrik. 'It makes you sick and it doesn't work very well.'

'I heard that,' came a voice from outside.

Erik eased himself down the side of the TARDIS with some awkwardness. His breastplate got caught on the corners and he cursed swiftly. As he made to follow Freydis inside, the Doctor held up his hand.

'Now,' he said. 'I don't know exactly what's wrong with my ship, but this air pocket will last about ten more seconds, then anyone standing out here is going to get crushed up by the pressure as every blood vessel in their body bursts and they die in hideous agony. Do you understand?'

Erik grunted.

'Are you going to behave yourself on board?' said the Doctor.

'Yes,' said Erik. 'Yes, I will.'

'And let us make it perfectly clear: by behave yourself I mean, do not, in any way, behave like a Viking?'

'On my blood,' said Erik, spitting on his hand and giving it out to shake.

The Doctor regarded it reluctantly. 'Um, just saying it will probably do,' said the Doctor. 'In you pop. No pillaging.'

*

The air bubble was shrinking and the light growing fainter, as the Doctor came back inside and shut the door. The TARDIS continued, slowly, to fall. Strange creatures flickered past the screens; a huge long body filled the screen, larger than anything any of them had seen before. Its tail nudged the TARDIS gently off course, and a loud beeping came on which made the visitors jump.

Text flashed up across the bottom of the scanner screen: '*100 metres.*'

'I know, I know. I never should have fitted that submarine warning system. Slow afternoon,' said the Doctor, looking around apologetically and pulling out some wires. 'What is *up* with you?'

The central column had completely stopped rising and falling. The lights were dimming. All that remained was the alarm warning.

'It will be our burial mound,' observed Eric, looking around him.

'Well, you're a cheery chap,' said the Doctor. Freydis was wandering around up and down the stairs, touching nearly everything in awe. Then something struck her.

'Loki,' she said, looking at him. 'Did I die?'

The Doctor looked at her shrewdly for an instant. 'You're not the first to think that here,' he said quietly. 'But no.'

'Well, good,' said Freydis. 'Because I'm all wet. I hate to think Valhalla would be wet.'

'You can change,' said the Doctor, indicating the

route to the wardrobe. 'How deep *are* these waters?'

Henrik watched Freydis leave to get out of her wet clothes, then came towards the screen.

'Ragnor says the west of the Isles is the deepest of trenches; that it goes down as far as the world itself,' he said. 'He says the fish men catch there are never otherwise seen and the cold will freeze a man, then the dark will close him in before he'd ever run out of breath in the waters.'

'It's true,' said Erik. 'There are whales here bigger than anything man could ever devise, and dark creatures that have never seen the sun upon them.'

'I wish the TARDIS had ears, so I could cover them,' said the Doctor. The beeping noise grew louder.

The text on the screen changed to: '*200 metres.*'

'Yes, I get it. We're falling down to the bottom of the ocean,' said the Doctor out loud. 'This was the stupidest warning system ever.'

The lights of the TARDIS seemed to dim a little more. It was becoming noticeably colder.

'I have been to frozen worlds and the surface of suns; through airless endless nothingness and negative space,' said the Doctor. 'This is not going to defeat us. It is *not*.'

'*300 metres.*'

'Argh, I am not going to die in metric!' he said out loud. 'Come on, come on, come *on*.'

'It's getting cold in here,' observed Erik.

Henrik had his face pressed up against the screen. From the fading glow from the TARDIS, he could make out the most astonishing things: fish that looked as though they had been made from rolled up leaves, so thin and delicate did they appear; creatures dancing with no eyes; a shoal of phosphorescent sea horses, shining brightly in the blackness.

'There is a world under here I could never dream,' he breathed.

The Doctor looked up from his efforts for a second. 'I know,' he grinned. 'Isn't it fantastic?' He returned his attention to the desk. 'Now, *come on.*'

'*400 metres.*'

There was a tinkling sound. The bulb on the top of the TARDIS had shattered. Now the screens were still working, but only a tiny amount of residual light remained. Henrik stepped away.

The Doctor flicked his screwdriver settings over and over in frustration. 'There is... She's not having any of it. I'm sure this is psychological. She's normally utterly impregnable.' He sat down cross-legged on the floor. 'Normally,' he added.

'*500 metres.*'

'What is your plan now, Doctor?' asked Henrik hopefully.

'I have an excellent plan,' said the Doctor. 'And we shall all be perfectly safe.'

'Oh good,' said Henrik.

'Don't you want to hear what it is?'

'No. Just knowing you are taking care of everything makes me feel better,' said Henrik.

There was a long pause.

'You know there is no plan?' said the Doctor finally.

'Yes,' said Henrik.

Freydis emerged back into the main console room. Gone were her fine, stiff clothes, sodden with salt water, her high, stiff collar and the many folds of fabric that lined the front of her skirts. Her tightly laced girdle and her kirtle had also been discarded, as had her fine jewels and hair combs. Instead she wore a long, very simple cream and brick-red shift that looked clean and soft and comfortable, and her hair was softly tied back, with damp tendrils still framing her face.

Henrik leapt to his feet. 'My lady,' he said.

Freydis shook her head. 'I am no longer a lady,' she said, delighted. 'Look at me!' She twirled around. 'I can move! I can sit! I don't look like a princess! I look like a girl!'

Henrik bit his lip. 'A beautiful girl,' he ventured.

Freydis smiled. 'Do you think so?' she teased. 'Even when all my gold is at the bottom of the sea?'

'I think so,' said Henrik.

'*700 metres.*'

'Looks like we're going to join the gold,' said Erik. But for that instant Henrik and Freydis did not look much fussed by the possibility of being at the bottom of the ocean.

A drip from the ceiling landed on the floor, then another.

The lights inside the TARDIS flickered and flared up and down. The Doctor had seemed to stop attempting to make something happen, and was simply laying his hands on the console.

'Oh my,' said Henrik, rushing to the screen. Outside in the ebbing and flowing glow on a screen that only just still worked, was a shipwrecked boat, its mast still intact, caught on an outcrop of rock on an underwater mountain. Eels slid in and out of polished-looking, reflective skeletons, tumbling cargo. And still the TARDIS continued to fall. 'There is a whole world down here,' he said.

'Not one we can live in,' grunted Erik.

'Full fathom five my father lies,' intoned the Doctor. 'Of his bones are coral made. Those are pearls that were his eyes.'

'What are you saying?' said Freydis.

'It doesn't matter,' said the Doctor. 'It's three hundred years away. And we are at the bottom of the ocean.' The droplets had become a trickle. The Doctor slumped to the floor, his long legs splayed out in front of him. 'Sea nymphs hourly ring his knell.'

As he said it, the entire room rang to the sound of the TARDIS's cloister bell tolling.

'Hark now I hear them,' said the Doctor, a hollow laugh on his lips. 'Ding dong bell.'

The TARDIS finally settled down heavily, billows of silt obscuring the screens, making a place for itself deep in the ocean.

The bell tolled once more.

'What does it mean?' said Henrik.

'Ha, well,' said the Doctor. 'Somewhat redundantly, the TARDIS cloister bell tolls when we're in grave mortal danger.'

He retrieved a saucepan from a cupboard and put it under the drip.

'One thing at a time,' he said. He went forward and stared at the screen. There was very little to see.

'Why can't you just dematerialise?' he said. 'Why can't you move? What's stopping you? It's not a little bit of fire, I'll tell you that for nothing.'

'Maybe it didn't like falling through the boat,' said Henrik. 'Recognised superior workmanship.'

'Thank you, Henrik,' said the Doctor. He patted the console. 'Come on, old thing. We can get out of this, can't we?'

The central console had gone dark and silent. The others looked around.

Erik sniffed. 'Whoever heard of a closed boat? No wonder she can't stay on the right side of the sea.'

'She's a fine ship,' said the Doctor fiercely.

'Oh, good,' said Erik. 'Get her to sail us away, then.'

'I will do exactly that,' said the Doctor, and he stormed away from the main console. It took a shout from Henrik to bring him back.

The lights from the TARDIS were nearly all faded; the console room felt cold and dank and very bleak. Freydis had gathered her cloak around her and gone to sit next to Henrik. She was frightened, of course she was; frightened half to death. They were leagues underneath the water, so far away from the possibility of safety. Yet, somehow, she felt slightly safer if he was there. But Henrik had got up, pacing back and forth, as if he could somehow stumble upon a solution. And pressing his nose up against the screen, he had seen something.

'*Dong!*' The cloister bell tolled again. And whatever it was, in the distance, glowed green and pink in response.

'*Doctor!*'

Chapter
Fourteen

The Doctor emerged into the console room somewhat more slowly than his usual long strides. His progress was impeded by the huge, heavy diving boots he was wearing. Over this he wore an old-fashioned diving suit, mustard in colour, that covered his entire body and buttoned with old-fashioned brass poppers at the wrists and ankles. Under his arm he carried a large round brass helmet, complete with bolts, that attached to a long tube at the back. He looked rather extraordinary.

'Fantastic, non? My friend Denayrouze gave it to me.' He looked down at it. 'I wish I'd made some new diver friends. I knew I shouldn't have turned down the invite to Jacques-Yves' wedding.'

The bell had stopped now, but the light still glowed in the distance.

'I think...' said the Doctor. 'I think these may be our flame-happy friends. Who made themselves known to us before.'

'Won't they burn you up?' said Freydis.

'Well, no,' said the Doctor. 'They don't burn underwater. Anyway, I only want to talk to them.' He peered at the screen again. 'Have you ever seen a light like it?'

Henrik shook his head. 'Not till I saw that little thing you carry.'

'Quite,' said the Doctor. 'There shouldn't be anything like that here yet. Not from Earth, anyway. So let me go and have a word.' He patted the TARDIS. 'Now,' he said. 'If I discover everything's all right will you take us home?'

The console did not respond at all.

'OK,' said the Doctor. He turned to Henrik. 'Now. Listen. This is very, very, very important. *Very* important. Important. Do you understand?'

'That it's important?' said Henrik.

'Exactly. He catches on quickly,' said the Doctor to Freydis. He took out the enormous pump system. 'This is an air pump. It pumps air down to the suit so I can breathe, do you understand? So if you stop pumping or fall asleep or decide to go wandering off, what is going to happen to me?'

'You'll die,' said Henrik.

'That's right! I'll die! Shortly followed by all of you. *So—*'

The Doctor demonstrated the correct pace and method for pumping. Erik eyed them sullenly from the corner.

'You can all take turns,' said the Doctor.

'I don't see the point of that,' said Erik. 'We're just

prolonging the inevitable.'

'Come on,' said the Doctor. 'Where's your Viking sense of derring-do? OK. Now there's only a tiny, tiny bit of power left for the air pocket. So don't go near the door, do you understand? Otherwise you're going to have a whole lot of ocean in here.'

Henrik nodded. The Doctor advanced to the door, and Freydis helped him screw down the huge, heavy helmet.

'One tug for yes, two tugs for no,' said the Doctor. 'Three tugs for "pull me back". Lots of tugs for "I am being savaged by a previously unsuspected jellyfish army".' He turned around and caught sight of himself reflected in the glass of the console. 'Hmm,' he said. 'Now I will go and terrorise Scooby Doo.'

'What?' said Freydis.

'It doesn't matter,' said the Doctor. 'Just keep the pump pumping, please.'

Henrik was already working on it. Very quickly, the Doctor pushed against the door. There was perhaps 30 centimetres of air pocket ahead. Enough for the door to remain open a crack to let the hose give out. There was barely a glow ahead, so the Doctor lit his screwdriver to point the way. He tugged once to let them know he was all right, then, feeling the weight of half a mile of water on his head, forced one heavy boot in front of the other and started his lonely journey.

The two points of light only highlighted the vastness of the territory. The Doctor could feel what a young ocean this was; boundless, infinite with life – with large life, he realised, as a heavy shoal of cod nearly knocked him off his feet. He bounced lightly through the sand, amazed as always how close it was to spacewalking; unable, even whilst he knew he must hurry, to stop from examining some of the more unusual species he came across.

'You are all so anxious to explore the stars,' he said. 'Don't have the faintest clue what an unbelievable world is right underneath your feet.'

He breathed comfortably through the tube. Nice work, Henrik; air was flowing at a good rate

The light ahead grew a little closer. Down here, it was very difficult to judge distance. The Doctor hoped he could reach it before his air hose ran out. Well, that was something to worry about when he got there. He paced onwards, ever onwards, turning back to glance at his TARDIS. It looked small and inconsequential, its light fading, as if it were deliberately trying to appear as insignificant as possible. The Doctor frowned. It didn't make sense. But he sensed the answers were ahead of him, not behind, and he trudged on; a small figure against the vastness of the ocean bed; heading from one tiny point of light on the planet to another.

Back in the TARDIS, Erik was angrily punching at buttons.

'Stop that,' said Henrik.

'Why?' said Erik. 'If these things make this ship work, then I'm going to try them, aren't I?'

'He said not to,' said Freydis.

'He said not to,' mimicked Erik nastily. 'I don't know when you turned into someone who always did what they were told.'

'As soon as he came and saved me,' said Freydis simply. 'From you.'

Erik twisted a lever. Something made a cranking sound. 'There we go,' he said. 'Turn a thing and something happens, look, whatever infernal machine it is.'

'No,' said Henrik. 'Oh no you don't.'

Erik looked up, fixing Henrik with a look through his shaggy brows. 'You want to fight with me, boy?' he said, quietly.

Henrik looked back.

'No,' said Freydis suddenly.

The Doctor stopped; with every step, sand that had never been stepped on whirled and flowed around him. The silence was deep and dark and absolute. He blinked and checked again to make sure he really was looking at what he thought he was looking at.

'Well well well,' he said. 'That really is quite something.' He leaned in a bit closer. 'Hello!'

While Henrik and Erik were eyeing each other up, Freydis had crept up on Erik's right-hand side, almost silent in her bare feet, across a floor now covered in water, and now she whisked the axe out of the belt pouch that went round Erik's generous middle.

She jumped back and held up the axe.

'It's not that Henrik wants to fight you, Erik. It's that we both do.'

Chapter
Fifteen

Seen up close, the light resolved itself into the shape of a fountain. It had a broad, round base, with several prongs leading up from it. The shape and the fountain itself were made up of what looked like a loop of blue-green light that flickered round and round upon itself, like a very peculiar art installation on the bottom of the ocean.

'You know,' said the Doctor, 'you would make a very fashionable table decoration for someone. With a gigantic table. In the future.'

The green lights pulsed.

'Ah, I'm only teasing you,' said the Doctor. As he got in closer, he saw what he had not noticed before, but confirmed his theory. The light was not in fact one unbroken beam, but constant streams of billions and billions of zeros and ones, running too fast for the normal eye to see.

'You are very beautiful,' said the Doctor, shaking his head in admiration. 'Look at you! People would come from miles around to see you. Well, we did.

DOCTOR WHO

Admittedly, it was miles *down*, which wasn't exactly what we wanted, but…'

Slowly, he circled round the fountain, which grew upwards and stretched out to let him see it, gradually altering into the shape of a magnificent oak tree under the ocean.

'Oh yes, very lovely. You're showing off now,' said the Doctor, his voice full of admiration. Then his tone changed. 'And what on *earth* are you doing?' he said, coming back to himself. 'People are dying! They're dying. You're killing them. And you *must* know you're doing it.'

In the deep, dark impenetrable silence of the bottom of the ocean, a whisper could be heard, a rustle and hum. The Doctor listened carefully.

'I know,' he said. 'I know. But it doesn't take away from the fact that you are becoming a monster. A big, beautiful monster.'

The green light stretched itself out and became an enormous sandworm, stretching back through the ocean.

'Enough of this,' said the Doctor. 'Stop it. Arrange yourself so we can have a bit of a chinwag.'

The light paused for a moment, then compressed itself into an exact replica of the Doctor in his diving suit, the light trailing off in a hose shape behind itself, the zeros and ones so close as to give the image of a real glowing figure.

The Doctor bowed. 'Of course,' he said.

The lights shimmered again then changed into the

Doctor's previous regenerations.

'Yes, yes,' said the Doctor. 'And you know me too. Well done. But you know a lot of things, don't you?'

The lights settled into a roughly human shape without detail.

'Consciousness of Arill,' he said, 'I am the Doctor and am pleased to make your acquaintance.'

He bowed, and the figure bowed back.

'You are a race of pure consciousness – you need networks to survive; limitless connections of power to race around. You live as ghost webs and trolls and throng cyberspace and endospace and any form of non-physical existence. Is that correct?'

The figure nodded.

'I know you! You love war planets; anywhere with huge government budgets and extra capacity and people not paying attention to you, where you can parasitise on energy sources without causing too much trouble. You can be a bit of a nuisance, but you don't normally cause trouble.

'But you are here. Why are you here? You can't do anything here! There isn't even going to be any electricity on this planet for a thousand years. There aren't going to be any networks or webs or zaguts or extended intelligence byorbs for centuries, millennia. You are ridiculously, embarrassingly early.'

The Doctor paused, as he listened to the breathy hisses and whispers.

'Yes, well, you should never trust satnav, everyone knows that.' He stood back. 'You've made a terrible,

terrible mistake and now you're stuck, all billions of you.' He shook his head. 'What on earth am I going to do with you?' His face was stern.

'We need to reach out. We need to continue the line.'

'Yes, down wires and connections and electricity and power lines. Which, as I keep telling you, this planet doesn't have yet!'

'We sense power. We sense electricity.'

'Yes, in their brains. Tiny amounts of electrical impulses. You've been experimenting with them, haven't you? But it's not going too well, is it? Not enough power for the billions of you. You keep burning them up.' The Doctor looked around the ocean floor. 'And all those poor turtles! How many have you killed already?'

There was a pause.

'We found the animals were not suitable to our needs.'

'But the humans?'

'We have only just begun. Sometimes we are too slow, sometimes too fast. We can wait. We can be patient.'

Poor, poor Eoric, thought the Doctor. To die for an experiment.

'You can't! You're a great big ball of rolling intelligence that can't stop moving!' he said, as the Arill rearranged itself into a giant billowing whale. 'You'll blow through them all, and you still won't find what you're looking for. And I'm not letting you pick them off whilst you get it through your huge and beautiful heads that it's not going to work.'

'But the humans can learn to do what we do; to think

from one to another; everything knowable at the one time. It is heaven.'

'No,' said the Doctor viciously. 'It is hell.'

There was a long silence.

'You must help us,' said the Arill. *'You must help us, Doctor.'*

'I know,' said the Doctor. He grimaced. 'Why can't you survive in air?' Then he answered his own question. 'Because you burst into flames. That's what you're trying to do. Reach out.'

'Continue the line.'

'Flames through solid air. Through people. Through everything, except water.'

'We must move.' It sounded as if the entity was in despair. *'We. Must. Move.'*

The Doctor thought about it. 'You're wanderers,' he said. 'But you also destroy. You swarm the circuits of a planet and get in everyone's way and slow everything down and feast on power lines and connections and suck up information until everyone gets sick of you and you travel on once more... you're like locusts.'

'We are merely travellers,' said the Arill. *'Those who travel are always despised.'*

'No, those who take and do not share are despised,' said the Doctor. 'All this knowledge and information you have... and you use it to try and steal electricity from the brains of a few islanders? Knowledge is nothing without wisdom, you know.'

'This costs us too. We have also sacrificed many sons.'

The Doctor meditated. 'Where could I even send

you? Who would want to take you in? All the planets developed enough to take you don't want you zipping up and down them.'

'Help us,' said the Arill. *'Help us. You can help us. You have something that can help us...'*

Slowly, the lights of the Arill began to pull together, and it shifted and became denser, squarer and tall and...

'No,' said the Doctor. 'Absolutely not.'

Then, suddenly, it became clear.

'No wonder she was playing dead. The poor thing. Trying to hide herself. She knows she's the only source of power in the world. You knew that the billions would feast on any source of power they saw. Oh, my poor TARDIS. So clever, but they spotted you. They targeted you.'

He squared up to the Arill TARDIS once again.

'You want my ship?'

'We want to leave.'

'When you've sucked the life out of her and left her for a husk? Not a chance.'

'Then we must travel through people.'

'You will fail.'

'We will experiment. They will adapt. Learn to live with us.'

'I don't think so.'

There was a long stand-off.

'Then you must help us, Doctor,' came the voice.

Inside the TARDIS, Erik had moved quickly. He shot

back with his left elbow and caught Freydis full in the stomach, then backed away from Henrik.

Henrik couldn't move; he was stuck, pumping at the same pace. He knew he couldn't stop, not even for a second. But if Erik advanced on Freydis... Henrik's heart was thudding painfully fast. He tried not to pump too quickly; he knew too much air could be just as dangerous for the Doctor as too little. But a tiny part of him knew he was trying to overcompensate; trying, on one level, to apologise in advance. Because if Erik moved on Freydis once more, he would leave his pump and defend her, even if it would lead them all to certain death.

The TARDIS was creaking and making noises, as if it wanted to move; as if she was trying to get away from something. She was firing herself up again. Erik moved round to the opposite side of the console and poked and prodded buttons at random.

'We'll get out of here,' said Erik. 'She knows when she's in the presence of a real captain.'

'No!' screamed Freydis, launching herself at him from the corner of the TARDIS. She charged over and jumped on his back. 'We're going to wait for the Doctor.'

Henrik pulled frantically on the air line. But it was too late. The TARDIS was already making a wheezing noise.

Sensing something, the Doctor turned round to see the wobbly lines of the police box in the distance start to ebb and fade.

'*Running scared,*' observed the Arill. '*I don't know why. We only want to make friends… Come and stay for a little while.*'

The Doctor gazed, helpless, then felt the pull on his airline. 'Yes, yes,' he muttered, impatiently. 'You're in trouble. I can see that. Go. Run for it, please. Escape. Don't stay here. Go for it.'

'*Without you?*' said the Arill. '*We are not the only ones who aren't wanted.*'

The Doctor smiled ruefully. 'Can you make yourself into the shape of a decompression chamber?'

'*The shape is not the thing,*' observed the Arill.

'No, of course not,' said the Doctor. 'It's just, two hearts… I run a lot of blood.'

'*And your brain,*' said the Arill ominously. '*You run a lot of brain.*'

Inside the TARDIS, all was desperate chaos. Freydis had leapt on Erik's back and he was biting her hand quite painfully. Henrik was trying to reach them. The TARDIS's central column had begun, tentatively, to move up and down. Henrik gave the tiny air pocket that held the pipe one final, pained look, then leapt from his post, diving for Erik's legs and bringing them all tumbling down in a heap.

'Freydis! Get the pump!' shouted Henrik, punching Erik as hard as he could in the stomach, but meeting with his heavy leather jerkin.

Erik wasn't letting Freydis go quite that easily; he

grabbed her foot again, and made her trip up.

'Gah!' shouted Henrik, sinking his teeth into Erik's leg. As Erik bent down to try and free himself, Henrik grabbed his hair and pulled it as hard as he could. This wasn't the most adult way of fighting, he realised. Lots of sword training hadn't exactly prepared him for this. But he would do what it took.

Freydis was kicking desperately, impeded by her bare feet, until Henrik managed to get a hand free and banged it repeatedly down on Erik's wrist, digging his nails into his wrist until, for a second, he let go. Freydis paused only to kick him square in the face then made a desperate dash to the pump, leaving Henrik and Erik desperately wrestling on the floor. But, just as she reached it and put up her hands, before she could press down even once, there was a sudden snapping sound, and the TARDIS doors slammed shut, breaking the air pocket and leaving a length of hose, severed, useless, and lying on the floor.

The hose, which had been pulled nearly taut, suddenly slithered down and skittered to the ocean floor. The Doctor looked at it. There was a pause. He looked up at the Arill.

'*How can you save us?*' said the entity. '*How can you save us now?*'

The Doctor spoke slowly, trying to conserve the remaining air. He could already feel the water starting to weigh him down; trickling into his helmet. 'You could try and save me.'

'*Under the water we are powerless,*' said the Arill. '*You cannot make the surface in time. The shape is not the thing. You are no use to us. We must extend the line. The line.*'

All of a sudden the lights started winking out on the form it had made for itself. It faded and faded and started to drift – and then it was gone. And there was nothing but heavy, freezing blackness all around, as the helmet filled with water, and the Doctor took his very last breath.

Chapter
Sixteen

The TARDIS dematerialised, then rematerialised almost immediately, still, Henrik realised, in the same place. With a final determined shove, he tipped up Erik and knocked him over, cracking his head on the stair.

'Quick,' shouted Freydis, throwing him the old leather belt from her wet dress. Before the stunned Erik realised what was happening, Henrik had tied both his hands behind his back to the metal balustrade. He added his own belt just to be sure.

'Shall I punch him unconscious?' asked Freydis. 'I expect I could.'

'I don't doubt it,' said Henrik.

They smiled at one another, but only for a second.

'We have to save him,' said Henrik, rushing for the doors.

'I'll... I'll make it go,' said Freydis, running to the console, and staring, completely flummoxed, at the buttons and levers. She tentatively pressed one and the TARDIS bounced to the side. 'Well, we're moving,' she said, trying to put a brave face on it.

But they were plunging through nothing. The TARDIS bounced all over the place.

'We won't be able to. We can't open the doors, Henrik. You have to realise, it's not possible.'

'But this is his ship,' said Henrik. 'Look how strange it is. It might even be able to find him. Go right!'

The TARDIS heaved and bumped. Freydis pulled up quickly. She looked at Henrik.

'When I fell into the water, down into the sea, before... Henrik, it is a terribly long way down,' she said. 'Terribly, terribly far. I do not know... no one could survive it.'

'Don't say that,' said Henrik. He peered at the screens, but nothing could be seen but great clouds of silt, as the TARDIS lurched here and there in confusion and Erik came round and started making angry threats from the other side of the control room.

The helmet had stood up well, the Doctor reflected. Not bad for something over a hundred years old. Its bolts had wobbled a bit, but it hadn't imploded. Of course, that would mean death took a little longer. He decided to lie down. He didn't have to breathe yet – as Martha Jones had once discovered his lung capacity was extraordinary, but a respiratory bypass system could only work for so long. The time was coming. The only sound was his pulses flowing, slower and slower. Apart from that there was silence; utter, pitch-black and total silence.

He wasn't about to give up, and things could be worse. He wasn't bleeding. Nobody was shooting at him. He could say his goodbyes to this lifetime from the comforts of a seabed... perhaps he could regenerate into something with gills... mind you they didn't go with his white hair... like those silmarillions... he didn't have white hair. Did he? He couldn't remember. He couldn't remember any colours, though he was sure he had seen them all. Some with names, some without.

He was being lulled... lulled and called home... full fathom five my father lies... of these the pearls that are his eyes...

'Ding dong bell,' he murmured with his very last vestiges of breath. 'Ding...dong...'

Vworp.

The stuttering glow was nearly gone, but it was enough.

'*Go ahead! Go ahead!*' Henrik had nearly screamed.

'I don't know how!' said Freydis, turning the handle this way, then that.

The TARDIS stumbled full length, then righted herself, then came to a halt mere paces from where the Doctor lay, pinned down by his boots and helmet, motionless in the sand.

They stared at the screens. The figure of the Doctor was prone in front of them.

'How...'

Erik looked down on them from where he was tied,

laughing. 'Well, there's a pickle,' he said. 'How long are you going to stay here looking at a dead man?'

'You close that mouth of yours,' said Freydis. 'Don't think I can't order Henrik to cut your head off.'

Henrik squinted. 'Well, actually, I don't think…'

'Ssh. We're wasting time.'

'I'll swim out,' said Henrik.

'You can't,' said Freydis immediately. 'You'll be crushed. It can't be done. I've been down there. It gets heavier and heavier until you can't move at all.'

'Only the dead walk the seabed,' said Erik. 'Mind you, you wouldn't mind if you were together, would you?' He made a noise that was somewhere between a cough and a guffaw.

'He must have another suit,' said Henrik boldly.

'Up there,' said Freydis. 'He has all manner of the strangest things I have ever seen.'

Henrik followed her finger to the wardrobe and charged up the stairs. The wardrobe was beautiful – he had never seen so many lovely things: the fine fabrics; the jewelled colours; the sheer careless riches of velvet and wool. But in his head it was a jumbled panicky dream as he desperately scurried around for something that would serve.

If the Doctor could possibly be alive… was it possible?

Chapter
Seventeen

Henrik had never been meant to be a Viking. That honour was reserved for the sons of the great and the good; the soldiers, the well born. He was a farmer's boy, tending the goats in the fields two days from Trondheim. His father was a man of few words, his mother from farming stock too; his brothers seemingly happy to chase every last minute of light through the long dark winter; to rise with the lark; to accomplish the same tasks from morning to night; season after season; moon turn to moon turn.

Henrik, though, was different; he dreamed his life away at the plough. He loved nights in the long hall when old men told stories of long ago battles; great triumphs and exciting voyages across the surface of the Earth. To be a Viking was the most courageous, the manliest and boldest thing one could do with one's life, and Henrik admired them intensely.

As his father pointed out, someone always had to tend the soil and milk the goats and care for the land the returning heroes would come back to; laden with treasure, and beautiful wives and stories of great escapes and unimaginable landscapes; worlds covered by rock, or sand; lands completely flat, or ripped by the highest mountains; great monsters slain.

But they had no need of farm boys.

Everything changed one day in the final days of light, just before the thick winter darkness enclosed them for months. He and his brother Johannes had gone ice fishing, hoping to catch some fresh mackerel; some to salt for the long weeks ahead, but some, they hoped, to grill for dinner, fresh and hot, with crackling skin and juicy eyes.

He couldn't remember how it happened. It wasn't quite midwinter, and they had had storms; the water had churned faster than usual, perhaps, postponing its full, deep freeze. Or perhaps he had not been as careful as he ought, in his eagerness to catch supper, the last chance at fresh fish. But he had grown up on the ice; was as nimble on it as a clawed beaver. He knew its depths and its polish, the tell-tale shades of lighter whites and greys that told you it was not strong; that there was danger and moving water nearby; when it could be cracked with a rock, or slid over on your cloaked knees, however much you knew your mother would tell you off.

That day, though, as he stepped out from his warm hearth, a good breakfast of meal and milk and honey in his belly, the white skies were still hinting at unsettled weather. And something had gone wrong.

By the time he heard the crack, his body was

already plummeting, halfway down; the crack a mere resonance in his head behind the desperate pain and shock of the icy water. It was like falling onto the point of a sword. He tried to scream, and water instantly invaded his throat, dirty ice clogging him up. After that, he lost the ability to consciously do anything. He was dimly aware, somehow, that there was a fishing rod above him, thrown, he realised, by his brother Johannes. He was, he knew, supposed to grab it. But the idea of being able to lift an arm that no longer seemed a part of him, that was no longer under his control… He could no more have lifted the riverbed.

Johannes was lying flat on the ice screaming at him, calling something out, trying to reach with his hand, but it meant nothing to him. He thrashed, a little, but then, suddenly from underneath, he felt the river reach up and grab him, like a huge hand, powerless to resist, that shoved him underneath the ice.

It was an odd experience, he found, to be underneath the ice. Even as he beat at it once or twice, and felt the terrible, terrible tightness in his mouth and throat, the panic as his gorge rose – even then, as the river pulled him on its way, he found himself regarding himself; in terrible pain, and the cold and the terror; this is it, he found himself thinking. And he tried, like a Viking, to face his death without fear; even as he tried to sob; to blink; to beat it back. He tried to take one more choking breath; to die a brave man, not a foolish boy who had fallen in the river. The pain and tightness in his chest was a terrifying brutal agony, for what seemed to be an endless time.

Then, nothing.

The sound of weeping awoke him. Inside, he felt as if he had swallowed a stone; a hard cold stone that could not dissolve. Later, Johannes told him when they brought him in, his eyelashes were separate and stiff, each individually frozen into a tiny icicle.

'And you were all grey and your skin was black,' Johannes said wonderingly, revelling in his role as witness to the terrible disaster. 'Mother shrieked like a Valkyrie.'

Johannes had alerted the first men he came across, in the fields across from the fjord, who had scrambled to his aid, even if they knew it was hopeless. A body in that river in winter would live less than five minutes. Nonetheless, they scrambled down the banks, one giving a great shout and pointing when they saw the unmoving figure.

The motionless form of Henrik had washed under the ice, coming to snag in the roots of a great old oak, by the side of the river where the ice had not yet formed. They hauled him out, crawling down a long log they carried to the side; shouting words of encouragement and hope, even as inside each they felt nothing but dread, carrying the stone-cold boy back home to his mother, wrapped in a rough jerkin.

His mother was having none of it. She put her boy beside the fire, in a cedar bath heated to the highest temperatures. The women of the village came as fast as they could, and rubbed and rubbed at his hands and his feet and his head, and refilled the water, and boiled the cauldron and closed the shutters and filled the room with steam and point blank refused to take the cold as a death.

Johannes always told proudly of how he stood at the back of the room, unnoticed, growing hot in his sealskin jerkin and knitted hat as, gradually, the miracle started to happen, and slowly, perilously slowly, the frozen boy twisted and jerked his fingers horribly; then his toes; the statue coming back to life like some twisted, unholy marionette.

Screaming with the pain of his nerve endings coming back to life, Henrik slowly opened his eyes and gasped for each breath, accompanied by the desperate hacking weeping of his mother.

Henrik always knew after that that there were many, many things in the world that nobody understood.

And even before his sore stiff fingers were properly mobile again, he became the miracle; the boy who returned to life. Stories were told, and word spread quickly beyond the village, with many people coming to see him. After two weeks of being confined to his bed by his mother, during which time he grew thoroughly bored of being poked and prodded and wondered over – he was desperate to move again. The great stone of ice in his heart that he had felt upon waking had almost melted to nothing – almost. There remained a tiny shard of flint that would never entirely leave him. And then he was summoned to Trondheim.

The physicians of Trondheim wore elaborate outfits in cloth of gold with high scarlet collars and plumed hats. They hummed and hawed and poked him. The priests of the new religion too came to see him, but his mother was having none of them. Finally, the physicians led him out to the fine jousting fields at the bottom of the orchards and bade him run and jump and perform gymnastic feats; and he was so delighted to finally be out of the house, that he did all of those things for all he was worth.

'You can do anything,' declared the head physician finally. 'What would you like to do, young man?'

And Henrik saw his chance, and he took it. No more farm. No more ploughing. No more goats.

'I want to be a Viking,' he said, as bold a nine-year-old as ever crossed the court.

At the sound of the startled commotion, the little princess, taking her morning constitutional with her nurse, turned suddenly in the direction of all the noise.

'What's that?' she demanded imperiously.

'It's just some farm scruff,' said her nurse, pushing her onwards. 'Nothing for you to bother your head about.'

'Is it the Miracle Boy?'

'There's no such thing,' scoffed the nurse. 'Now, hurry up. If you're late for your dancing master, he'll make you quadrille from now till Tuesday.'

Princess Freydis had scowled and stamped her

little foot, as was her wont, and her nurse ignored her, as was hers.

Back in the TARDIS, Henrik stumbled over an enormous crinoline – which he did not recognise – and was on the point of giving up in despair when he spied a huge orange suit – a spacesuit, although he could never have known. To Henrik's eyes it had the same big, all-encompassing head as the diving suit, and a strong body cover, and that was good enough for him. He hurried back to the console room, working the unfamiliar zips and poppers as he did so, Freydis dashing to help him

'The sand has run out of this hourglass,' commented Erik occasionally, but they tried to ignore him, their fingers sweaty and clumsy in their haste. The enormous helmet came last. Both of them were nervous putting it on.

'I'll just hold my breath,' said Henrik. 'I don't know how it works or anything.'

But in fact, as soon as the helmet plugged in, it automatically connected to the air supply on the back of the suit.

'I can breathe!' said Henrik excitedly. 'I can breathe in here! I can't see, though.'

The visor was totally black. Fiddling with the buttons, Freydis pressed one which cleared the visor. Then another that opened it.

'Oh!' she said in surprise. She closed it again. As she did so, a light beam came on on Henrik's helmet.

They all jumped a little.

'Never-ending marvels,' gasped Freydis, as Henrik moved his head to and fro, fascinated by the stream of light.

'Quick, open the door,' ordered Henrik. The TARDIS helpfully lit up the lever. 'As quick as you can. Go. Now. Now!'

Freydis blinked quickly. Then, just as quickly she pressed his visor twice again, leaned up on her tiptoes and kissed Henrik quickly on the mouth.

'Gods be with you,' she whispered, then as Henrik lumbered to the door, she threw the same lever the Doctor had before.

Immediately, a great wall of water collapsed inside the TARDIS. Henrik bent his head and pushed his way through it, heavy in his astronaut costume. The water coursed through, a great waterfall pouring in.

Freydis closed the door; to her amazement it slammed shut without difficulty. The water sluiced away. She watched it vanish into cracks in the doors and down the corridors. How big was this strange place? Where did it go? Then she ran to the screens. Henrik was walking towards the prone figure of the Doctor, slowly and carefully. He bent down as he reached him. Freydis and even Erik watched, holding their breaths.

Suddenly there was a massive flurry of activity. The silt rose up, making everything difficult to see, but something was moving. Freydis blinked, trying to make it out. The figure of the Doctor seemed to be jerking and moving about. In fact… he was fighting him off.

'It's Henrik!' screamed Freydis pointlessly at the screen. 'He's *saving* you, you idiot.'

Erik gave out a hollow laugh.

'Doesn't get much right, your young sweetheart.'

Freydis whirled on him. 'He's braver and better than you could ever be,' she hissed.

There was a pause.

'And he's not my sweetheart,' she added, but not before Erik gave a knowing laugh again.

'I'm sure your father the King will be delighted with this news,' he said.

Freydis grit her teeth, watching the struggle onscreen, her heart pounding. 'I am leaving you at the bottom of the sea,' she spat.

'Well, I'll have company,' said Erik.

'This is why I never sleep. No one ever *lets* me sleep.'

The Doctor had felt – for the first time in a long, long while – relaxed. That was the word. Relaxed. He wasn't tense, on the run, shouting, saving. He was comfortable. A little cold, but even that didn't seem to matter. Whatever happened next, this was the most comfortable, most relaxing feeling he had ever known. Nothing could scare him or chase him; nobody even knew where he was. He had tried opening his eyes, experimentally, just to see if he still could; at first it was hard to tell if he had his eyes open or not; the darkness was numinous; without stars or definition; almost as pure a void as deepest space.

Then, suddenly, without warning, a great beam of light swept across him. His eyes blinked and his reflexes all strained – all of them – to take a breath. Yet somehow he managed to override them, as he noticed behind the light the figure of an astronaut.

No. He thought. Not here. Not again. Astronauts coming from the sea he hardly dared remember. And he must not, because the need to think suddenly brought awareness that his lungs were burning and his chest was filled with a terrible tightness.

He lurched towards the figure and attempted to bring it down. But Henrik, bolstered by his air supply and no stranger to men panicking in the water, was too delighted by the Doctor's signs of life to give it much credence. He put to the back of his mind the thought – not the thought, the definite, absolute knowledge – that there was absolutely no way that any man could have survived without air for as long as that. He would think about that another time. Now he had to do one thing and one thing only. He picked up the weakened Doctor, ignoring his waving arms and legs, and carried him back to the TARDIS, like a tantruming child.

The now useless hose from the Doctor's suit billowed behind them as Henrik turned back towards the TARDIS, gently lifting his hand to indicate that they were safe and coming home.

Almost instantly, the Doctor went floppy in his arms, and Henrik started to move as fast as he could under the pressure and his heavy suit.

*

'He's got him,' said Freydis, gasping in relief.

'He's got a corpse,' grunted Erik.

Henrik was lumbering his way back to the TARDIS.

'What do you mean?' said Freydis.

'You know,' said Erik. 'Who could be alive after that?' He paused. 'So what is he now?'

The knock at the TARDIS door, even though she was of course expecting it, startled her much more than it should have done.

'You're going to let it in?' said Erik. 'The man carrying the monster.'

'He is not a monster,' said Freydis.

'He is *not* a man,' said Erik.

'He is a God,' said Freydis, her voice sounding doubtful.

'And you're sure he's on your side, are you?'

Freydis paused. Henrik knocked again. Freydis shot her eyes to Erik, who was leering at her.

'On your pretty head, your highness,' he said.

'Oh! Thor take you,' she shouted, and slammed on the door-opening mechanism.

This time, the wall of water swept the two figures into the TARDIS on a great wave, catching Freydis too, who was standing in its way. She just managed to press the door-closing mechanism before rushing to the two figures, getting caught up in the freezing water swirling around them, sliding into the room and collapsing on the floor.

Chapter
Eighteen

Freydis found blankets in the wardrobe, and they crouched round the console, on the far side from Erik. Henrik had stayed dry in his suit, but both the Doctor, whose suit had started to leak, and Freydis were soaking.

'Hem,' said Henrik, clearing his throat. 'You know, in Tyholt… when one is very cold… it is considered the best thing to do to warm up a cold person is to put them close to a warm body…'

His face was pink and he was stammering. Freydis gave him a very distinct look. He may have got to know her better since the shipwreck, Henrik reflected, but she was still a Princess of Trondheim. He deeply regretted having mentioned it.

'Go to him, then,' said Freydis with a chill in her voice that had nothing to do with the state of her dress.

Henrik swallowed hard and turned towards the figure on the floor. As he knelt down beside him, the Doctor slowly stirred, spluttering and coughing sea water onto the floor. When he saw where he was he just, for a moment, looked ever so slightly rueful – then he smiled. Then he fell asleep again.

When he awoke once more he was wrapped in blankets and Henrik was scouring the place looking for something to make a fire.

'How on earth does he manage?' he complained. 'How can he make a fire when he's cold? This is a terrible ship.'

The Doctor coughed a little croakily.

'Um… bit warmer, please,' he said.

The TARDIS console glowed orange and the temperature in the room immediately became noticeably hotter.

The Doctor looked around. Then his face lit up as he realised what had happened.

'You didn't *save* me?' he said.

Freydis and Henrik tried to look modest, and failed.

'You did! That's amazing!' He leapt up, seemingly completely recovered. 'Here you are, down at the bottom of the sea, all the way from the Dark Ages…'

'The what?' said Freydis. 'You mean the modern ages.'

'Of course,' said the Doctor. 'You live in the most modern of modern times.' He lowered his voice. 'Everyone thinks that, you know,' he said in a stage whisper. He looked around again. 'Thank you from the bottom of my hearts.' His gaze alighted on Erik, tied to his post. 'Oh, Erik. Have you been doing naughty Viking stuff again?'

'He tried—' started Freydis.

'Hush, hush, no tales,' said the Doctor, jumping up and trying, ineffectually, to get the water off his clothes.

'Can we leave him here?' asked Freydis eagerly. 'Can we go somewhere in your ship and leave him here?'

The Doctor jumped up to the console, carefully wiping up any remaining seawater.

'I know,' he said crooningly to the TARDIS. 'I know you hate the wet stuff.' He pulled a lever and the console lit up again, the threat of the Arill having disappeared. 'Yes! Now let's get you somewhere dry – and out of sight. I wish you'd told me you were hiding from the Arill.'

He checked a screen readout which displayed a three-dimensional picture of the Arill; a connected stream of binary light, just as they had been underwater; constantly shifting and moving; never still. The display showed them infiltrating the systems of a distant world, taking over their connections, their air space, their communications networks; gorging themselves on its power, taking every iota of its knowledge and information and leaving it a husk. There was almost no power source it couldn't drain; no reactor so strong; no power resources so seemingly limited.

'They would suck up a sun,' said the Doctor wonderingly. 'And yet they're here. What a wrong turn. But they can't stop being hungry. They'll feast on anything and everyone they can get. Unless we all start living underwater. But that doesn't happen till the year 3000.'

He turned to face the others.

'They say that knowledge is power. Well, they don't say it yet. Someone will say it. And they'll be right.'

'Pliny said it,' said Freydis.

'Did he? You know, he drones on so I never listened to half of what he said. Anyway. Great. Yes. Knowledge is power. And to these guys, the Arill, that's all that matters. Evolution; maintenance of the species. It all requires power. And they'll get theirs from any source available. Continue the line, you see. But in your world – fabulous though it is, don't get me wrong – the most powerful weapon; the most powerful minds; the most powerful computational machines; the most powerful lifting equipment – it's all you. It's all people at the moment. And they'll feed on that if they have to.'

Freydis blinked trying to take it in. 'You mean… the thing that sets things on fire…'

'It's not a thing,' said the Doctor. 'It's a species. Just like you, only with less interesting hair. But instead of living off the land, or domesticating animals, it lives off power. The electrical impulses that power many worlds. There aren't many here… but the strongest are in your brains.'

'Are they in everything's brains?' said Henrik.

'To one extent or another.'

'Hence the dead turtles?'

'Yes. Hence the dead turtles. Now. We have to get back—'

'Are we leaving him?' Freydis pointed at Erik.

'No,' said the Doctor wearily. 'We're not leaving him. You're not half bloodthirsty, even for a Viking princess.'

'He has done me wrong.'

'That's what Vikings do,' said the Doctor. 'If only there was someone who could make it up to you. From a Viking perspective.' He coughed meaningfully.

Freydis deliberately didn't look at Henrik, who was trying to stop his face going pink.

Erik snorted. 'And you're going to get us out of this funeral pyre are you?' he said, deliberately looking at the overflowing saucepan. 'In case you haven't noticed, there's water still getting in.'

'Is it?' said the Doctor. 'I thought the swimming pool was leaking again. OK!' He whirled round, all his positivity restored. 'Who's ready?'

'Are we going to defeat these... Arill?' said Henrik.

'Well, we'll have to think of something,' said the Doctor. 'They can't hang around here, that's for sure. But they're not evil as such. They just have a problem distinguishing humans from turtles, but they're not trying to be bad. Well. They steal and ravage planets and plunder all their power and leave them for barren waste. But some people think that's quite romantic.'

And with a dramatic flourish, he floored the TARDIS's handle and she dematerialised with a great,

happy wheezing noise, leaving the great black expanse
of the ocean floor as quiet and deep and alone as it had
been for millennia before.

Chapter
Nineteen

Underneath a massive, thick springy bank of heather near the great white beach of Uig on the very western coast of Lewis, on the outer Hebrides, there is a small sandy cave.

If you didn't know it was there, you would never find it. Perhaps if you were walking your dog, on one of those glorious, heart-stopping mornings when you forget your entire holiday so far has been wet and cold, even though you knew it probably would be wet and cold but you came – or were made to come – anyway, and have stopped even trying to dry out your coat in the evenings, and, secretly, you're rather enjoying playing Scrabble (the TV reception is absolutely rubbish and they don't even have a satellite dish) and huddling in front of the wood-burning stove your friendly host lights for you each evening.

Then one morning, just as you had all started half-laughing about the ridiculous amount of rain you get up here and how maybe next year you would holiday in Antarctica, you wake up and the entire world looks fresh off a washing line.

It's a great big sprawling canvas that doesn't use the normal palette, but has as many shades of grey and green and white and blue that can fade in and out of each other; the sky is bigger and wider than you can ever remember seeing before, and the world smells of warm gorse and bright sand and salt of course; always salt. The salt carries on the breeze, but the sun, even now, shines warmly on your back like a benediction, or a reward, earned through enduring the ceaseless rain.

So you take the daft dog, who is the reason you couldn't go to Spain in the first place, and you head out early and by yourself, much earlier than you would wake at home to the alarm and the bus stop and the traffic; and you head out across the endless beach – there is just one other group of people there; a man in a very long scarf who appears to – he can't be, surely – throwing sticks for a small metal dog whilst a young brown-haired girl in a miniskirt and knee high boots claps and bends over laughing, but that cannot possibly be the case, so you decide to just give the crazy people a wide berth on this perfect morning, and follow your own real dog, and breathe in the air, and feel the daft cares and worries of the rest of the world fall right away; you can't even get a mobile signal.

Then your daft dog disappears up into the dunes and, even though you know he's unlikely to get eaten by rogue hares, you follow him up to make sure. You can hear him barking his head off – it must be the rabbits, surely – but you can't see him at all, so you scramble down the sand and prickly gorse, trying to follow the sound. Nothing; where is he?

And then, unexpectedly, you find yourself tripping over a tiny cairn of white stones outside a great outcrop of heather. Nothing to see at all; except you can still hear your dog barking, right in front of you. You push your hand forward… and find it pushes through the heather; that there is a tiny cave, under the dunes, that no one would ever find unless they knew about it or had a really dumb dog.

Excited, you push your way through.

Inside the cave, it is sandy and shaded; a perfect place to hide.

But there is nothing there. No litter, no footprints, no markings on the walls. By the looks of things there has been nothing and nobody there for hundreds of years. The dog is chasing his tail, sniffing round and round a square, but there is nothing there and no sign that anything ever has been. For a moment… for a moment, you admit to yourself, you were a bit excited. You thought there might be something inside… an adventure. Buried treasure. But that is silly. It's just a cave; an empty cave. You tell the dog to hush.

And anyway, it is a beautiful, perfect day on Lewis, and there are bacon sandwiches for breakfast and beach cricket to be played, and a real holiday to start, and it's time to get back to the croft before everyone wonders where you have gone.

*

The Doctor finished building the small cairn out of stones. There was a big arrow pointing towards it. Next to it, he'd spelled out, again in stones, 'THAT THING IS HERE. YOU KNOW, THAT THING.'

'What's that for?' said Henrik.

Even Henrik had been grudgingly impressed when the TARDIS had materialised out of the bottom of the sea into the little sandy cave. He hadn't wanted to let Freydis go out on her own and had tried to go before her. She had given him a look, and darted forwards anyway. Then they were under the waterfall of heather and plum in the heart of the island.

'It's so I don't forget where I hid her,' said the Doctor. 'It's very important the Arill don't get a grip on my ship. She's the most powerful thing in this solar system at the moment. Well, at any moment. But right about now, a few Chinese fireworks aren't going to prove much distraction against a neutron flow simulator. She can protect herself, of course.' He patted her. 'But they would bombard her; bombard her with an endless fire. They wouldn't win, but it wouldn't be very pleasant. I won't have it. I shan't.'

Henrik was a quick study, and had already found it easiest to nod along to the fifty per cent of the Doctor's conversations he didn't understand.

The Doctor let his hand rest on the TARDIS. This was the right thing to do, he was sure of it. He didn't dwell on the fact that from now on he would forget her very existence; might never find her again. If you didn't risk everything then you risked nothing at all.

He had lived by that for long enough now.

He turned to face the others, smiling, and ushered them all outside, even Erik.

'He's not coming,' said Freydis.

'Well, you shouldn't have broken my ship, then, should you?' growled Erik.

'You,' said the Doctor, manoeuvring himself about. He turned this way and that, then licked his finger and stuck it in the air. 'Your men,' he said. 'They're washed up over… *there*. Go see to them.'

Erik wrinkled his forehead. 'And how could you possibly know that?'

'Oh, you know. Seasonal tides, phases of the moon.' He winked at Henrik. 'It's useful for pub quizzes.'

Erik muttered, but headed south in the direction the Doctor had indicated.

'I hope he is eaten by a bear,' said Freydis.

'There aren't any bears here,' the Doctor pointed out. 'Look. No trees. No woods. Bears require woods for their… ahem. Anyway. Now. To work.'

He took a deep breath, then hung a perception filter on the TARDIS's external phone.

Henrik blinked. 'Where's your ship?' he asked blankly.

'What ship?' asked Freydis.

The Doctor finished off the little tor outside, then followed them to the path. 'West,' he said. 'We must go west.'

All the villagers were standing on the beach, in silence.

They wore their newest robes, and even the little children were quiet, cowed by the import of the day.

Hayn, the town Elder, had closed his eyes and dressed him – though the body was in such a terrible state, it had proved very difficult. How difficult, he would never tell Corc. He put iron coins over his eyes and swathed the whole in hessian.

Corc stood at the front, his hand on his sword. He had shed no tears, but his eyes were drawn and anguished, white with tiredness and lack of sleep. Luag had been staying with Brogan; he made absolutely no pretence at hiding his feelings, and had cried almost continuously. The women of the village had muttered that the boy needed his family – the only family he had left – at a time like this, but no one would have dared mentioned it to Corc.

And now it was nearly time. The other Viking had been quickly buried in a shallow grave towards the heart of the island, unmarked. But Eoric had people to mourn him.

Four of Eoric's young friends, considerably more cowed now than they had seemed before, carried the bier down to the ship. No one wanted to comment on how light the corpse was. It barely needed two to carry it. Gently, and reverently, the young men placed the body onto the already prepared longboat.

Although normally the longboat burial was kept for chieftains, it was generally accepted that, as Corc's heir, and the boldest and the bravest of the young men of the settlement, it would have come to Eoric eventually. And as such, anything less than the highest of send-offs would do a disservice to their leader and to their homeland.

Dyed cloth was placed upon the boat, and a clasp of finest worked bronze. Everything they had that looked glorious and was of value was there to bear Eoric to the land of the Gods; to ensure he was placed there as befitted his status.

Corc had made it clear that there could be no doubt that he had died in battle, protecting them all. His own private doubts about how much of Eoric had been in that horrifying, walking thing he kept entirely to himself, as he lay, sleepless under the star-lit sky.

All the riches did not detract from the sorry state of Eoric, but nobody mentioned it. One by one, all the settlers came forwards, starting with the women and children – some more willing than others – and gently kissed him. Then the men came, raised their swords and bowed their heads, saluting a warrior. Finally, Corc stepped forwards.

He stood at the top of the boat and bent his head. Then he clasped the forehead of his ruined son.

'My boy,' he said, his voice cracking, unsure if he could go on. 'My son… you were the pride of me and of our land and our seas and the joy and the swell of my heart. As the sun breaks the horizon of our Samhrains and the moon rules the depths of our Beltanes, you will be in our minds and in our—'

His voice went completely and he could not continue. He looked up, his eyes ghastly and red rimmed.

'Take… take him away,' he gasped, as the four bearers came forward to cover the boat in light, combustible straw and launch it.

Behind them, however, a tiny figure was flying down.

'Eoric! Eoric! I never got to say goodbye! You didn't let me say goodbye!'

It was little Luag, who had not joined the procession. Corc caught him in his arms.

'Let me go! Let me go! I hate you! You killed Eoric! Set me free.'

Luag kicked and pushed frantically against him, till Corc set him down then he splashed into the shallow tide and jumped up on the side of the boat.

'Take me, Eoric,' he said. 'I'll come with you! We'll sail to the gates of the Gods. And we'll have mead together and play and you can teach me how to fire arrows and it'll be great.'

He was weeping steady tears, his voice desperate.

'And you can be my brother and we can play again.'

Finally, Brogan took pity and splashed into the water after him, gathering him up in her voluminous chest and soothing him as if he were seven months, not seven years.

'There, there,' she said, shooting a look at Corc, whose face was so twisted in pain it was as if he hadn't even noticed what had just taken place.

The Elder was still intoning the rituals and muttering as the boys got the boat launched out on the water, though not too far; they were still mindful of its dangers. The burning torch was brought forward from the bonfire and silently handed to Corc, who took it, his own fist trembling, and stepped forward into the waves.

For a second, everyone paused. The only sound that could be heard was Luag's quiet sobbing.

The Doctor, Freydis and Henrik had arrived and stood respectfully at the back of the mourners, patiently watching. For an instant, it looked as if Corc might, like Luag, attempt to jump on the funeral bier. But, after staring at his son's ruined form for a long time, he turned his face away, and gave the boat a shove. At the same time he hurled the torch into it.

The alcohol caught at once and sent a billowing rush of wind into the sail, which started to blow the boat off into the greater depths of the sea.

The villagers stood back watching, as the sun set over the distant horizon, and the longboat, now a trail of fire, grew smaller and smaller; heading north west, out to, they fervently hoped, the long happy lands where everyone feasted and hunted and loved and was merry and sat at the high table; and their plate was always full with meat and fruit and bread and honey; and their glass never emptied, and warriors enjoyed eternal victory over death.

As the fire faded, crackling more and more quietly, it was clear that the settlers were watching the boat for another reason too. There was a tension in the air, as she was allowed to pass unmolested almost the entire length of the bay.

Almost.

When it came, it was quick and merciless. A line of fire joining itself to the already lit ship. Fast, indiscriminate, utterly without mercy.

'No!' cried the Doctor, unable to help himself. 'No! We *talked* about this! There's nothing even there!'

He strode to the beach, furious.

'You do not despoil our dead,' he shouted.

'He has joined his Gods,' observed the Elder.

'They're not Gods!' shouted the Doctor, exasperated. 'They're... they're stupid blithering idiots!'

Everyone watched as the funeral bier suddenly, against the heavy grey skies, showed a perfect, charcoal outline of itself, holding, just for a moment, the very memory of its shape in smoke. Then, suddenly, it collapsed like powder, the ashes blowing here and there; coming to rest, gently, and bobbing on top of the waves.

Corc approached the Doctor, pain heavy in his face. 'You said you can help us. Can you help us? I do not want to lose anyone else's sons.'

The Doctor bit his lip. 'Of course I can,' he said. He looked out to sea. He had an idea. Whether it would work could only be reckoned in carrying it through. 'When' was, at the moment, the far more pressing question.

Henrik stood beside them. 'A storm is coming,' he said gently, looking out to sea.

'Oh yes,' said the Doctor. 'Oh yes.'

*

There was no funeral feasting. Corc had forbidden it. This was not a glorious ascendancy. He could find nothing to celebrate in a life that had hardly begun.

Also, they were running low on food. They had not, in the end, salted much of the turtle meat. It was not as good as fish. And their trading partners were still warned off by the two braziers on the eastern shore. Which meant that they could be safe, but also that they lacked the trade from the inner isles and the mainland. No wood, no wool, no meat, no barley. And no fish; now the animals had stopped washing ashore and they dare not fish. And it was Beltane; the world was on the turn. The long summer was at an end, and the long winter, where it was dark for many months; would soon be here, and they had nothing salted, nothing stored.

There were no good winters. But this one looked to be as hard as anyone could remember. Anything they could keep back, they should. Or perhaps, thought Corc grimly, it didn't matter. Perhaps the fire would take them all before their bellies did. At least they'd die warm.

The Doctor and Henrik took over the long hall.

'I need pacing space,' said the Doctor. 'The low-roofed stuff, it's no good for me.' He glanced at Henrik.

'Look how tall you are,' he said happily. 'Best diets humans ever had, your lot. You're about to move into larger conurbations and go really tiny for centuries.'

Henrik frowned. 'So, this thing...'

'The Arill, yes.'

'You say it can't survive in the open air?'

'No. It overheats. Supercombusts. Bursts into flames. That's what we're seeing. It's not deliberate. Well, not really. It's just looking for an escape passage. Unfortunately, it tends to use anyone who comes along.'

'So can't we just lift it out of the water somehow? Fish it out?'

The Doctor reminded himself that Henrik had not truly seen the scale of the thing, nor understood it.

'Well we could,' he grumbled. 'If we had one of those outlawed OMNEEFEESH planet-sized net rigs they banned in Calissima. It turned their oceans from teeming with life to devastated sandscape in point four of a parsec.'

He thought about it some more.

'Doctor?'

'Yes?'

'Can I ask you... What Freydis says...'

'What *does* Freydis say?' said the Doctor. 'I am, of course, an expert in matters of the heart.'

'The way you talk...' Henrik started to say.

'Is perfect, actually,' said the Doctor. 'And old Norse is very, very difficult. Second only to Calprinthina Upper, and that is spoken entirely by squeaking your hand under your armpit to a variety of subtly different pitches.'

'The way you talk,' continued Henrik, determined to get to the end of a sentence, 'about things. And when Freydis keeps saying you're a God… You don't exactly say yes, but you don't exactly say no.'

'Hello, Doctor,' said Freydis, entering the hall with her head bowed. 'Oh, that poor boy. That poor family… what's left of it.'

The others agreed, nodding silently.

'I cannot *believe* these clothes,' Freydis said eventually, to change the mood. 'So comfortable! I'll be baking bread next.'

She glanced at Henrik.

'The Doctor and I were just talking,' said Henrik.

'About women!' said the Doctor jauntily. 'I know loads.'

'Really? Her captors must have had better locks on their longboat cages,' said Freydis.

'Well, that's just plain rude,' said the Doctor. 'Anyway, we've finished now. So give me some space here, I need room to pace up and down.'

Freydis and Henrik watched him for a while as he walked from one end of the room to another, occasionally muttering words they didn't understand, like 'connectivity' and 'electrical charge'.

'What's he doing?' whispered Freydis.

'He says he's thinking,' said Henrik.

'Did you ask him?'

'Um, I was just about to.'

'I'll do it.'

Freydis stood up and stepped directly in front of the Doctor, breaking his stride.

'We need to know,' she said.

Her large eyes blinked, and her strident confidence suffered a little now they were face to face, as he turned to look at her. This Doctor had a very peculiar habit of being suddenly able to give you total attention, as if there was no one else he would rather be talking to; as if everything and anything you could possibly say was of the utmost importance to him. Suddenly she found herself uncharacteristically a little tongue-tied.

'With everything you do… everything you have…' Her voice wobbled off. To say it out loud now sounded impossibly rude. She quickly cut her eyes to Henrik.

'She thinks you might be dead,' said Henrik, coming to her rescue.

'What kind of a God are you?' said Freydis at the same time.

'Dead or a God? Are those my only two options?'

'Don't you think we deserve to know?'

'Yes,' said the Doctor. 'Yes, you do.'

He stopped pacing, and leaned against the space in the wattle and daub wall that was open to the sky. The salt smell blew in, and the Doctor took a deep breath. The air here, unpolluted by anything worse than a few peat fires… it was so fresh it was intoxicating.

'You know the stars in the sky?'

'Those points of light?'

'Yes.'

'Well. Those points of light are other star systems… like your sun. That big orange ball that you see up here once or twice a year. Well. Other planets are out there. And people, and other species, and things, and entities and all sorts… Oh, there is a *lot* out there. Really. A lot.'

Freydis frowned. 'And is it really, really small?'

'What? Oh. No. No, just far away.'

'How far?'

'Far. Far far far far far far far far far far far… oh, it is really terribly difficult to explain this to pre-Galileans. You live on something called the Earth. It is a planet. There are many planets with many different people living on them.'

'And they aren't all like us?'

'You catch on fast. No. They aren't all like you.'

The Doctor waited to see if the penny would drop. Freydis's mouth opened in amazement. Here it comes, thought the Doctor.

'So you *are* a God.'

'No! Well… in a manner of speaking.'

'Why won't you say one way or the other?' asked Henrik.

'Because…' said the Doctor, wriggling his foot. 'Well… Because… I suppose… Once upon a time… I might have been messing around in the sixth century and helped out some of your Icelandic friends and, well, I was a lot younger then. A *lot* younger. You should know that. And perhaps Edda the bard was watching, and, well, I had a few nights out and maybe I played a silly trick on him.'

'What kind of trick?'

'It was late, there was honey mead…'

'Doctor,' said Henrik.

'Well, maybe I shot him.'

'You *shot* him?'

'With mistletoe. Well, to be quite honest, I persuaded this other chap to shoot him. A blind chap. Was an amazing shot actually. No one could believe he'd pull it off. Hilarious.'

'Of course,' he added, 'totally irresponsible, I wouldn't do it now. Very much my younger days. And Edda never did see the funny side.'

'The funny side of being shot with mistletoe?'

'Maybe you had to be there.'

'And he thought you were a God?'

'He never could get my name right.'

'So he sang you in? To the sacred rhymes?'

'It appears so,' said the Doctor, blushing slightly.

'But wait,' said Freydis. 'The Gods are as old as time.'

'Well, we come and go a bit.' He straightened up. 'I'm not a God. I am a Lord. I'm a Time Lord. I can travel in time. But I'm not a God and I don't live for ever or have magic powers, apart from my astonishing brain, thank you very much. There is no such thing as magic. I am a traveller. I travel through worlds and through space…. just not much through sea.'

'Not at all through sea,' said Henrik

'Thank you, Henrik,' said the Doctor. 'But over all the universe and throughout all time.'

Freydis looked him up and down. 'Well, that's good,' she said coolly. 'Can you destroy that thing under the sea, then, please? Is it also from another world?'

'Ah,' said the Doctor, taking out his sonic screwdriver and fiddling with it. 'Well. Yes, it is. And no, I can't.'

'Why not?' said Freydis. 'If you're a Lord. Lords are powerful.'

'I am' said the Doctor. 'So I try not to destroy things. Ahem. More often than is strictly and morally necessary.'

'So you can travel all over the universe and impersonate a God and you know all this and you cannot save this place?' said Freydis.

'I could figure it out,' said the Doctor. 'If you would just let me get on with my pacing.'

Freydis looked at him. 'You're no less of a slave than I was,' she said.

The Doctor looked back at her. 'We all have our code to live by, Princess. And for as long as you are here, you are free to choose your own. But if yours is vengeance, you must know that we cannot be friends.'

Freydis took this in. There was a long silence.

'You know,' she said finally, 'how Loki dies?'

'Just Edda's little joke, I'm sure,' said the Doctor, looking out of the window. 'You know, I think I'm going to try some pacing outdoors.'

'How does Loki die?' said Henrik, who'd had little schooling and found the workings of humans were quite puzzling enough for him most of the time, without having to worry about the Gods as well.

'He doesn't,' said Freydis, watching the Doctor lope down the muddy pathway. 'He is condemned to swallow poison from the tail of the great snake of the world. For ever. Or till Ragnarok, the end of everything.'

Henrik glanced out of the window. 'Well, he seems reasonably cheerful about it.'

'Not everyone screams and shouts when they are sad,' observed Freydis.

Chapter
Twenty

'VENGEANCE.'

To the chilled, damp and hungry men huddled together on the south side of the island, burning gorse twigs to keep warm whilst Olaf, who was a bit of an idiot, pranced around trying to catch a rabbit, the reappearance of their old captain didn't inspire as much confidence as Erik would have liked. 'He's the one that got us into this mess' seemed to be the general consensus, as well as the unavoidable truth that if he hadn't offered to fight the native people, then ordered them to kidnap that hellcat, they would be sitting cosily round the blazing village fire right now, eating barley stew and bread and maybe even charming a young lady.

But instead, here they were, shipwrecked for the second time in as many days. It was a miracle they'd all made it to shore alive; the boat had stayed just about afloat, even with a massive square hole in it, to transport them all, kicking wildly, back in with the tide. And round this side of the island, nothing seemed to have set them alight yet.

'Come on, little rabbit,' bounced Olaf relentlessly, who was convinced that running about was the best way to get warm, not huddling. A drizzle had commenced, and the sky was grey and murky, with no sign at all that the weather might change or the clouds might lift in time for anyone to get some sleep.

'WE SHALL STEAL UPON THEM WHILST THEY SLEEP,' continued Erik mercilessly.

'Well, we'll have to,' observed one of the Vikings, Lars, to another. 'We won't be.'

'AND GET OUR REVENGE! WE SHALL FIND THAT DEMON THEY CALL DOCTOR AND WE SHALL PURGE HIM! WE SHALL DELIVER THE PRINCESS IN CAPTIVITY TO GISSAR! WE SHALL SAIL AGAIN TRIUMPHANT.'

'Didn't he notice the enormous hole in our boat?' said Lars.

Erik fixed him with a beady eye. 'Do you have something cowardly to say?'

'No,' said Lars hastily, unhappy to be under the gaze of his tempestuous captain.

At that moment there was a yell from Olaf. In chasing one rabbit, he'd inadvertently stepped on another. It wouldn't be much between nineteen men, but it was definitely a start.

Erik looked at his cold, hungry men, and cursed. This wasn't how Vikings should be. But he had been a boat captain for a long time and knew that raiders needed to be fed. He divided them up into one or two hunting groups, and sent the others to forage for dandelions and anything else they could find in the harsh land that might boil up. Eventually, they came up with five strapping rabbits and enough edible leaves for a salad, rigged the sail up over some bushes to form a makeshift tent to protect them from the rain, and set them up to cook over the fire.

'Now,' said Erik, once everyone was a little cheered by the fire and was getting some meat inside them. This is what we're going to do...'

The Doctor was taking a thinking stroll just as the drizzle began. He couldn't bear the inaction.

If he really was a God, he reflected, slightly crossly, he could control the weather. He blinked the rain out of his eyelashes and decided just to ignore it. Everyone was inside, out of the way. He wondered if the long winter was spent mostly like this: indoors as much as possible; spending the summer trying to get as many provisions together as possible. Life was so hard, almost impossibly hard. And yet it prevailed. He allowed himself a half smile.

Down by the water's edge, he saw a small seated figure. At first he wondered if he was seeing things, but no. There was definitely somebody there. He advanced.

'Hello?'

The figure turned round. It was Luag.

'What are you doing?' asked the Doctor, politely ignoring the fact that Luag was clearly having a massive cry.

'I was trying to draw the headland,' said Luag, showing the Doctor his flint and slate. 'But the rain keeps washing it away. And that's why I'm sad,' he said crossly, rubbing at his face.

'I understand that completely,' said the Doctor. 'But I wish you wouldn't sit so close to the water. It's not safe. Did nobody say?'

Luag shrugged. 'I don't know where my dad is. And Brogan is busy. I haven't seen her.'

'I thought she was looking after you.'

'I don't need anyone to look after me.'

'Of course you don't,' said the Doctor. 'You are, after all, seven. So we both know that.'

Luag bit his lip and stared into the distance.

'Shall we sit here for a bit?'

'Won't you get wet?'

'Time Lords love getting wet. It's one of our things,' lied the Doctor.

'I don't mind it either,' confessed Luag. 'Sometimes it's like being alive.'

'Just like it,' said the Doctor.

'Storms are even better,' said Luag. 'I think one's coming.'

'Do you know when?' the Doctor asked eagerly.

'Nobody knows *when*,' said Luag. 'When your ears do popping usually.'

'Yes,' said the Doctor. 'Come and tell me if your ears pop, all right?'

Luag nodded seriously.

'Why do you like storms so much, anyway?'

'Well, when it's storms or raining, you can run and scream and nobody can hear you.'

'Shall we do that?'

Luag eyed him carefully. 'Grown-ups don't run about and do screaming.'

'Who says I'm a grown-up?' said the Doctor. 'Perhaps I'm just unnervingly tall. Come on!'

And they both stood up and screamed their injustices to the sky, and ran around. The Doctor showed Luag how to pull up his outer clothing, as the Doctor pulled up his jacket, over his shoulders to catch the wind and make them run faster, and they charged in circles at each other, laughing and growling and rumpusing in the fast-fading light.

Henrik was cleaning his sword, carefully, with a square of fabric he'd found in the room for just this purpose. Freydis was still at the window. He looked up as the rain came on, a great grey curtain pulled across the land.

'Back home,' she said, gazing at the dull haze, 'they'll be getting ready for winter, don't you think?'

Henrik smiled and nodded.

'They'll be taking the wheels off the carts and putting on the runners... My ladies will be finishing up fresh stitching on the furs.'

Henrik raised his eyebrows. 'Indeed.'

'Well, what would you be doing? If you weren't at sea?'

'I'd be breaking the ice off the cow's water barrel, milady,' said Henrik. 'Our lives are not the same, yours and mine.'

'Nonetheless,' pouted Freydis. She sighed. 'These muddy souls don't even care.' She had seen Luag tramping out earlier in the heavy rain, all alone, and had called to him but, by the time she'd got outside, he had gone and she had thought, getting drenched, that he would have been on his way to another homestead.

'You know it never snows here,' she said. 'I cannot imagine, can you? A world without snow? Just this eternal fog of grey. No bursting bright days when everything crackles and the town houses shine and the reindeer trample through the undergrowth, and onto the old road and into the square. They wear cloth of gold,' she reminisced, 'at holiday feast times. They look so very smart.

'My nounou makes the best honey cakes,' she added. 'They are sweet and bright and we eat them warm in the morning in front of the fire, then put on our skates and go and play on the stream. One year it froze solid from Beltane to early Mars. They roasted a boar on the ice. And there were races, flanked by the hot wine sellers, do you remember, at the Frost Fair? It was *such* fun. We sponsored the young men with dyed gull feathers.'

Henrik didn't say anything. His life had not allowed many visits to frost fairs.

Freydis sighed dramatically again. 'And now I will be here for ever.'

Henrik didn't say anything.

'Although,' she went on, 'it was not always parties. I worked too. I would be forced to sew, and to sing, and talk politely to the fat old men who visited the court, even though they stank to Valhalla itself and bored me to crying.' She smiled coquettishly at Henrik. 'Would you make me sew and sing, Henrik?'

Henrik continued polishing his sword, the tips of his ears turning very pink; he had found a stone, too, and was sharpening it as best he could.

'You don't answer me,' said Freydis, displeased. 'Why not? You are my only friend here.'

Henrik looked up. 'Do not coquette with me, milady,' he said, quietly but with utter determination. 'We can be friends, perhaps. And if I can help you, I can and I will. Always,' he added fiercely, almost to himself. 'But do not tease me with your honey cakes, and sleigh bells and for something that can never be.'

Freydis felt her heart pounding furiously. She moved away from the window. 'But...' she said. 'But why do you say it will never be?'

'Because,' said Henrik, 'either we shall all be killed by the fire, or we shall recover, and fix up the ship, or make a new one; something must have been washed ashore. And then you shall continue, or go home, and I shall continue, or go home, and we never more shall meet and you shall forget you ever met me. So do not toy with me.'

Freydis took a step towards him. Her voice now was serious too. 'I do not toy, Henrik.'

He looked at her. 'You are teasing me,' he said. 'You are rich and high born and you are teasing a farmer boy who was lucky enough to be chosen.'

Freydis shook her head in dismay. 'The handsomest, bravest boy,' she whispered, 'who was ever born on a farm.'

And she stepped up till she was standing right in front of him, and tilted her head towards his and suddenly he felt, in his hands, the weight of the beautiful hair he had dreamed of; her pale throat and the line of her jaw, and her soft mouth, the palest pink; the shade that haunted his dreams; and then he kissed her, fiercely.

Raining or not, there was still food to find. Braan had left at first light, and Brogan was on her own in the homestead, pounding meal in front of the fire. Luag had been sleeping in the alcove – he had been awake half the night; she had been dimly conscious of him there, tossing and turning. Dozy from her broken night, she found herself staring into the fire as she wondered about one day having her own little boy to cuddle and hold – one as sweet and as smart as Luag, but never, ever so sad. Braan could teach her own little boy how to hunt and fish and forage, and she would make him sweet rabbitskin slippers and make sure he was cosy and warm tied in his bag all the long winter, close to his mother. It was a happy reverie. At first, she barely heard her name being called.

'Brooogannnnn,' the voice hissed. She thought it

was Luag, unaware that he had slipped out, pained and unsleeping, moments before.

'Brooogannnnn,' the voice came again.

'Why?' she found herself thinking, woozily. 'Why is the fire speaking to me?'

'Luag! Come here, Luag! It's time! Come to me! Come and eat!'

The Doctor and Luag stopped running about, and Luag tilted his head.

'Is that the woman who's looking after you?' said the Doctor.

Luag shrugged. 'She never comes and calls for me,' he said. 'We just eat what is in the pot whenever we like. She doesn't really mind.'

'Well, she's obviously worried about you,' said the Doctor. 'It's nice. She'll have something nice and warm for you.'

Luag bit his lip. 'I'd rather stay with you.'

'Run along,' said the Doctor. 'Get a good meal in you and get dried off. It's not good for you to be in those wet clothes.'

Luag gave him the look of someone for whom wet clothes were as much a part of life as day and night, but still lingered reluctantly, unwilling to leave his new playmate.

Afterwards, the Doctor could never think of how close he had come to ushering Luag off cheerily to his death with a word and a wave.

*

If it hadn't been such a grey, miserable wet day, they probably wouldn't have noticed right away. If there had been some sunshine in the air, her glow wouldn't have stood out against a bright day. But it was not a bright day. It was grey and damp and chilled; it was funereal. And night was coming on. In that sombre atmosphere, Brogan's eerie iridescence was immediately obvious.

The Doctor blinked twice, his heart sinking. 'Oh,' he said. 'Oh, Brogan. I am so very, very sorry.' He put Luag behind him.

Brogan moved towards them. Her eyes were strange; no longer the blue-grey common to all the islanders; they now looked orange, reflecting the flames dancing behind them.

'Come on, Luag,' she said, her voice hissing and strange. Inside, she felt warm and powerful; wonderful. She needed to share it, to pass it on. The voice from the fire had told her what to do. 'Come and join the line.' She stretched out her wide, comforting arms towards him.

Luag poked his head out.

'Don't you dare,' said the Doctor sharply. He was startled by how nearly he'd made Luag go to her. 'Don't you dare. You stay behind me, OK? You stay here. You keep me between you and her.'

'He needs to join the line.'

The Doctor marched up to Brogan.

'Come, hold my hand,' said Brogan. 'Or perhaps a little kiss?'

'What are you trying to do?' he shouted at Brogan's eyes. 'I know you can see me. This is *idiocy*. Humans are not a network.'

'They can be,' said Brogan. 'We can join their brains. Jump from one to another.'

'But you burn up the host! Faster and faster! You can't get it right!'

'So we must keep jumping. Moving on. What happens to those left behind does not matter, as long as we keep moving. Surely you understand that, Doctor?'

'Let me help,' said the Doctor. 'Please. Let me help you.'

'What can you do for us?'

'You are a huge, powerful and intelligent omnipresence!' said the Doctor. 'Against a small island of mud, spears and two thousand, four hundred rabbits! It's not exactly easy!'

'That is why we are making our own arrangements,' said Brogan, stepping forward again.

'Oh no you don't,' said the Doctor, leaping backwards.

Arill-Brogan shot out a hand and set a patch of gorse on fire.

The Doctor shook his head. 'That won't help you.'

His attention was drawn suddenly to a figure standing high on the dune. Slowly, carefully, Arill-Brogan turned her head to where he was looking.

The figure stood there, outlined. It was Braan. Her young man. Her beloved.

'My love,' she called out. 'Come quickly! Help!'

Braan started to run down the dunes towards her.

'Nooo!' screeched Luag. 'It's not her! It's not safe!'

Braan pulled up as Luag tried to get in his way.

'It's not her.'

'Help me!' screeched Arill-Brogan. 'He tried to attack me.'

The Doctor put his hands up in an expression of surrender. 'I did nothing of the kind,' he barked. 'I didn't touch her! And Braan, listen to me. Neither must you. You *mustn't*.'

Dripping with sweat, Braan stood in front of them, making a third point of the triangle between the Doctor and Brogan. The Doctor had shouted at Luag to return to the village, but he was still there, keeping well back.

'Look at her,' said the Doctor. '*Look* at her. Really look at her.'

Blinking, uncomprehending, Braan turned to look at his beloved.

And then he understood.

'No,' he said. 'No no no. Brogan, my love. What have you done? What have you done?'

His eyes filled with pain, he turned to the Doctor.

'Help me, my love,' said Brogan in an imploring tone, in that odd, husky voice. 'Please help me. Please just hold me.'

'You can't,' said the Doctor, fixing Braan with a look. 'If you do, the same thing will happen to you. Do you understand? The same thing. Then to another, then to another, then to another, until everybody is dead.'

'Please,' said Brogan. 'Please.' She stepped forwards.

The Doctor also took a step towards Braan then, shook his head; put his arm in front of Braan's chest.

'I must go to her,' said Braan

'You must not,' said the Doctor. 'You must not. Please. It is not her. As soon as the fire took her, she was already gone.'

Braan's eyes filled with tears.

'It hurts,' said Brogan suddenly in the choked voice, as if her vocal chords were withering like dry leaves. Suddenly, though, she sounded like herself and not like the Arill. 'It hurts, my love.'

The glowing in her grew stronger, and her foot started to smoke. She let out an unearthly scream as the three stared at it.

'No,' said Braan, lurching forwards. 'No!'

'You cannot!'

Brogan fell, writhing in agony, to the ground. The Arill were moving through her far faster than they had through Eoric. Now the burning could be seen through her flesh; her shrieks were becoming demented.

'THE LINE! THE LINE! WE NEED THE LINE!'

Luag had crouched on the sand several metres away and had covered up his arms and ears.

The Doctor was holding himself in front of Braan, who looked half-crazed, to stop him trying to save her. 'She is gone,' he said.

Braan shook his head and straightened up. 'She is not,' he said, drawing his bow at the tortured figure.

'Please, my love.' Brogan continued screaming in

211

agony, as flames shot forth from her hands and feet.

The Doctor understood. Slowly and carefully, he took a step backwards.

When Brogan saw him pull back his bowing arm, she nodded vigorously, her eyes signalling desperately. 'Yes.' She could barely speak, only beg mutely with her eyes to be put out of this agony. 'The line. No. Yes. The line,' she croaked.

Braan blinked the tears from his eyes once, twice, then, like the huntsman he was, drew back the string on his bow and shot once, cleanly.

The Doctor found he could not watch, and instead knelt down next to Luag, shielding his face and holding him tightly in his arms.

Chapter
Twenty-One

Corc stood in front of the assembly, his voice still pained, but his demeanour steady and his presence solid, despite what had taken place. Every islander was there in the great hall, sitting, or standing; their faces pale with shock and fear; some trembling; some unable even to take in the grave danger they were in.

'There can be no more fires,' declared Corc. 'We must eat what we can forage, nothing more. Fires spread this evil.'

'No fishing and no fires?' said one of the young men, drawn and furious at the back of the room, still utterly unable to credit what had happened. 'A starvation is a longer death than a burning, Corc. It pains more too. Is that what you wish for us?'

'Nothing that has happened is anything I have wished for you,' growled Corc. 'But I am still your chief, and if you do not want that, then we must deal with that as a separate matter.'

The room went quiet, with a few mutterings. Nobody, it appeared, wanted to take on the challenge of Corc. And no one appeared to have any solutions.

'We must fight it!' shouted Freydis, suddenly, in the local tongue. She was flushed and frustrated, standing with Henrik at the back of the room, struggling to understand all they were saying. The mutterings grew louder.

'You,' said someone, 'are another mouth to feed. And you brought the trouble.'

There were many assenting noises to this.

'Maybe we could sacrifice you,' someone said. 'Maybe that would make it go away.'

The Doctor had been trying to make himself inconspicuous in the corner of the room. They had learned they could conduct through the fire, but fires burnt out. They needed more.

'Oh, not human sacrifice,' he said. As the room looked at him, he threw up his hands as if it was a trivial matter. 'What? They've tried it. It doesn't work and it's really boring. Trust me, it's rubbish, you wouldn't like it. Come on, let's think of something else.'

Corc put up his hand to stem the flow of conversation.

'She did not cause it,' he said. 'We know now that the bounty of fish and the loss of our brother must have been the work of this fire monster, before the fighting ship was ever spied on the horizon.

'We do not know how to fight it,' he went on. 'But the Doctor tells us it can be spoken to. Perhaps it can be bargained with. Perhaps it can be reasonable.'

'Yes,' said someone. 'Reasonable like all our invaders.'

'He can fight,' said Freydis, pointing at the Doctor. 'He is powerful! Why won't he fight?'

The Doctor looked up mildly. 'When I can think of a way to deal with the Arill without killing every single one of you, believe me, you will be the first to know.'

'But when, Doctor. *When?*'

The Doctor looked around. 'Um, if anyone feels their ears pop, could they let me know?'

Chapter
Twenty-Two

There is a shape to hunger, when it comes. It is not like drowning, where the dread is worse than the end itself. It is known. Deep in the DNA of every human being; the need to be fed, constantly, underpinning every thought and every move and every word. The worm of pain that beds down in the stomach; the clench of fear.

Not just for yourself. It is never just for yourself. It is for your partner, having to rise and face the day and find food, something so very, very important, without more than a small bowl of meal to sustain them. It is the look on the face of your child when he asks for something more that you do not have to give. It is the awful feeling of debilitating exhaustion and failure, as you queue for your share, your portion of what is left; the tiny pieces of fish, from the time of plenty; disintegrating with salt, gobbled down so fast they barely register. Waking again from dreams of great fresh crabs, their sweet skin sucked from its claws; sea trout prepared with chestnuts brought from the great shore; neeps roasted deep in the embers of the fire. Without trading with the other islands – who had obeyed their imprecations to stay away – there was not enough meal; and in any case bread could not be baked; nor vegetables. Nearly everything they lived on, everything they relied on in their diet was from the sea. The sea was barred to them. Their hearths were barred to them. And every day became colder and colder and rabbits became harder and harder to catch; and gradually, all the families moved together to the great hall, and sealed off its windows and gaps from the howling wind; even its chimney was covered over with great rushes. At night, all huddled together. There was little talk; even that energy needed to be conserved. And, as nobody needed to mention out loud, every day the children grew quieter and quieter.

The Doctor sat down with Luag to distract himself from the difficulty of safely removing a multi-dimensional multi-being consciousness from a civilisation that had only just invented the spade. Every few seconds, he glanced at the grey sky.

He found this so hard; every day the same length; every night unbearably long. He wasn't used to a problem he couldn't solve in less than an hour. Every hour that passed here, as the people became more worried, more drawn, more frightened, felt like a year. He felt so frustrated and glanced at the sky again, for the fifteenth time in five minutes.

The children of the settlement were receiving the largest rations possible; everyone had brought forth all they had in store, as was custom during hard times, and it was being carefully stored and guarded in the long hall, rations strictly imposed. All other work was futile and immediately abandoned – mending sails, building and repairing dwellings; weaving and whittling, in favour of spending most of their days roaming over the island in search of game, and edible roots. It was a balance, always, not to expend more energy hunting than was required to replace it. The Doctor, though enthusiastic to help, had shown himself little more than a liability on expeditions, unable to stay quiet for the necessary periods of time. He also had, as Corc said, his work; he had to make a plan; formulate a way to save them. Quickly. He shared out his food ration amongst the children carefully, so as not to arouse suspicion.

'This,' he said to Luag, pulling out the beautifully carved piece, 'is a pawn.'

'A prawn.'

'Many, many people think that. I have no problem with you calling it a prawn.'

But the boy's attention was already distracted. 'This looks like Freydis.'

'It is Freydis. This is her as a queen.'

There were two carved likenesses of the princess, one in red and one in white. They were marvellously detailed, showing the thick braids of her yellow hair, and the long arc of her neck. In both she had her hand over her mouth.

'Why?' asked Luag.

'I'm not sure,' said the Doctor. 'Perhaps to remind her that where she was going, her conversational skills were not strictly necessary.'

'But she's the best piece on the board.'

'She is. I imagine the carver had met her.'

Luag picked up the King.

'Now, he is the most important piece,' said the Doctor. 'He needs to be protected at all times. He can't move very fast.'

'Because he's too fat,' said Luag.

'Hmm. You might have something there,' said the Doctor. 'Anyway, you protect your own king.'

'With prawns.'

'Yes. And you try and attack the other person's.'

'With these horsies.'

'It's quite hard to win with just the horsies.'

'I am only going to move the horsies,' said Luag. 'They're the best ones. Hip hop jump!'

'Hip hop jump,' said the Doctor, staring at the board.

'I love Chest,' said Luag. 'This is the best game ever. How do you win?'

'You try,' said the Doctor, 'to think a few moves ahead.' He looked up at the sky. 'This time of year...' he said to Luag. 'Do you get a lot of storms?'

Luag nodded. 'It's great. Sometimes they wash up dolphins.'

'Oh no,' said the Doctor.

'Licious,' said Luag, his little face clouding over as he thought of it. 'When I was the littlest I used to get the eyes. But I'm not the littlest any more.'

'Do you get seaweed?' said the Doctor.

Luag nodded. 'Licious,' he said again.

The Doctor smiled. 'Well, perhaps we will have a storm and it will throw up some seaweed and some other good things.' He thought for a second. 'Oh, Luag. I would *so* love to let you taste a fish finger.'

They put their heads back to the board.

'The thing is, when we only play with horsies, it can turn into quite a long game,' said the Doctor. 'Not that I'm complaining, I'm just pointing it out.'

'But the prawns are very boring.'

'I know.'

'And I don't want to move Freydis. I'm too scared I might lose her.' Luag picked up the rook carefully. 'What's this?'

'It's a tower. A great thing made of stone that keeps humans safe.'

'We need one of those,' said Luag.

'Humans think it makes them safe,' said the Doctor. 'Doesn't always. Useful piece to play with though.'

'Will we ever be safe?' said Luag, quietly, as if pretending he wasn't asking the question.

The Doctor paused. He hated lying to children. But not as much as he hated scaring them.

'Of course,' he said, just as, from over the other side of the dune on which they were perched came a scattering of sand, blown by heavy feet advancing across the heath.

*

Henrik and Freydis were foraging together. Giggling, occasionally touching hands, picking up seaweed and tiny cockles from the rocks; taking care not to touch the water. Then into the heart of the island itself. Freydis for the first time allowed herself to appreciate that, even though it had no great forests or magnificent cities, it had its charms. The great soft heather was a deep shade of purple that contrasted with the low grey sky; Henrik strode across it boldly, looking for mushrooms. She enjoyed watching him walk.

'Come on, farm boy,' she teased. 'You should be great at this.'

Henrik looked at her. He didn't like it when she teased him like this. But when he saw her face, laughing, her cheeks pink in the wind, her hair flying behind him, he realised suddenly that he didn't mind. Not at all. He held out his thick rough rower's hand and she placed in it her delicate white one. He was about to start to kiss her again, when she froze, and indicated over his shoulder. They were at the top of a tiny tor. Just over in the distance could be seen, burning faintly, the two separate pyres of the braziers, warning off passing ships and other islanders.

'They're in there,' said Freydis in a fury. 'This threat. It's in the fire. He could put it out just like that. You've seen the way his ship moved. He has power but he won't use it.'

'Hmm,' said Henrik.

'His odd clothes, the way he talks, the things he knows. He's a *God*. Do you doubt that he could defeat

222

these invaders?'

'I've never seen him with a sword,' said Henrik.

'Don't be ridiculous. He's a coward. It's not that he can't protect us. It's that he won't.'

'I'm sure that's not true,' protested Henrik. 'He was not a coward when he came to save you.'

Freydis looked at him. 'You did most of that,' she said.

Henrik would have liked to have believed that were true, but was an honest person on the whole.

'It was all him,' said Henrik. 'He's really... he's really quite amazing.'

'Yes!' said Freydis. 'Well, if he's so amazing why is he mooning about walking up and down with his hands behind his back instead of bringing his power down to smite our enemies? Whose side is he on? What kind of protector spends his morning playing chess? What can chess teach you about fighting?'

'Well,' said Henrik, 'it teaches you about when to advance... when to defend...'

'When to retreat and knock over all your men,' said Freydis, fiercely. 'It's ridiculous. Maybe we should force him to help us.'

'We should do nothing of the kind,' said Henrik, horrified.

'Why not? Don't you have the stomach for it?'

They stood staring at each other. Henrik hated arguments and wished they hadn't got here. Freydis knew she shouldn't wear her frustrations so close to the surface. But they were all so meek! They needed to fight their enemies and here they were gathering mushrooms!

'I hope the heather keeps you warm,' she said to Henrik. 'In the five minutes before he lets the fire get you. He's a trickster, Henrik. You don't know what side he's playing! Don't trust him.'

Henrik looked unhappy. 'I don't know what else to do.'

And Freydis, because she didn't either, sniffed mightily and turned round to storm off, just as they heard the horn.

The Doctor poked his head out, at first pushing Luag down in the gorse. He was confronted with the figure of Erik – looking a little thinner and more bedraggled than he had the first time – charging over the distant dunes with a motley collection of fellow Vikings in tow.

'Oh, for pity's sake,' grumbled the Doctor. 'You know, insane human persistence isn't always the virtue it's made out to be.'

He took out his screwdriver.

'This is one of the more arcane settings,' he explained to a terrified Luag, then put it to his mouth and blew. The screwdriver made the noise of a perfect horn, sounding the alarm. From all around where the villagers were gathering seaweed or searching for turnip roots, heads popped up; from his high vantage point the Doctor could see quite far. He also saw, to his horror, something he had not noticed before. One of the Vikings was carrying a lighted torch.

'Oh, no,' he said, scrambling down the sand. 'Oh, no no no no no.'

As the two sides faced each other once more, outside the long hall, the Doctor saw at even closer range that the Vikings were faring even worse than the islanders were. Their faces, bristling with whiskers, were gaunt and grey; their swords dull, their eyes wild. Hungry men were terribly dangerous, the Doctor knew. And they were all hungry men here.

'Hello, Erik,' he said, sauntering down to the group as if he hadn't a care in the world. 'Have you lost weight? Suits you.'

'Are you still here?' grunted Erik. 'I thought you'd have been off with your underwater friends by now. You know he's one of them,' he said to the villagers unhelpfully.

Corc stepped forward. 'He is standing shoulder to shoulder with us,' he said. 'I cannot imagine anyone choosing to do so.'

Erik snorted. 'Let me tell you what we want,' he grunted. 'Either we kill you all—'

'I'm hungry,' said Olaf.

The others shushed him.

'No one is eating anyone,' said Erik. 'I'm a Viking captain, not a Finn.'

His men laughed sourly.

'We need your food stores and the wreckage of Ragnor's boat. We can fix the hole in our boat. We'll take the woman and be on our way. And this time nobody chases us. This place is cursed.'

'You can have none of those things,' said Corc, calmly. 'We will keep our food stores, and Freydis is under our protection.'

'You will fight and die to save the Viking princess?' sneered Erik.

'We will,' said Corc.

There was a long silence.

Freydis was standing there, very serious and poised, watching the goings-on. Henrik glanced at her, uneasy. He was completely in thrall to her, but wary too; she was so unpredictable. Was she toying with him, cold and lonely, facing an uncertain future? Was he simply a diversion; or a pawn in some greater plan?

For a moment nobody moved. Then the Doctor stepped forward. 'First,' he said. 'Put out the light.'

Erik glanced back at it. 'Why?' he said. 'Is it going to go on fire? Oh no, look. It's already on fire.'

The Doctor shook his head. 'You saw what happened to that boy. It will happen to your men, too.'

The man holding the torch glanced at it, confused.

'But how can you live without fire?' said Erik.

Nobody could answer that. The Viking carefully, and a little shakily, kicked a divot of earth over with his heel and buried the foot of the torch in the sand so it stood up, looking like an oversize match, still burning. The Doctor kept his eye on it.

'We just want to go,' said Erik, in a wheedling voice.

'Give us her, give us the first boat to patch up ours, and some tools, and some food… then we'll leave from the other side of the island, skip that monster of yours. Once we're out on the open sea we can fish. It's best for everyone. Some of you can even come if you like. Come, live the life on the open sea with us. Young men only. Or you can stay here and starve to death like the rest. It takes a long time, though.'

'It will take a lot less if you take our young men,' said Corc. 'No.'

'Then it is stalemate,' said Erik. 'Talking is done.' He drew his sword.

'Hang on, hang on,' said the Doctor. 'Talking is never done. Why don't you come and join with us, help us gather food.'

'Whilst you do what?' sneered Erik. 'Have a lie down at the bottom of the sea?'

Freydis stepped forward suddenly.

'Hush, boys,' she said. She faced up to Erik. 'You will take no food from the mouths of these people,' she said. 'You may take the wood – the wood for the boat that was built to carry me – and you may take me. And you will leave and you will trouble nobody here again with your poxy, paltry fighting ways. You impress no one, Erik.'

She held up her wrists towards him in a gesture of surrender.

Henrik's heart plummeted. His hunger, his fear, his anxieties all forgotten he strode forwards.

'No,' he said. 'No. I forbid it.'

Freydis turned her heavy-lidded eyes on him. 'Oh,' she said. 'Another man who wishes to tell me what to do.'

'You cannot put yourself back into captivity.'

She stared at him. 'Can you think of another way that he will let the island go free?'

Henrik threw up his arms in frustration. 'You can't do this.'

'You could come,' she said. 'Heaven knows, they need decent sailors. This lot look like they'd sink their own shoes, if they had any.'

Henrik blinked rapidly. 'But then I would be your guard again.'

'Better that than dead.'

'To stand by… to watch you become a bride. But not my bride.'

'Henrik, my love.' Freydis's voice was very quiet and sad. 'I have to.'

'You don't,' said Henrik.

Corc stepped forward. 'My lady, there is no need to sacrifice yourself in this way. The trip may be suicide; the marriage may be grave.'

'I would rather live free with you for a short time than as your jailer for ever in the Ice Kingdom,' said Henrik.

'It's all the same to me,' grunted Erik. 'Just depends on how many of you I have to kill to get her in it.'

'You start here,' said Henrik, and drew his sword.

The Doctor had crept away, carefully, to the hall, and

picked up one of the rough clay bowls, filling it with water. Now he attempted to sidle up without being noticed and use it to extinguish the torch, still burning away; still filling the air with a threat more deadly than any between the two groups of men. Just as he was nearly there though, Freydis suddenly yelled at Henrik to stop it, and everyone drew their swords, and Lars grabbed up the torch. The Doctor was torn between watching him and watching Erik and Henrik, who had charged at each other, swords drawn.

'*Stop it!*' Freydis was screaming, loudly and angrily.

Henrik, though weakened through lack of food and fear, was still light on his feet, with the same cunning aptitude with a sword the Viking chiefs had spotted when they'd recruited him from his lowly birth. Erik had force and a far better sword, but was heavier, his age and bodyweight showing against him. He parried Henrik's pointed thrust at his leather jerkin, pushing the lighter sword aside, and advancing quickly. Henrik jumped back, slashing at his arm, but Erik was quicker than he looked and not born yesterday, and he twisted and turned 360 degrees, lifting his weapon as he moved. He lifted it high above his head, but, taking advantage of the split second, Henrik put his head down and charged it into Erik's belly. Erik immediately stumbled backwards, off balance, and Henrik slashed sideways and managed to catch his right thigh. Erik let out an enormous bellow, and staggered round, hitting Henrik in the side of the head with the flat of his sword. If it had been the sharp side, it would have opened Henrik's skull like someone knocking the top off a boiled egg.

As it was, he was badly winded, and staggered back, gasping for breath. Freydis tried to put herself in between the two men, but Henrik pushed her down and out of the way immediately.

Meanwhile, Lars had thrown the Doctor's water to the ground and was holding him at bay with his sword. His hand was trembling.

'Are you shaking because you're hungry or because you really don't want to kill me?' asked the Doctor politely. 'If it's the latter, why don't you just put that down? You'll ruffle this...' He felt around his mouth. There didn't appear to be a word for bow tie in their language, so it came out as: '... twine thing.'

Lars sniffed. 'I'm starving, in I? If you think a Viking is afraid to kill, matey, you haven't met many.'

'Oh,' said the Doctor. 'What about if I can talk you round with a word on the sanctity of human life, and the beauty of this amazing planet you inhabit and have practically to yourselves? You have all the space, all the resources you could ever need or want. Why take everyone else's? Why all the bloody slaughter and devastation?'

Lars shrugged. 'Issa laugh, innit?'

'You know,' said the Doctor, 'I think I'm beginning to figure out why ASBOs were never really going to work.'

'Ssh,' said Lars. 'Or I might just kill you anyway.'

'OK, hang on, appeal to self-interest... Lars, if

you don't put out that fire, it's... it might turn into a monster.'

Lar's thick brow inched slightly upwards. 'Yeah?'

'Yeah!'

'Størr!' said Lars.

'Cool?' echoed the Doctor. 'How on earth do you have a word for "cool" and not one for "bow tie"? The two are basically synonymous. And it's not "cool".'

Lars was glancing at the torch now, as if daring it to do something. It was just then that Freydis threw herself between the two men and Henrik pushed her to the ground. The Doctor took advantage of Lars's distraction to duck out from under the sword, then, swivelling around, gave Lars a rapid Chinese burn that made him immediately drop it.

'Hey!' called out Lars, outraged. 'That's not fair.'

But the Doctor was already brandishing the sword in his direction. 'Wow,' he said. 'Look at this.'

Erik changed his focus to him. 'You don't know what to do with that,' he sneered.

In response, the Doctor tossed the sword up, caught it lightly by its hilt and performed a series of thrusts and parries with near-perfect fencing balance.

'D'Artagnan taught me it's all in the legs,' he mused, as the others stood watching this display of skill. He slashed a 'Z' into Erik's leather jerkin. He looked at the zed, puzzled. 'Or the other one... They all wear masks, those chappies. Very hard to tell them apart.'

With a vicious backswipe behind him, he knocked

the torch flame on the head, holding the sword down till it went out.

'I have,' he continued in a conversational tone of voice, 'met a lot of people on my travels. And *you*, sir...'

Erik was watching him.

'... I hate to be insulting, but you do remain one of the most pig-headed, dog-breathed specimens of what is generally quite a sensible species. Put that sword down.'

The adrenalin of the fight draining from him, and becoming sensible of the wound in his thigh, Erik slowly – as if to maintain his self-respect – lowered his sword. The remaining Vikings also lowered theirs, returning from a gang of frightening fighters back to a collection of sorry-looking scrawny specimens.

'Good!' said the Doctor, glancing round the circle. 'Now let's hold a sensible conversation, shall we? About human beings working together? Corc.'

Corc cleared his throat. 'You can have the wood and restore your boat,' he said. 'That is no problem to us. We would like you to leave. If you spare men to help forage for food, you may repair it with whatever help we can give you. But you will not take our food, and you will not take the Princess.'

There was some muttering among the Vikings, but a general air of assent.

'Otherwise,' said the Doctor, 'you will feel my wrath. AHA. That sounded quite good, didn't it? RRAH!'

He took the sword and balanced it rather well on his chin, then realised everyone had gone quiet and was looking at him, so stopped and let it drop into his hand. 'So are we agreed? Friends?'

Everyone spat onto their hands.

'Ugh, I hate this bit,' said the Doctor.

'Get *off* me!' Freydis was shouting.

'I don't understand,' Henrik was protesting. 'I was getting you out of the way of a sword fight. Why are you so cross?'

'I don't need rescuing,' said Freydis.

'That's right,' said Henrik. 'I remember when you unlocked that cupboard all by yourself.'

She heaved him away. 'You think I'm some weak woman.'

'I thought you were someone in the way of a sword fight,' said Henrik.

'Who do you think you are, anyway?' said Freydis. 'To push me around.'

'Someone trying to have a *sword fight*,' said Henrik.

'Well, if you'd let me go with them, you wouldn't have had to have a fight.'

'Yes, but now you don't have to go with them,' said Henrik, glancing over at Erik, who was mopping up the blood from his leg wound. 'So why not stop being so angry?'

'Because I am just tired of everyone else making decisions for me all the time,' said Freydis. 'My entire life I am told where to sit, what to do, who to marry.

233

And I'm not stupid. I see this doesn't happen to men. But I don't think I'm much stupider than men. Do you?'

'Nooo,' said Henrik.

'And then I get a new chance. Somewhere afresh. Where women aren't necessarily just to be bought and sold. Even he...' She indicated the Doctor, who was trying to wave politely to people instead of shaking their spat-on hands. 'Even the God treats me with respect. So I thought you might listen to me.'

'I did listen to you,' said Henrik. 'I listened to you make an awful suggestion that would mean separation and certain death, and I acted on it.'

'You pushed me out the way.'

'You were being stupid!'

'Nobody calls me stupid!'

'There you go again, pulling the "princess" card when you don't get your way! It's always going to be like that with you, isn't it. You won't stop reminding me that you're better than I am, even when you're facing certain ruddy death.'

Freydis scrambled up. 'I'd probably be better off with fat Gissar.'

'Maybe you would,' said Henrik. 'Maybe you're more trouble than you're worth.'

As soon as the words escaped him, he could have cut out his tongue. Her face fell immediately – then, just as quickly, stiffened, with the automatic self-preservation of a girl raised at court, until it was impassive as the chess pieces that bore her likeness.

'Freydis,' said Henrik, but he knew it was like talking to a mask. He cursed inwardly. Why did she have to be so unbelievably stubborn?

'I'm going to gather mushrooms,' Freydis said to Corc. 'Do you have someone who can divine which are good and which are poisonous?'

Corc nodded briskly. 'Our Elder can,' he said.

'Mostly,' said the Elder. 'My eyesight's not what it was... still, it is a quick death, they say. A terribly painful one, going by the screaming, but...'

'I can,' said the Doctor.

'Everyone,' said Corc, looking at the collection of people in front of him. 'We're going to split up. Half to look for mushrooms, half for seaweed. But not too close to the water, do you understand?'

'You're not going to eat seaweed without fire?' said one of the Vikings.

Everyone turned to look at him.

'What?' he said. 'I just think you're crazy, that's all.'

'And you're lucky to be alive,' said Corc shortly, turning away, as one of the other village men came forward and collected up all the swords.

'Yeah, so are you,' muttered Lars, but only to himself.

The Doctor caught up with Corc. 'This should keep us going,' he said.

Corc grunted. 'As long as the peace holds. And when we've eaten every living thing on the island,

235

Doctor. What then?'

The Doctor said nothing. Then he asked, gently, 'Where's Luag?'

Corc tried to shrug, tried to show that mention of his youngest son hadn't come as nearly a shock to him. In his own pain, wrapped up in the concerns and tribulations of his people, thinking about individuals hadn't really come into it.

'He'll be around,' he said. 'Like a baby goat that loses its mother. They find one eventually.'

'He could do with a father,' said the Doctor, as carefully as he could.

Corc's mouth twisted. 'I think there's lots of things everyone would like right now,' he said, realising his guilt was making him harsh. 'But I have bigger things to worry about.'

'Do you?' said the Doctor.

The group started to break up, Freydis striding out in front, Henrik – shoulders bowed, wishing vigorously that he had fallen in love with a nice farm girl and never left the farm – trailing up the rear, and not one of them noticing that just under the extinguished torch, a cinder had fallen, and even now, in the thick gorse, had started to smoulder and give out a tiny wisp of smoke, practically invisible against the great grey sky.

Chapter
Twenty-Three

Eating raw rabbit is a messy business. It's not something you would choose to do under normal circumstances. But when you are very, very hungry and tired, and a bit wet, and have spent the entire afternoon picking up mushrooms, only to be told that most of them would kill you instantly and you have to throw them away again, then you look at the mushrooms you can eat and the rabbits that the big Viking managed to catch, and think what a delicious stew it would make if you could brew it up in a cauldron with some simmering herbs and radishes... Well, if you don't think about that, you just get on with what's in front of you, even if your sword has been taken away, leaving you nothing to cut your dinner with.

Everyone ate quickly, and in silence. With the added muscle of the Vikings, and the villagers know-how, it was the largest meal they'd eaten in days. Huddled together inside the long hall in the fading light, it felt dark and cheerless after they'd all eaten and washed (washing raw rabbit off you, in the dark, without any soap is also on the nasty side). They huddled together under all their furs collected to try and keep warm, nervously close to their new neighbours.

Freydis and Henrik made it their job to be on opposite ends of the group, as far away from one another as they possibly could. Freydis was telling herself that she had done the right thing; she couldn't be pushed around by a man for another single minute. But another, deeper part of herself was wishing he would turn round, look at her just for a moment, the way he'd looked at her that day they'd been alone in the Long Hall. And then she could tell him she wasn't really horrible; just terrified – for her life, for her future and for how much she loved him, and then their silly quarrel would be forgotten. But she wouldn't tell him first. He'd been the one to boss her about; he was the one who needed to apologise. Also she didn't really want him to have to watch her eat raw rabbit. Henrik's thoughts ran along very similar lines, though he was less bothered about the aesthetic appeal of the rabbit.

As night fell, its thick blackness covering them all like a cowl, the moonlight unable to penetrate the rushes that now covered the windows, there wasn't a single person in the room who didn't wish for the cheer and warmth and light of a fire as never before.

After a period of prolonged silence – no one had anything much to say – a low, deep voice suddenly started to sing. It was Olaf, the slow-witted Viking.

He had a surprisingly beautiful baritone, rich as thick honey.

He sang a long ballad about a journey home. Although not everyone understood the words, there was absolutely no doubt about their meaning; it was the homesickness, the utter melancholy in his voice, the sound of a man so far from home he didn't know if he would ever live long enough to see it again, or if his loved ones would even recognise him if he did.

Gradually the other Vikings picked up the melody, familiar to them, and joined in; the villagers too, sang or gently beat upon the ground. For their home too, as they knew it, was gone; their notions of safety, of comfort, of a place and a meal to call their own had vanished, and they too did not know if they could ever return to the way they had been.

In this tiny dark hovel, under a shroud of the great northern night, at the very western tip of the known world, they became, briefly, a group of souls united as one in fear, in longing, in hope.

Olaf sang:

> *Sá einn veit*
> *er víða ratar*
> *ok hefr fjölð um farit*
> *hverju geði*
> *stýrir gumna hverr*
> *sá er vitandi er vits*

The Doctor lay, slightly separate from the group, his

long body stretched out on the floor, his head resting on his right hand, his eyes closed, listening. It was a song he knew very well.

By dawn, the Doctor was staring out over the waves and looking at the sky. The waves were white-tipped today, frothy and high, and the clouds were scudding quickly.

'Good,' he said. 'That's good.'

Henrik had joined him, unable to sleep, tortured by thoughts of Freydis. The idea of never speaking to her again made him feel utterly terrible.

'Hello,' said the Doctor. 'Come to me for love advice?'

'No,' said Henrik sullenly.

'Oh. Probably just as well,' said the Doctor. 'Anyway,' he glanced at the sky once more, 'I think today is the day. I am going to try talking to them one more time. But after that…'

He paused ominously, but Henrik was hopelessly distracted, sighing and throwing stones into the water.

'… *after that*…'

Henrik didn't stir until the Doctor took from his pocket an earthenware jar, tightly stoppered with a cork.

'Hey!' said Henrik. 'That's ours! That came from our ship!'

'It washed up,' said the Doctor. 'Law of the briny deep. Anyway, I need it.'

Henrik held it reverently. 'This carried oil,' he said.

'It comes from Gaul.'

'I know,' said the Doctor. 'Looks like fantastic Lecrusus workmanship.'

Henrik looked at him. 'You always have to get the last word, don't you?'

'That's not part of my love advice,' said the Doctor.

'No' said Henrik. He shook the gourd. 'There's something inside.'

'There is,' said the Doctor. He uncorked it and unrolled the sheet of paper. 'Psychic paper,' he said, displaying it with a flourish.

'Why has it got a picture of you on it, except with big monster teeth?' said Henrik.

'Does it? No, it's got writing on it. Well, binary Transmuting Xtensior, actually, but you don't need to worry about that.'

The psychic paper rearranged itself into a series of tiny blue symbols which appeared to dance across the surface.

'It's a language they can read,' said the Doctor.

Henrik looked confused.

'It's... it's talking. But on paper.'

Henrik squinted. '*Those* are runes?'

'Yup. It's a way of putting words down on paper so someone who can't hear you can understand you.'

'I know what runes are.'

'Of course you do.'

Henrik thought about this for a while. 'What's paper?' he asked eventually.

The Doctor left him to his pebble throwing, and

waded into the water. His message to the Arill was clear. Leave this place. He understood it would take them considerable use of their energy reserves to do so; he was, in effect, asking them to sacrifice some of their number. The weather was not going in his favour. But diplomacy might.

He knew a way to help them, that was the most important thing now. But they had made a mistake. They had come to the wrong place. *If* they stopped their attacks, they would manage this together, in the best way possible. If not… well, he would do what he must. It was a warning. He only ever gave one.

Rolling up his trouser legs, he walked into the freezing surf, standing, surveying the dim horizon of the bay. Then he took the gourd and, with a practised bodyline throw, hurtled it far into the great surf. The gourd went so far that they could not hear it breaking the surface of the water.

'And I want that back when you've finished with it!' the Doctor shouted.

'Will the monster get that?' Henrik asked.

'I would think so,' said the Doctor. 'A message in a bottle. They always work. Now all we have to do is wait.'

He sat down cross-legged in the damp sand.

'So you're just going to sit and wait?' said Henrik.

The Doctor glanced again at the sky. Great grey clouds gathered there. 'Oh yes,' he said. 'We'll know soon enough, one way or another. Chess?'

Henrik shook his head and stared at him, sitting

there, looking completely at peace. Perhaps Freydis had been right. Why wouldn't he fight for them? What was all this nonsense about bottles and runes and sitting when people were dying all around them? Unconsciously his hand went to his sword hilt.

'*Doctor,*' he commanded. 'This is... this is not the Viking way.'

'I'm aware of that,' came the voice.

'They are our enemies! They must be crushed. They have killed us! They are trying to kill us all the time! How can you sit there and do nothing?'

The Doctor looked up at Henrik with tired eyes. Up until now Henrik had thought of him as a man just a few years older than himself. Suddenly he realised he could not be. The eyes he was looking into were far, far older than that. Older than anything Henrik had ever seen, since that cold day long ago when he had felt the rivers pull and realised he was in the grip of something more ancient and powerful and permanent than he would ever be.

'They aren't trying to kill anyone, Henrik,' he said. 'It's happening as a by-product – that's why it's taking some people such a long time to die, and some such a short time. They're just trying to get through. To survive, just like us. Every time they set a fire, they sacrifice their own life force; many of their own souls. They are not without casualties. And when they sent a hundred dead turtles, nobody minded.'

'But this is different!' said Henrik. 'These are people.'

'And when you land on settlements,' said the Doctor, 'when your blood lust is up and you berserkers are rampaging through the town, putting people to the sword, laughing, stealing, taking... what do you think then?'

Henrik hung his head. 'But it is the Viking way,' he said stubbornly. 'I'm proud to be a Viking.'

'And they are proud to be the Arill,' said the Doctor. 'What's it for? I will never understand it. For example, if I were to slaughter all of you...'

He stilled Henrik's sceptical look with one of his own. It was a look which convinced Henrik immediately and beyond any shadow of a doubt that he could immediately do so if he so chose.

'What would that help?' he went on. 'What would that prove, except to hand on misery? So I have explained the situation to them in full. I have spelled it out very clearly. They must wait for civilisation, or make their own way back to the stars without harming any one of you. Now they will understand. Do you think what you do as a Viking is wrong?'

Henrik thought of how he had only ever thought of the glory; had barely thought of the people they fought at all. As little more than turtles, in fact.

'Perhaps,' he said.

The Doctor stared out to sea. 'Then take that as your warning. No more. But everyone deserves a warning.'

He picked up a stone and hurled it into the grey waves, then sat down again.

'But only one.'

Henrik took his hand off his sword and sat down to wait with him.

'No,' said the Doctor, closing his eyes. 'You don't wait. You go and say sorry to the girl.'

'But it wasn't my fault,' said Henrik.

'I may not know much about women,' said the Doctor, opening one eye, 'but I do know *something*.'

Freydis was just outside the long hall, braiding up her hair. It was not something she had ever done herself, and she was not finding it particularly easy. But something in the rhythmic twisting of the strands was comforting and, as she tethered up her unruly locks, it felt like she was stiffening herself up too; making herself once more distant; formally untouchable and royal.

More prepared, at any rate, for whatever may come next; whatever she was facing, she would face it alone. Henrik hadn't been there in the long hall when she had awoken that morning; after tossing and turning most of the night (as well as thinking about Henrik, it was also difficult to get away from the Vikings, who smelled a lot better at sea), she had finally dozed off just before dawn.

When Henrik had arisen, he had thought she looked as comfortable and peaceful as an infant, which had made him markedly grumpier. Now, though, stomping back from the beach and seeing her carefully tending her hair in the dull morning light, she looked to him like something from a story; exactly like someone who would tempt a God from the sky.

'Freydis,' he said, softly.

Freydis stiffened; at first she did not want to turn round or give any indication that she had heard the sound of his voice. But inside her heart leapt; the sense of relief was huge and palpable. Slowly, she turned around, her eyes wide, her face open, and blushing, with relief and shyness and happiness... when she caught sight of someone, or something, just behind Henrik's shoulder. And suddenly, unable to speak, her eyes widened even further, as she stared out at the sea.

'Look,' she said in awe. 'Look at the water.'

The sea had changed. Something was there; something was in it. It was all lit up with an extraordinary bouncing glow, tiny pinpoints of green light.

Henrik and Freydis turned back and ran to the sea, where the Doctor was standing with this arms wide apart.

'Look at it!' he was saying. 'Look!'

The lights gleamed and glistened on the tops of the waves, tiny dots as far as the eye could see. They lit up the grey waves like a celebration, right across the bay.

The other villagers came forward in amazement. It was very beautiful.

'Look at that!' breathed Henrik. 'What's happening?'

'They're dispersing,' whispered the Doctor. 'They've read our message. Look, isn't it beautiful? And so noble.'

'What are they?' said Henrik.

'That's the Arill,' said the Doctor. 'Together they form a power. Apart, like this, they are just... well. Aren't the lights pretty?'

The tiny lights bobbed up and down on the waves, dancing in and out like iridescent snowflakes.

'How could they cause all that horrible fire?' said Henrik. 'They're so small and beautiful.'

'Strength in numbers,' said the Doctor. 'Always.'

He bowed his head.

'Thank you,' he said to the Arill. 'Thank you.'

As if in response the lights shimmered right across the bay, then, sliding further and further apart, gradually began to wink out.

'That's it?' said Freydis, doubtfully.

'They have done the bravest thing,' said the Doctor. 'They have sacrificed themselves to save you. They knew this world was not for them.'

'Just like that?'

'They're gone?' said Corc, wonderingly. He put his hand tentatively into the water.

'Isn't that amazing?' said the Doctor. 'They did the right thing. Well, I'd be a bit careful for a day or so.'

Corc nodded and swiftly removed his hand from the water. 'They came from another place?'

'Very far away,' said the Doctor. 'And alas, they can never return.'

He turned and walked slowly up the beach.

CHAPTER FOUR

Chapter
Twenty-Four

The little leftover cinder from the torch had smouldered on, unnoticed beneath the gorse, at the spot where the Vikings had appeared over the tops of the dunes. Sheltered from the wind, it had taken root there; not quite bursting into flame, but nonetheless ticking over, finding enough fuel in the roots and the wind-dried grass.

Almost anyone in the little community who might have found it would have known immediately what to do. They had all been warned sternly and often enough by now; they had all seen the results with their own eyes. Braan, partner of Brogan, had been unable to speak of it, but the blackened remains of his sweetheart told their own fearsome story. The stranger said they were safe now, but was it true?

Almost anyone would have immediately quenched the flame with seawater, or at least run and told Corc about it. Anyone except Lars and Olaf, out on an early-morning quest to find a goat, or something that could be milked, or laid eggs, or in any way would provide them with something that was more of a breakfast than cold seaweed and leftover rabbit kidney.

Olaf smelled it first. 'Olaf smell breakfast,' he said, mistakenly.

Lars ran round immediately. 'You're right,' he said. 'Smell that! We could roast those kidneys and no mistake!'

'No fire,' said Olaf. 'No fire. Man said no fire.'

'Yes, well, that was our enemies, innit?' said Lars. 'They're going to tell you that, aren't they? Mess with your head so you get so weak they can kill you in their sleep. You know, they probably have a great big fire out the back that they hadn't told anyone about. And they're laughing at us. They're cunning, islanders. It's all finished now, anyway, didn't you see those pretty lights?'

Olaf frowned, confused. 'I like pretty lights,' he confessed. 'But fire eat man. Corc said...'

'Yeah, so he *said*,' said Lars, who prided himself on always being able to get one over on people. 'But why would you listen to those earth-eaters?'

Olaf frowned again.

'Are you a Viking, or are you an island slave?' said Lars. 'I'm not scared of some stupid little fire. I'm not going to touch it, am I? I'm not an idiot.'

Had Lars been patrolling with any single other person on the island at that point they would immediately have pointed out the obvious – that Lars was indeed a terrible, terrible idiot and therefore probably a bad choice to investigate their new-found security. But he was with the only person possible who had never accused anyone of anything.

Olaf hung his head. 'Olaf idiot,' he said.

'You are,' said Lars. 'Now, watch this for clever, right. It'll never get near us.'

He picked up a stout root from the ground and pushed it through the leftover rabbit. Then he knelt down on the ground next to the smouldering earth, and slowly, gently, coaxed it into life, the tiny wisps of smoke growing thicker; the tiny orange tongue beginning gradually to crackle.

If Lars had been with anyone else that day, they could have rushed back and shouted a warning. They could have held Lars back, perhaps, or knocked him to the ground with a rock; anything to prevent his gaining power, but no one came as the flames spoke his name and the warm, strong power of the Arill felt like a million suns exploding inside of him.

Arill-Lars hissed, his eyes flickering the strange orange-yellow, 'Olafff... Come, join the line...'

Olaf, whose father had sent his slow-witted son off on his first voyage with trepidation, patted on the arm by Olaf's mother, who had always refused to recognise her son's limitations, and thought it might well be the making of him – and, with his usefulness and sweet singing voice, until disaster had struck had been well on the way to be proved right – Olaf, who would never hoist another sack, or sing another ballad, was, with one touch, connected to the fire that burned between them; that needed an outlet to move, to expand, to rush its connection along; for without the outlet, it was too much for humans to bear. There could be no line.

Olaf lurched this way and that way. The promise of extraordinary power and knowledge meant nothing to him; no more than it had to Brogan; only he knew something was very wrong. And every time he lurched, and jumped, and turned around, then another bolt of flame would come out from him, setting on fire grass and stems and bushes all around.

The wind was whipping higher and higher around them, feeding the flames. But, although the clouds looked pregnant and heavy with water, the rain did not start to fall, and the flames grew in strength as they raged. Olaf ran, still holding Lars's hand, hither and thither. And Lars laughed and shouted out in the maelstrom that the line would be joined; the line was coming!

And so they marched to the settlement, setting alight all that could burn on the way, until a great wall of fire banked the dunes, like an army of warriors, dancing out of the shadows, who would fight till they had consumed them all.

The lights had been a trick. A lulling. The warning had failed.

'Do not touch them!' was the first thing Henrik shouted as they appeared, shocked and bitterly disappointed to his very core. There was a pause.

He and Freydis looked at each other, both with nerves jingling on the very edge. Both were utterly adrenalised, poised for fight or flight. Henrik was about to bark an order at her to get to safety – then, suddenly, at the very last second, he changed his mind and kept quiet. And Freydis saw it. She understood immediately what he had done, and what it had cost him to do so. And she cursed the Gods to the very heavens.

'Tricks!' she screamed. 'All tricks! I'll fetch water.' She charged out of the back door.

What had been Lars and Olaf stood in front of the village, the flames now raging high behind them. From one of the huts, a woman started to scream; screams of fury as well as fear.

The Doctor came charging back from the sea and shouted hoarsely at the villagers to fetch water; as much as they could carry, in anything they could. Every house had a pot, though the Doctor had never wished so much for the simplest of things – a bath; a hose; a tap. But there was nothing. The wall of fire was making a terrible noise now, blown by the ever quickening wind towards the little village which had suffered so much already; the figures emerging looked browbeaten, too tired to counter this later threat. And in the Doctor's breast there beat the refrain: you were wrong. You were wrong. They have tricked you.

But Lars was marching on, unstoppable, laughing, his orange eyes full of joy.

'*This is not the worst way, Doctor,*' he called out in the breathy, unearthly tones. '*Do you see? We can get out! We can be free!*'

'You dispersed!' said the Doctor.

'The shape is not the thing,' said the Arill. *'And now we have you all together, your guard down. Now we can truly build a line.'*

'But for how long?' implored the Doctor. 'For a day? Hours? Minutes? And it is murder. What you are doing is murder.'

'It is bandwidth,' sneered the mouth of Lars.

The first buckets of water were being thrown on the men, but Olaf shook it off like a dog. Lars barely noticed, and blinked.

'My fire is inside,' he sneered.

'The land!' shouted the Doctor. 'Concentrate on your land! We cannot help them now.'

But Lars continued to advance.

'I am here for all of you,' he said. *'We will refine our way with the humans now. We will come to an arrangement. All we need is a line.'*

Lars smiled, a ghastly rictus, revealing a glowing light within.

'And then, dear Doctor. Then you. You shall keep us alive for much longer, no? Long enough… to travel? To find a ship? To spread throughout the world?'

'No,' said the Doctor. 'No.'

'But that is what we do,' said the Arill simply, implacably. *'That is what we do. That is what life is. And it is* wonderful.'

As if galvanised by the voices and the flames, suddenly one man was standing in front of the Doctor, holding his sword high. It was Erik.

'Don't be stupid, Erik, don't try and fight it,' said the Doctor.

Erik, his red beard reflected in the flames, making his face already glow, turned, and laughed heartily in the Doctor's face.

'Fight it?' he roared. *'Fight it? It is taking over the world! A Viking knows power! A Viking knows strength! My dear fellow, I'm going to* join *it!'*

And, holding up his sword, he ran into the arms of his fellows; the spark immediately jumping, taking root in him. His face took on a wondrous, horrible glow as the power and the knowledge of the Arill swept through him, hand tightly held in Lars's fist.

'Ah…' said Arill-Lars. *'That feels wonderful! Look, how we grow ever stronger! Ever more powerful! We are the future! Join us now! You will never be cold! Never be hungry.'*

But even now, it was evident that Olaf remained in much distress, still twisting and turning unhappily; his feet had begun to smoke.

The Doctor continued to shout at the islanders to concentrate on putting out the fires that were growing ever nearer, but his voice was more and more choked in the thickening smoke.

'No more!' he shouted, impotently – just as another man passed the line in front of him, moving like a sleepwalker towards the group of Arill.

The Doctor grabbed him.

'Aren't you listening to me?' he shouted. 'No more!'

Corc looked up at him with dull eyes, as villagers

ran back and forth behind them, fighting for their homes and everything they had ever owned. One, with a sharp scream, was brushed by the flames. Instantly she took the glow upon her, marching forward and taking Erik's hand. Ragnor, the first Viking captain, who had been through so much, was also pawed by a distraught Olaf, and found himself, in an instant, drawn towards the line and joining the legion of flames.

'But why not?' said Corc, his voice a husk. 'They have won. Look at them. They are happy. They are warm. I have failed. I have failed to protect my people; I have failed to protect our land and our homes; I have failed to protect my son.'

'You have another son,' said the Doctor urgently. 'You can't do this, Corc. You can't. Your people need you.'

'My people are doomed. We are all doomed,' said Corc. 'You're all doomed!' he cried out into the billowing smoke and deafening wind. He turned to the Doctor, sheathed his sword and spat on his hand.

'Thank you for trying,' he said. 'Thank you for doing your best. But the Norse people when they come… there is always death, there is always bloodshed, there is always fire. It just took a little longer this time.'

'For the last time, I am *not* spitting on my hand,' said the Doctor. 'One strain of Iberian prune flu round here and you won't need the Arill to wipe you out.'

He grabbed Corc by the shoulders.

'Get behind me and help with the water, man. They

need you.'

'They needed me. I failed,' Corc intoned again, and with enormous strength, tore himself out of the Doctor's arms and ran towards Lars, who was laughing and showing his teeth. As the Doctor launched himself after him, he was beaten to it; just as Corc lumbered into the embrace of the Arill, he was hurled to the ground by Henrik, who hadn't heard their conversation, but had realised the gist of it; enough, anyway, to whack Corc solidly in the head when he jumped on them.

'Stay out of it,' Henrik shouted, pushing a stunned Corc backwards and trying to roll him across the ground.

Lars continued to advance, smiling, even as a crying, bellowing Olaf twisted his arm back again, winning them several crucial seconds.

'Quick!' shouted Henrik, but the Doctor was already there, hauling Corc away as far as possible like a large sack of potatoes, to dump him behind a copse.

But Henrik had not factored in the presence of Erik. The vengeance of what had once been Erik, whom he had bested in armed combat, remained in the depths of a consciousness now also full of the glory and wrath of the alien. Gathering his strength, equal to that of poor, burning Olaf, he hurled himself at the scrabbling, scrambling figure on the ground. Henrik desperately tried to scuttle backwards like a crab, as the line of flaming, bright people swayed and veered like a gigantic snake.

For a split second, it looked like he'd made it and

got away. Olaf stumbled once again, jerking the line back once more, as he started to cry hot tears, which steamed on his cheeks. Henrik made it several paces backwards and turned round, his face full of hope, to face the Doctor, and Freydis, who had run back from where she had set up a line of people passing pots from the well to the wall of fire they could do so little to quench. For a moment, everything paused, held in stasis, and it was as if even the flames themselves went quiet.

And then Henrik blinked. And when he opened his eyes again, they glowed.

Chapter
Twenty-Five

Freydis gasped. But she did not hesitate, not for an instant. She whipped off the cloak Brogan had given her, and she wrapped it round her hands.

'Don't,' said the Doctor, with a warning note in his voice. He realised it was useless. Freydis was deaf to that, now.

As Henrik blinked and felt the power flood through him, his head began to turn, slowly, inexorably, towards his fellow sufferers.

'*The...line...*' he rasped.

'By Odin's fists,' screeched Freydis. 'Absolutely no way.'

And, covered in the cloak, she charged at him, pushing him and tugging him down towards the water's edge.

The Doctor, quickly covering up with his jacket, went to help, whilst knowing deep down it was futile. But Freydis would not be halted. Henrik recoiled from her and tried to pull himself round, but through a sheer effort of will, she pushed him on, down the path, across the sand. The Doctor helped.

Even through the thick tweed of his jacket, he could feel the heat coming off him. Behind him, a horrible scream announced that Olaf's poor body, made of flesh and blood, had finally given up the fight. He knew there was nothing that could be done; the Arill's power sparked through the electrical connections of the brain. Once those burned out, there would be little left to save.

But that would mean nothing to Freydis. Her hair had come undone and she looked wild; red and furious and as full of fire as the Arill itself, as she pushed and hurled and physically forced Henrik down the beach to the ocean and into the sea.

'*Nooo!*' he cried. '*We shall not return.*'

'You shall,' said Freydis, grimly. And under the welter of black clouds above, she kicked away at his knees until he fell over. She motioned the Doctor to hold back, for no one else could do it except for her. Still cloaking her hands, she took Henrik's head, and she held his entire body under the waves.

Time stood still.

Freydis was holding the back of Henrik's head, as one would caress that of a lover; tenderly, almost. The Doctor found it difficult to watch. He did not know what to say. She pushed away his help – she had to do this herself. Freydis was counting very quietly under her breath; the same five numbers, over and over. As the Doctor watched her hand though, he noticed, even as it held Henrik – and he was not struggling – even as it held him under, it continued to caress his hair; caress his head.

He felt the warmth radiating from Henrik's body still pulsing through him – although was he imagining it or was it growing less? – and at the same time, a large drop of water plopped on his forehead. He glanced up at the sky, black with clouds.

'Good,' he muttered to himself. 'Oh, good.'

Freydis looked at him fiercely. 'Nothing is good,' she hissed. 'Is it long enough? Is it long enough now?'

The Doctor felt Henrik. At last, the terrible heat had gone. The water had quenched it – but they both knew at what cost. Was this a kinder death? At least a death on their terms? He felt for a pulse in Henrik's neck. There was nothing. The body felt cold. He was gone.

'Yes,' he said gently. 'Yes. It is long enough now.'

Freydis lifted up the motionless form, and crouched in the water, heedless to the soaking she was getting from the surf and the rain above.

The water poured from Henrik's mouth and lungs as she turned him over. His face was now as white as the belly of a fish, except for a huge mark, right across his right eye and forehead, which was black and dead-looking. The mark of the Arill.

'My love,' said Freydis, gathering him close in her arms; putting her pink cheek next to his stone one. 'My love,' she crooned. 'My darling. They will not have you.'

*

The Doctor tried to help, but Freydis was having none of it and pushed him away. With a heavy heart, he left them in the water and hurried back to the settlement. It was as he had hoped: the heavy rain was already damping down the fire, which was licking at the side of the outmost homestead. And there, slumped on the ground in a row, blackened and twisted, tragic to see, was the line-up of victims, burnt up and burned out; nothing left now but ashes and cinders fading away in the rain.

Alone amongst them, Erik had kept his red beard to the end, and his sword in his hand, teeth bared in a grin. In this case it wasn't, the Doctor noticed, the rictus of death; Erik genuinely was smiling. The Doctor shook his head. Once a Viking, always a Viking.

The Doctor stood amongst the ruination of the dead, arched his back and gazed up at the heavens pouring down on him; soaking every fibre of his being without his noticing.

'You had your warning!' he shouted. 'I offered to help you – remember that!'

But he was shouting it to an empty, pitiless sky.

He found Corc behind a rock, his head burrowed in his son's neck.

'Well done, Daddy,' Luag was saying. 'They didn't get you! You and Henrik stopped them! You're the bravest ever.'

Corc did not trust himself to speak, but gave himself over to the feeling of his son's hands around his neck;

his soft hair in his face; his enormous, enormous gratitude to life, to the rain, to everything.

Luag jumped up. 'Doctor!' he said, pushing a finger in his ear and wriggling it hard. 'My ears popped! My ears popped!'

The Doctor simply nodded briskly. His face was grave, set in his purpose. Above the horizon, the clouds were blacker and darker than ever.

'They had their chance,' he said, his mouth a tight line. 'They didn't start out a bad race, you know. But they seem to have got a taste for it. Like children playing with matches.'

He held out his hand to Corc.

'I will need your sword. I will need all the swords. It is past time.'

Chapter
Twenty-Six

Freydis didn't know how long she sat there, rocking. She knew she was chilled to the bone, or she should be, but she felt nothing. At one stage she became aware of the silhouette of the Doctor standing, watching her from the top of the dunes. He moved towards her and gently helped her out of the water.

'You will freeze too,' he said.

'Help me with him,' said Freydis fiercely. 'I want to take him indoors.'

The Doctor nodded sadly. 'You know... Freydis... it was very brave what you did.'

'You're a God,' said Freydis. 'Why couldn't you...'

'I'm not...' The Doctor, his heart so heavy, couldn't face getting into an argument. Freydis's face looked carved out of ivory and, as she passed her hand over it, he saw immediately the melancholy present in the chess set.

Without another word, he raised Henrik by the shoulders, carrying most of the weight, although Freydis insisted on taking his legs. Clumsily stumbling through the sand, through the pouring rain, Freydis drenched, her teeth chattering without her even realising it, stalked forward, her jaw clenched.

In the long hall, she laid him down, and immediately started to strip of him his wet garments, and herself. Then she drew him as close to her body as she could manage, pulled around them both every piece of cloth in the room, in the building, and started slowly rubbing each of his fingers between her own. The Doctor watched for a second then turned away. This was a private mourning, and he had a battle ahead.

Outside, the rain was growing ever heavier; although it should technically still have been daylight, it was in fact almost pitch dark, the clouds rumbling and thickening, pile upon pile of dark grey and black. Corc was shaking his ears to relieve the pressure, waiting steadily for the Doctor in a barn, with every sword in the village and the twine the Doctor had requested.

'What are you going to do with these?' he asked. 'You only have two hands. Or do you wish to take my men with you? Every man I have is yours.'

'You have lost more than enough,' said the Doctor, gently, picking up the twine. 'OK, before I do this one last time; you have no welding equipment or superglue, right? Or, say, a stapler?'

He frowned at himself.

'I have to ask… I'm sure I had something with a

stationery cupboard in it. I just… it just slips my mind for a moment what it might be. It's almost as if my perception is being filtered somehow. It's a kind of bluey-greyey-sky-at-the-precise-moment-of-no-stars-nightfall colour. I think.' He tutted. 'What is it?'

Corc looked at him uncomprehendingly. 'Is there anything else I can do?' he asked awkwardly, still horribly ashamed of his behaviour.

'Yes,' said the Doctor, as if it had never happened. 'Fetch me the coracle, there's a good chap. And hold the end of this.'

He had lined up the swords in a great row, metres long, and he painstakingly went up the line of them, using his sonic screwdriver to link the one to the next, hilt to tip. Corc watched him without commenting on his extraordinary tool, or the fact that they would probably need those swords back at some point. It was at the very end that the Doctor stopped.

'OK,' he said. 'This is what they call the weakest link.'

Very, very carefully, he took the twine, and used it to lace the sonic screwdriver very tightly to the end of the long chain of swords.

'Look at you,' he said to it, pleased. 'Leading the charge! I wish you could sonic yourself, though.'

When he had fastened it as tightly and as well as he knew how, he stood back and looked at the long pole, pleased with himself.

'What is it?' said Corc. 'Is it a weapon?'

The Doctor regarded it sadly.

'Yes,' he said. 'It is. Of a sort. But the only person it's going to work against is me.'

Corc carried one end of the chain of swords, the Doctor the other. They had to really push against the weather now. It was wild and woolly; a full storm. Night was falling, even at such an early time of day. Black waves pounded onto the shore with incredibly violence. Their roar drowned out all possible conversation. Braan, stone faced, brought the coracle up behind them. Fragile enough to begin with in normal seas, it looked positively ridiculous in this; flimsy, like a paper boat set out upon the ocean.

'Let me come,' said Corc.

'No,' said the Doctor. 'Do not ask me again. Turn now and go back to your homes. I promise, all I can do, I will do.'

Braan said nothing. The Doctor felt, once again, how much he had failed these people.

'It stops,' he said. 'It stops now. We have had enough.'

'Aye,' said Corc eventually, shouting to be heard over the howling wind. 'We have.'

The Doctor lashed the long spear to the upturned base of the coracle. It stretched out far in front and behind in, like the hands of a great clock.

'Gods' speed,' said Braan.

The Doctor stepped forward with his hand out. Just as he put it out to grasp Corc's, he stopped, suddenly, lifted it to his mouth, and spat.

'I don't think this is going to catch on,' he grumbled, as they shook hands. 'Not past the black plague anyway.'

He turned into the dark, dark sea, paused for a moment, watching the pounding waves. Then he took the coracle, floated it ahead of him, still capsized, then, with barely a splash, plunged underneath the waters like a seal.

Chapter
Twenty-Seven

The Doctor had hurriedly stripped off his jacket. But he kept his shoes on and, taking a deep breath, plunged into the frigid foam, ducking his head immediately. He found his way more through touch than sight; it was almost impossible to see anything through the churning black water. Coughing and spluttering from the cold, he moved into the underside of the coracle, twisting his body so he was lying on his back, holding on to the rough plank seats, breathing with as little of himself above the water as possible, the tide buffeting the boat here and there. He went on beneath the water, where he was not pushed too swiftly by the tides, but the roar of the surf in his ears made finding his bearings very difficult. He slowed his breathing, deliberately; feeling his body become at one with the water, allowing himself to feel the wind direction. The vibrational frequency of the wave crests allowed him to calculate, when he relaxed enough into swimming, exactly where he was in relation to the shore, to the distant isles, to the spot he had calculated was the location point of the Arill, down below – shimmering; shifting; waiting; a million, million souls; pinpoints of evolved consciousness; so, so hungry.

Not all monsters, the Doctor reflected, came with guns and claws.

Another breath, and he sensed the deepening of the ocean beneath him, its ancient powers waning and waxing with the moon; many, many types of life teeming beneath him. A huge shoal of enormous cod swam in and out of his legs, silvering and flickering past him. The Doctor closed his eyes. Another species he longed to save. One thing at a time he thought, placing one arm over another, just one over another, pushing the coracle always a little ahead. One thing at a time was not an easy concept for him. But now it was all that mattered, in the crashing, heaving wet darkness of the ocean. All he could do, one thing at a time.

There was nothing to be seen overhead except the dark toiling clouds; the pattering of the rain on the water drowned out by its roar. Eyes closed was better; easier to feel the wave pattern; concentrate on the wind direction. He counted down in his head. And when he felt he was there, holding a long piece of twine attached to the end of the coracle, he dived.

There they were, he thought, the only points of light that could be seen for miles around. A sparkling constellation reflected deep in the water. The tiny flickering zeros and ones were not only green today; they flickered and sparkled through every different shade, some weaker, some brighter. It was clear, from the way the lights coalesced, and started to move up towards him, that he was expected. As soon as he realised they'd noticed him, he turned up and shot for the surface again, confident that they would follow.

He hauled himself into the small boat. At the mercy of the terrifying seas, sitting shivering in the tiny coracle, the Doctor struggled to focus himself. He crossed his legs, put his hand on the great steel spear, and waited.

He exclaimed in delight when the Arill arrived. He couldn't help himself. They were just so delightful. They had made themselves into a huge, iridescent field of dancing jellyfish, shimmering and twisting just under the water.

'Look at that!' he said. 'You're so very beautiful and clever. Why did you have to go and ruin it by attacking humanity?'

The Arill shimmered and swayed.

'Nobody seemed to mind when we were attacking fish. How were we to know?'

'No,' said the Doctor. 'Sorry about that, fish. Valid point. But then I told you to stop.'

'Yes. We got your message.'

The Doctor looked down. 'I felt I owed you a warning. I was wrong. You tricked me. And it gave you a chance to attack, again and again without mercy.'

'They call you the trickster. And they loved the fire.'

'You sucked the juice from them and let them lie

where they fell.'

'We must continue the line.'

'And I will help you,' said the Doctor. 'I said I would. And I will.'

The jellyfish pulsated expectantly. The coracle tossed and turned in the water, thrown hither and thither in the gale.

'I will help you!' shouted the Doctor over the rain. He leant over the side. 'Take me.'

He held out his hand.

'Take me. There is enough power in my brain to give you all that you need. You can take it, take it all. You can use it to get away. You can escape. You know who I am. Nihophogas is running a level 9 systems intelligence pass right about now, and their nebula is passing right above us. They have defence programmes in the trillions of gigawatts. You can gorge yourself on their power; they have billions and billions of lines of code, all echoing and throbbing away; you can surf on pure electrons; gobble up bandwidth to your heart's content. And I can get you there. You know I can.'

The lights fluctuated and flickered in excitement.

'I will give you the charge,' said the Doctor. 'All you must do is promise to leave.'

'But you will die,' said the Arill.

'Well,' said the Doctor, 'at least I won't have to eat any more of that rabbit. Although I would have liked one last game of chess.'

The Arill gathered itself together till it was pointed exactly at the Doctor.

'I thought the shape was not the thing,' grumbled the Doctor. 'You've just made yourself look totally like a torpedo.'

The Arill did not answer. Their time for talking was over. The Doctor, shakily, stood up in the coracle and outstretched both his arms.

On the shore, Corc and Braan watched with sinking hearts as, in the pitch black of the howling maelstrom, a bright shot of light outlined in orange, yellow and red the clear shape of a man.

'Well, that's that then,' said Braan, kicking at a rock on the shore. 'It's all over. They've got him.'

He turned and went back to the village. Only Corc stayed, desperately trying to work out what was happening.

The fire flooded the Doctor's nerve endings and synapses. His eyes flew open; showing immediately the orange glow. He had not received a dose of the Arill; he had received them all. There was no sign now of the jellyfish pinpoints of light.

Inside, he felt their multitude, and their confidence. The fast-flowing network of information; the sensation of the world at his fingertips; an imprecation to hurry on, faster, quicker, more, again. He could understand the attraction to the Vikings and the islanders; he supposed he could understand its attraction to anyone. To burn brightly in the universe.

At first, too, the warmth inside had felt wonderful;

ecstatically good after so long feeling frozen, or damp, or uncomfortable, or all of those things. It felt like the sun on his back on a May morning in the Florentine palatinate; or the second sunrise of the Erentos.

But he knew, he knew he could not let them take hold. He could not allow the billions of particles charging through his system, consuming him; they could not consume him. He had a plan. It had to take shape. And yet. He could see the appeal. Let the heat and warmth take him over. It was comfortable and… suddenly a great peal of thunder cracked out. It seemed to shake the very sky above him, and the Doctor remembered instantly what he was there for and why. A lone point of light.

With a very great effort, he bent down and slowly, carefully picked up the mighty spear, grafted from the swords of the brave and the fallen. With painful, burning slowness, he activated the screwdriver, attached carefully to the very top. Then slowly, taking great care, tossed here and there in the little coracle, desperate not to drop it or be tipped overboard, he raised it up to his chest, his hands shaking, sweat dripping off his forehead as he tried not to let the burning overwhelm him.

The great spear wobbled ominously, ten metres in the air, the glow from the Doctor glinting off its intricately carved length. The tiny green light on the screwdriver blinked once, blinked twice, and with a great, final effort of will, the Doctor managed to lift the entire thing over his head, ten metres in the air. His hair started to smoulder.

Inside his skull, his brain was screaming; a million, million tiny strands of consciousness feeding; using, dragging from him the very fibres of his being. His head wanted to burst, was desperate, in fact, to burst into flames. The force of will to keep the pressure down as the Arill invaded every cell of his body became almost more than he could bear.

But still he held up the spear.

The storm crashed again, getting ever closer. The screwdriver bleeped, slightly altered its course. All around, the boat was being thrown over the waves; the darkness was roaring; the Doctor fighting against an entire race invading his brain; a fight no one had yet won.

And then it came.

CRAACK.

The lightning lanced out of the sky. The screwdriver beeped. This was what it had been programmed to look for. The large metal spear sticking straight up was the tallest point for miles around. Every sinew in his body strained to keep it upright, but the Doctor was failing, his arms beginning to give out, the fire forcing him down to the ground... when CRAACK. The screwdriver found its target, and the lightning lanced down the metal pole faster than the eye could follow it.

'GAAHHHH...'

The second influx of power was even worse than the first; in his already weakened state, the Doctor was nearly blown back by the punch of it. Through the searing agony, the Doctor knew this was it. The time to take his split second and use it.

For unwittingly, unavoidably, as unstoppable as a nuclear reaction, every particle in the Arill, every tiny mote of consciousness was designed towards one clear objective: CONTINUE THE LINE.

Without thinking, without any conscious choice, the charge ricocheted as it hit the rubber soles of his desert boots and rebounded back out of his body, up through the great metal spear – carrying the consciousness of the Arill with it.

Their harsh scream carried over the noise of the storm, as the lightning bolt split the sky apart. The clouds were blown away by its force; the sky stuttered and cracked, and the lightning flung the unwanted hitchhikers hither and thither through the upper atmosphere.

Still watching, hypnotised by the side of the bay, Corc stared at the place the lightning had been; its shape imprinted on his retinas. Incredibly, the sky had cleared; the storm had calmed with remarkable speed, to reveal underneath it a dark cold sky prickled with stars – and, for the first time, something else. A great undulating line of lights – mostly green, but with pink and some blue – shook and shimmered in the sky. It was like nothing Corc had ever seen before. He shook his head; the lights looked to form lines and patterns, as if dancing amongst themselves. It was extraordinarily beautiful, half filling the sky. Corc watched it for a long time; all the while, too, looking into the blackness, to see if there was any sign of a coracle heading back to shore. There was nothing. Chilled to the bone, Corc watched and waited for a long time as, gradually, the other villagers crept down to stand beside him and marvel at the new lights.

Had he done it now? Had it gone, finally? The whispers went up and down the line of villagers. They had thought they were safe before. And they gazed at the staggering chords of lights in the Northern sky for hour after hour, until the hope began to truly take root: he had done it. He had succeeded.

But nobody came back to shore.

Chapter
Twenty-Eight

Exhausted, the Doctor came round to find that dawn was breaking. It took him a little while to realise that he was still in the coracle; that he was still alive, that the storm was over, and that it was gently, steadily, bobbing him back to shore.

One thing struck him, though. Something was wrong. Something felt very strange. What was it? Something out of place that he couldn't quite put his finger on. He picked up his hand. Then he saw it. He wasn't cold. He still felt warm. There was some residual energy; some leftover effort from what remained of the Arill. He blinked several times.

Freydis was unaware of what had happened. She hadn't noticed that everyone was down on the shoreline, tentatively throwing things in the water, and, when dawn came again, putting toes here and there in the water. When nothing happened, one of the bolder young boys had lit a fire on the beach. Standing well back, the villagers had eyed it warily. But nothing had happened.

Immediately they built another, much bigger. And another. And the same young man, whose name was Gren, and whom Corc immediately had his eye on, jumped into another of the fishing coracles and paddled out a little way; then threw in a hook and almost immediately pulled in a big fat cod. Then another, then another, then all the young men of the village threw caution to the wind and ran to their little boats and jumped in; and the women started to boil up soup and tea, and someone ran round to the back of the island to douse one fire to alert their neighbours that Lowith was once more open for business.

Freydis barely heard the crackle of the flames at the far end of the long hall, as one of the women came and laid a fire there. She was still with Henrik, wrapped in blankets still desperately trying to rub life back into his cold, pale limbs.

The woman looked upset and sympathetic at the scene.

'It's all well again, ma'am,' she said in Freydis's own tongue. 'He did not return, but he has made it right.'

Freydis showed no signs of having heard her, and the woman crept out again. Of course it was not well again. How could it be well again? The world could go burn for all she cared.

Suddenly, she felt something. She was sure of it. She was sure she had felt something – a tremor. A flicker. She glanced down. As if stirred by the crackle of the fire, Henrik twitched. Then he twitched again. With a sense of horror, Freydis for the first time thought he might indeed be dead; that his corpse might be twitching into rigor with the change in temperature.

Then Henrik opened his eyes. Freydis stared deeply into them. Was it him? Was he still possessed by the evil from under the sea? Or was he gone completely, with nothing left of his essence; of what made him him? What he had been through had been… even the Doctor thought he was dead, thought Freydis. No one else had survived. Not even the Doctor himself by the sounds of things. She swallowed suddenly, thinking of herself here alone. Then she looked again into Henrik's eyes. They were as bright as ever.

'When I was a little girl,' she said, 'there was a rumour of a boy… from the farmlands, they said, I forgot where. But they brought him up to court. They called him the miracle. They said he had fallen in cold water; had lain in cold water, like someone dead, for a long, long time. Then he had come back to life. And he was just as he was before.'

Very, very slowly, Henrik blinked.

'He was not just as he was before,' he said, hoarsely. His vocal cords still sounded charred, ruined. He coughed, suddenly, which turned into a coughing fit. To Freydis's utter amazement, he sat up.

'He was not just as he was before,' he said, wobbling slightly as he sat up. 'Because it was then that he realised that more things were possible than he had ever dreamed of.'

Freydis stared at him, her Henrik, given back to her by the sea.

Henrik held up his hand to his extremely sore head.

'And he realised he could survive for possibly longer than average in extremely cold water... My head hurts.'

Freydis moved him closer to the fire, her mouth still open in awe. Henrik tried to stand up, stumbled, then caught his feet again. He leaned heavily on Freydis and they limped towards the fire.

'There is a stone inside of me,' he tried to explain, then realised it was coming out wrong. 'But I realised... I realised... I need the love of a good and slightly terrifying woman.'

Freydis was still staring at him.

'What?' he rasped, then held his hand up to his face. Half his hair had gone, and he felt a large, painful scar across his eye. As the blood started to circulate again to his extremities, he felt, suddenly, how painful it was.

'Argh,' he yelped. 'Odin's eyes, do I look awful?'

Freydis smiled, suddenly. His handsome blonde features had changed, that was for sure. Everything she had thought she had admired about him – his fine frame, his beautiful face, so different from Gissar – suddenly became completely unimportant. It was him she loved, after all.

'You look perfect,' she said, trying to blink away a tear. Freydis never cried. She put her hand up to her mouth and her face was, once again, as implacable as ever. 'Perfect,' she said. And they embraced in front of the fire.

Gren was the first to discover the coracle bobbing in to shore. At first he had thought it was empty; then, he saw with a terrible shock the Doctor, glowing brightly, lying down within it.

'It's all right,' the Doctor had pleaded. 'I'm all right really.' He could see Gren in two minds about whether to sink him there and then. Young men, he thought. 'I promise,' he said. 'I'm not dangerous. As long as you don't touch me.'

Gren had no intention of touching him, and beckoned the others over. After taking assurances from the Doctor that the Arill were well and truly gone and that he would not harm them, they lined up their little kayaks by the side of his coracle, and gave him an escort to shore.

Seeing them coming in all together, and not knowing quite what to expect, the villagers lit bonfires all along the line of the beach, as a welcome party. Corc, who had seen the Doctor silhouetted in fire against the sky, believed they were bringing back a body; hopefully, Gods be praised, the very last of them. He had ordered the braziers lit, then the entire village lined up either side of him, as the little boats slowly brought the coracle into land.

Corc stepped forwards, then jumped back in shock, as the Doctor lifted himself up off the floor of the boat.

'Hallo!'

Everyone shrank away.

'I know. I know. Residual short circuits. Lighting up. It's all right, it's all right.'

Still, everyone stayed well back.

He blinked, his flame-jumping eyes trying to avoid setting light to the nearest bush.

'It's very unpleasant on the eyes.'

He sighed.

'Do you know what might help? A cup of tea.'

'So it's gone?' said Corc, glancing out at the ocean. 'Or is it you?'

'It's nearly all gone,' said the Doctor. 'I've sent them into the upper atmosphere. Now they're a line of charged particles, circulating endlessly. *Aurora Borealis*. They won't be unhappy, you know. But now they're out there, there's nowhere else for them to go. You'll see. You'll be able to check on them whenever you like.'

'Thank you,' said Corc. 'Thank you.'

'I am sorry...' The Doctor stopped himself. 'I am not sorry for offering mercy. I am sorry it was not accepted.'

He looked down.

Corc shrugged. 'Man inflicting pain on his brother, for the most of it. As usual.'

They thought about it.

'And all those poor turtles,' said the Doctor.

Corc grunted in a way that indicated that he was slightly less concerned about the turtles.

'And your planet is so young. You'll learn to trust

me. I hope.' The Doctor frowned. 'You'll still never listen, though. Which is of course your prerogative as a free people.'

Corc took a step forward. 'But will you… will you have to stay like this? Can you never be touched again?'

The Doctor smiled ruefully. 'Sometimes,' he said, 'I'm not sure that would make much difference.'

Then he snapped out of it.

'But no,' he said. 'Nope. There is a way I can get rid of it. It takes a bit of hopping though. And I need you, Corc. And Luag… Where is he?'

'I'm here!' came the shrill little voice from the back of the dunes. He bounced forward.

'My indefatigable Luag,' said the Doctor, smiling. 'Now, come here. But not too close, OK?'

Luag ran up to him and the Doctor crouched down. Luag was carrying the two horses from the chess set.

'Don't lose those,' said the Doctor. 'Now. Can you listen very carefully?'

Luag nodded importantly. 'I had four breakfasts,' he said.

'Good' said the Doctor. 'Breakfast is very good for memory retention.' He bit his lip. 'You'll need,' he said, 'to go and get your dad. To hold his hand. He's going to be very frightened, so he'll need you to help him.'

'Yes,' said Luag. 'All right.'

He went backwards and took Corc by the hand. Corc looked down at his son, and, smiling a little awkwardly, let the boy take his big hand in his little one.

The Doctor addressed his comments to the child, but glanced at Corc and, occasionally, Braan, to make sure they were following him.

'Now,' he said. 'I have to get rid of this fire inside me, don't I?'

Luag nodded.

'I spoke to the Arill about it. Well, I say spoke to them. More of a command really. An order. Anyway, they agreed to it when they thought I was sending them off to play in an military defence trilabyte wireless infrastructure. But never mind about that for now.

'All you need to know is this: the Arill were legion. But they were also every tiny point of light on the waves. And all you have to remember – and you do have to remember – is this: don't touch.

'Also, I don't know how long it will last. So if you have anything to say, please say it quickly.'

Chapter
Twenty-Nine

The Doctor started to jump up and down and twist himself in a most peculiar way. It was entirely extraordinary to watch but, slowly, it seemed as if the orange glow that had been a part of him was starting, in some odd way to separate. It maintained the shape of a person, but was no longer intrinsic or connected. First one, then, as the Doctor continued to writhe, another shadow seemed to twist itself out of him until it looked like two people dancing.

The line of people on the beach moved backwards. Except for three figures.

Corc was suddenly very, very glad to feel his son's fingers tight in his, and squeezed. For, walking away from the Doctor, who was now whirling like a dervish, was the slight, but unmistakeable figure of Eoric.

Corc stared, heart in his mouth. The one thing he had longed to see, had longed with every fibre of his being. But he knew his son. He had loved him and raised him and given him his first sword. He had taught him how to fish and how to tend the soil; how to mend an axe and given him his first cup of ale. He had tried to console him after he had lost his mother; and fought with him bitterly as he had grown. Then he had watched his boy die, horribly, by fire; and he had set the brazier alight and sent him to join the Gods.

This could not be Eoric. So what was it?

'Doctor,' he said hoarsely.

'Don't worry!' shouted the Doctor above his caperings.

Luag had no such misgivings. He was delighted. 'Eoric!' he screamed, tearing his hand out of his father's.

'What is it?' said Corc, trying to keep the trembling from his voice.

'They invaded him. They took him,' said the Doctor. 'That means, they had a big part of him as part of their… well. It's very complicated to explain right now. But a part of him is there. The shape can be the thing. It can. And they have very kindly, albeit without much of a choice, agreed to let him say goodbye. But you can't…'

'I can't touch him,' nodded Corc. As the figure grew closer it could be seen that he was made up of flames; oddly contorted into Eoric's shape. All his features could be made out, but he flickered, in orange and yellow, in front of them.

'But it is him,' said Corc, asking one more time.

'It is,' said the Doctor. 'And you must realise that even after he has to go – they are sacrificing power to hold him… but you must also realise that he is also still with them. We are many parts. We too are legion. He will still be there, up amongst the stars after they have gone. After they have gone, after you have gone, after everything you know has gone, but as long as there are stars.'

Corc blinked several times. 'With the Gods, then. After all.'

The Doctor lifted a hand wearily. 'If you like,' he said. 'Yes. If you like.'

Corc stepped forward. Then he reached down and took Luag's hand and they walked down towards the strange figure on the rocky shore.

The Doctor moved on and watched from a respectable distance.

Corc was nodding vehemently; it was clear from their gesticulations that both of them were desperately trying to apologise for things they'd said; for things they didn't mean; to use their unexpected chance, their extra moments to say all they had ever wanted to say. Then the figure knelt down in the sand so it could talk to Luag, who jumped up and down in excitement. Perhaps not quite understanding the gravity of the situation, thought the Doctor; it was fairly clear that he was showing Eoric his two little ivory horses from the chess set and making them jump up and down and chase one another. And the Doctor could also see that the fire-Eoric was laughing. He turned away. It was right, he thought to himself. It was right that fathers and sons got a chance to say goodbye. All fathers and sons should get a chance to say goodbye.

But he was not going to think about that today.

He turned. There was Braan, bent down in front of the flaming figure of Brogan. They were not touching, but as each uttered again and again their love for one another, they moved their hands together, mirroring each other, as if they were on different sides of a glass.

'I will see you,' Braan said. 'Every night. Every night in the sky.'

'Oh yes, my love,' Brogan said. 'Oh yes.'

'That sounds better than it is,' said Braan. 'I'd rather have you tucked up beside me at home.'

'I'll be in your fire too,' said Brogan. 'I'll keep you warm.'

Suddenly the Doctor stopped writhing. The orange glow had entirely left his body; his eyes took back their normal grey-green colour. Quietly, over the noise of the now rippling sea, came one final voice; the last trace of Olaf, singing his own way home:

> *… betra er ósent*
> *en sé ofsóit*
> *svá Þundr um reist*
> *fyr þjóða rök*
> *þar hann upp um reis*
> *er hann aptr of kom*

'I am sorry, Olaf,' the Doctor said to himself. 'That was all I had left. And I am sorry, too, Lars. It is harsh to judge young men. And you too, Ragnor. And even you, Erik.'

The flame that was Eoric was starting to splutter a little and grown fainter. It was time. The end of the burnings. In a way that, the Doctor hoped, had brought a consolation.

He walked slowly towards the groups.

'It's time,' he said.

Corc nodded gruffly. Then he turned his head. 'Thank you,' he said.

The Doctor nodded his head. Flame-Eoric could barely be seen now, he was wavering in the wind; going out like a guttering candle.

'Son,' said Corc for the last time. 'I just want you to know. I was – I am – so very, very proud of you. My brave warrior boy.'

And flame-Eoric smiled, gently, sadly, glanced one last time at Luag, then flickered out and was gone.

Luag skipped up to the Doctor. 'He's going to be in the stars,' he said gravely. 'He's going to watch us and everything! He said he'll send us a sign.'

'I'm very glad to hear it,' said the Doctor. He was quite back to normal, but he gave himself one last quick shivery shake, like a wet dog. 'That is excellent news.'

'Thank you,' said Corc. 'I don't know how you did it, but from the bottom of my heart, thank you.'

'That's all right,' said the Doctor. 'Now, don't go turning it into an annual event and burning people in some big wicker thing to commemorate it. I *mean* that.'

Corc looked perturbed. 'Why would we?'

'If I knew why anyone ever did anything,' said the Doctor, 'I would retire to a hammock with a rather excellent hat and read a lot of novels with pink covers.'

Chapter
Thirty

'But you can't,' said the Doctor. 'You can't just play with horsies all the time. Honestly. Trust me, I know about these things. You know I was once the highest seed in the Quatronial, and they play the 256-square board.'

The sky was clear today; cold, with squalls almost certain to move in later on, but at the moment it was a sharp clear almost translucent pale colour. The islanders were busy; there was much to do, and their trading neighbours and friends had been visiting, anxious for news, when they relit the brazier on the eastern tip.

'Well, I just like the horsies,' said Luag.

'Yes, but it means I'll just keep beating you and beating you and you'll never get any...'

The Doctor glanced down at the board.

'Oh,' he said.

He squinted at it again.

'How did you do that?' he said.

Braan stopped by on his way hunting and looked

at the board. 'I don't know that game—' he started.

'Well, that's good,' said the Doctor. 'Want to play me?'

'But that little fellow looks like he's winning.'

'Well, he *looks* like he's winning, oh yes. He *looks* like he's winning.'

'I am winning,' said Luag.

Braan smiled. Then he looked thoughtful and sat down for a second. 'There's more out there, isn't there?' he asked the Doctor, looking up at the sky.

'Oh yes,' said the Doctor. 'Oh yes.'

'I thought… I thought it was just a cloth. With the light beyond for Valhalla. And holes in it, so we could think of Valhalla.'

The Doctor blinked. 'There are many things behind it, Braan.'

'Will they come back?'

The Doctor shook his head. 'I think you're safe for now.'

Braan paused. 'And you. You're from out there too, aren't you?'

The Doctor nodded.

'How do you get there?' said Braan. 'How do you get back?'

The Doctor thought about it. He was sure he knew, if he thought very hard about it. He was sure he had a way. It was elusive, somewhere, a stray thought lying dormant in the corner of his mind.

'Do you know,' he said. 'I was wondering about that. I mean, I think I must have a ship. I mean, that would seem likely, right?'

Braan nodded. 'Well, you turned up here out of nowhere… I mean, we were a bit busy at the time, but if we'd thought about it, I'm sure we'd have been surprised.'

'Yes,' said the Doctor wonderingly. 'Me too. I wonder if I've left it round here anywhere?'

'I can help you find it!' said Luag. 'What does it look like?'

'You know, I can't remember,' said the Doctor. 'I'm sure I've got a… no. I thought I knew what colour it was, there, but I can't find the word. How annoying.'

'Does it have a sail?'

'I don't know. Maybe.'

'Well, I'll look out for it,' said Braan. 'Anything that doesn't look like something of ours.'

'Thank you so much,' said the Doctor, waving him on his way.

'Does it have buttons?' said Luag.

The Doctor took another one off his tweed jacket. 'This is absolutely your last one, OK?'

Luag nodded, putting it carefully in his rabbit skin pouch. 'Oh,' he said. 'I can't help you look. Dad wants me to help Henrik and Freydis, then come hunting with him.'

'Does he now?' said the Doctor. 'So are you two chaps…'

Luag smiled. 'He likes me around all the time now. It's brilliant.'

'It is. You watch out for him, OK? He needs you.'

Luag nodded.

The Doctor got up.

'Hey!' said Luag. 'We haven't finished the game.'

The Doctor smiled. 'I hate saying this,' he said. 'You did win. I lose. Checkmate.'

Down by the shoreline, Henrik, Freydis and the two last of the Vikings – who were a very changed and sorry crew – were working hard, honing planks, heating pitch and mending the second of the Viking boats.

'No cupboards,' Freydis said.

'Fine by me,' said Henrik.

The Doctor watched them for a while. 'She's a beauty,' he said.

'Thanks,' said Henrik. 'Hopefully she'll run well.'

'It's a funny thing,' said the Doctor. 'But I had a ship around here. You don't... you don't happen to have seen it, do you?'

They both looked confused.

'Like the coracle?' said Henrik. 'No, how would that get you anywhere? Surely you need something bigger?'

'I don't think it is bigger,' said Freydis. 'I don't think it looks that big at all.'

'But it is big,' insisted Henrik.

Freydis gave him the look.

'Stop giving me the look.'

'So,' said the Doctor, 'I'm looking for something I can't remember that's of indeterminate colour that is either very big or very small?'

Everybody nodded.

'OK. Great.'

In the end, it was Luag who found it. Jumping and leaping about the gorse, having been let off helping with the boat by both Henrik and Freydis, who weren't entirely sure they wanted caulking rendered by a six-year-old, he spotted a tiny white cairn on the ground, scattering rabbits as he went.

'What's this?' he asked.

The Doctor glanced down. 'It's writing,' he said. 'Like runes.'

'I want to read runes,' said Luag.

'Get Henrik to teach you before he goes,' said the Doctor. 'It's handy. You can write stories.'

'I'll write one about you,' said Luag.

'I'd like that,' said the Doctor.

'I'll write all about the chess set and how it came here and what happened and who everybody was so everyone will know all about it.'

'That will be absolutely incredibly useful,' said the Doctor, stilling inside himself the deep and certain knowledge that Luag never would write his history, or if he did it would never be found. It was time to leave these people alone. He would not know why not. He would not find out.

He crouched down.

'"This way"?' he read out, looking at the arrow. 'Well, that must have been me. I wonder why?'

They pushed on nervously, tentatively pushing aside the great long leaves covering the entrance to the sandy cave. Inside was something, he was sure of it. Just a feeling. Something that kept slipping off the edge of his range of vision. Suddenly, he remembered what must be making it like that.

'Luag,' he said. 'Turn sideways. Very slowly. Like you're not fussed.'

Luag made a parody of someone pretending not to be fussed. 'Like this?' he said, slinking to the side, his eyes wide.

'Good,' said the Doctor. 'Now, look to the side. But very slowly and in a relaxed fashion.'

There was a pause.

'Wow!' said Luag. 'Doctor! You won't believe what's there! It's a really, really strange colour!'

'Brilliant!' said the Doctor. 'Perception filter. Fantastic. I wonder what it's hiding?'

He took out his screwdriver, adjusted the settings, and pointed it straight in front of him.

The TARDIS appeared in his field of vision. The Doctor's grin threatened to split his cheeks.

'My TARDIS! Brilliant! I am so glad it was you.'

'Is that your ship?' said Luag. 'It looks rubbish. Where's the sail?'

'It is not rubbish,' said the Doctor. 'But I'm not going to take you inside for a look. I don't think it would do you any good. You are perfectly good as you are, Luag.'

Luag squinted. 'Of course I am. Why wouldn't I be?'

'Oh, sorry, forgot,' said the Doctor. 'They don't invent self-doubt until the mid-nineteenth century. 'Of *course* you are.'

He paused.

'But stay here, though. I've got something for you.'

He disappeared inside the TARDIS and rummaged around for quite some time.

Luag stayed outside waiting patiently. When the Doctor did reappear, he was clasping something in his hand. Something orange.

'What's that?' said Luag.

'You put it in a pot and put it over the fire,' said the Doctor. 'Or maybe put it on a stick and toast it. Maybe that would be better. It's hard to make fish fingers without grills.'

'Do I eat it?' said Luag

'Yes,' said the Doctor.

Luag tentatively licked the package. 'Hmm,' he said.

'Not that bit,' said the Doctor. 'That's the box.'

'I knew that,' said Luag quickly.

'The bit you eat is inside.'

'I knew that.'

'Come on, let's go find your dad.'

Chapter
Thirty-One

Henrik and Freydis and the rest of the Viking band were nearly finished. Corc had given them as large a portion of the new mainland supplies as he could manage; their neighbours had been generous, as they were with one another in times of hunger and trouble. An island still needed its friends.

The Doctor tried to plot a course for them, but neither of them had seen a printed map before and, anyway, they didn't exactly know where they were going.

'Just not Iceland,' said Freydis, with a shiver, squeezing Henrik's hand. His scar would not fade, but the joy that shone out of their faces burned brighter than any fire.

The Doctor looked pensive. 'Normally,' he said, 'I never interfere in history or in the technology or development of other races,' he said. He glanced around. 'So don't tell *anyone* about this, right?'

Henrik did what he normally did, and nodded along with the Doctor, who produced from his pocket a tiny round device, no larger than the tip of his thumb.

'What's that?' said Freydis.

'Um…' said the Doctor. 'I'm not telling you. In case
it all gets passed on or something. It's… it's a gift from
the Gods.'

'What does it do?' said Henrik, watching the little
arrow spin this way and that as he turned it around.

'It tells you where to go,' said the Doctor. 'And you
must keep it exactly, exactly pointing to *here*.'

He turned so the arrow pointed to north. 'And head
south south west. South south west, do you hear?
Exactly. You'll get picked up by the Gulf Stream. You
won't even have to row, you'll surf there.'

Henrik looked interested.

'Where?'

'By my calculations, Martha's Vineyard,' said the
Doctor. 'Ooh, it's lovely. You'll like it. Plus, the real
estate is going to be very, very valuable one day.'

They looked at one another.

'I remembered all about your ship, by the way,'
said Henrik.

'Oh yes!' said the Doctor. 'Perception filter. Isn't
she a beauty?'

'Well,' said Henrik. 'She sank to the bottom of the
sea and let in a lot of water. I hope we do a bit better.'

The Doctor looked peevish. 'She's a wonderful
ship.'

'Whatever you say,' said Henrik. Then he smiled.
'I'm teasing. She's the best… colour I've ever seen.'

'She's brilliant!'

'That's what I said.'

'But she is! She is amazing. Do you want another ride, so I can show you what she can do? No, come with me, it'll be great, we'll go do the Festtofian nebulea and charter water ponies!'

For a second, Henrik looked briefly tempted. Then he turned to Freydis.

'My love,' said Freydis, 'we have to catch the turning of the tide.'

Henrik smiled. 'Thank you, Doctor. But I can't. I think we probably have enough adventures ahead.'

'My ship is, like, completely brilliant, though,' said the Doctor quietly.

'If you love your ship, that's all that matters,' said Henrik, gravely. Then he let out a guffaw and he and the Doctor embraced quickly.

The Doctor and Freydis simply acknowledged one another.

'The monsters that tricked us?' said Freydis. 'You tricked them back?'

The Doctor shrugged. 'I might have intimated that… well that they might have been going somewhere else, yes. No mistletoe, though.'

'The trickster.'

The Doctor winced. 'My lady,' he said. 'I am so glad you are delivered. You are very brave.'

'Thank you, Loki,' said Freydis. 'Thank you for my life. Even with your tricks.'

The Doctor nodded.

'I hope you do not live the end the poet wrote about you,' she said.

305

'Well, it's really an issue of translation,' said the Doctor. 'The great snake eating its tail is simply the wheel of time, rolling around and around, ever on. And the poisons of the snake are the wounds of time. And yes it is my destiny to endure them, and to find them, and to fix them, if I can. But I don't think of it as a terrible destiny. It doesn't make me sad.'

Freydis looked at him closely. 'Then what made you sad?'

The Doctor paused. 'That would be as long as the longest saga, and take the harshest of winters to tell,' he said, glancing out to the bay. 'And, like you say, the tide is turning.'

Freydis nodded and inclined her head.

'The queen,' said the Doctor, making a bow.

'But I will never be a queen,' said Freydis.

'And yet you will be remembered as one for ever,' said the Doctor. 'It does strange things, the wheel of time.'

Only Luag glanced back at the TARDIS, rather than, like the others, ahead at the Viking boat beating westerly towards the horizons. He waved furiously, smiling, his hand still tightly clasped in his father's. The ship starting to dematerialise didn't faze him in the slightest; Luag had seen a lot in his short life so far, and he turned back to his dad as the villagers began to scatter, finally, from the waterfront; to fix, to mend, to plough, to dig; to hunt, to catch, to survive.

It was the Doctor, in fact, watching through the

screen at them, who lingered a little while longer, just to enjoy their relief and joy at the returning normality; their return to the circle of seasons and land and living; glancing up at the sky, from time to time; watching for the lights. He looked and then, out of respect, turned off the repaired blue light outside and, finally, holding up his screwdriver, switched it off too; watching its light wink out, and sat in the dark; returning this world to the way it deserved to be – lit only by fire.

Then, after a moment, he pushed forward on the accelerator, and with a breathy, repeated sound, made the TARDIS vanish far beyond the night.

Acknowledgements

Special thanks to the Whoviennes, particularly Naomi Alderman, and Caitlin Moran, both of whom opened my eyes to a few things; Gillian Shaver; Doug Segal for friendly help and input; my family and friends, particularly my lovely husband for occasionally having 11 other chaps in this marriage; Ali Gunn; Justin Richards for editing, being the fount of all knowledge and having a good birthday; Albert DePetrillo, Ed Griffiths and all at BBC Books; Jake Lingwood ('Ja-ake...') at Ebury; and all at Little, Brown.

DOCTOR WHO

The Encyclopedia

Gary Russell

Available for iPad

An unforgettable tour of space and time!

The ultimate series companion and episode guide, covering seven thrilling years of *Doctor Who*. Download everything that has happened, un-happened and happened again in the world of the Eleventh Doctor. Unlock even more content by purchasing Ninth Doctor and Tenth Doctor bundles.

◊

Explore and search over three thousand entries by episode, character, place or object and see the connections that link them together

◊

Open interactive 'portals' for the Doctor, Amy, Rory, River and other major characters

◊

Build an A-Z of your favourites, explore galleries of imagery, and preview and buy must-have episodes

BBC DOCTOR WHO

The Angel's Kiss

A Melody Malone Mystery

On some days, New York is one of the most beautiful places on Earth. This was one of the other days…

Melody Malone, owner and sole employee of the Angel Detective Agency, has an unexpected caller. It's movie star Rock Railton, and he thinks someone is out to kill him. When he mentions the 'kiss of the Angel', she takes the case. Angels are Melody's business…

At the press party for Railton's latest movie, studio owner Max Kliener invites Melody to the film set of their next blockbuster. He's obviously spotted her potential, and Melody is flattered when Kliener asks her to become a star. But the cost of fame, she'll soon discover, is greater than anyone could possibly imagine.

Will Melody be able to escape Kliener's dastardly plan – before the Angels take Manhattan?

£1.99 ISBN 978 1 448 14133 3

B|B|C

DOCTOR WHO

Devil in the Smoke

An Adventure for the Great Detective

Madame Vastra, the fabled Lizard Woman of Paternoster Row, knew death in many shapes and forms. But perhaps one of the most bizarre of these was death by snow...

On a cold day in December, two young boys, tired of sweeping snow from the workhouse yard, decide to build a snowman – and are confronted with a strange and grisly mystery. In horrified fascination, they watch as their snowman begins to bleed...

The search for answers to this impossible event will plunge Harry into the most hazardous – and exhilarating – adventure of his life. He will encounter a hideous troll. He will dine with a mysterious parlour maid. And he will help the Great Detective, Madame Vastra, save the world from the terrifying Devil in the Smoke.

£1.99 ISBN 978 1 448 14147 0

BBC

DOCTOR WHO

Summer Falls

Amelia Williams

'When summer falls, the Lord of Winter will arise…'

In the seaside village of Watchcombe, young Kate is determined to make the most of her last week of summer holiday. But when she discovers a mysterious painting entitled *The Lord of Winter* in a charity shop, it leads her on an adventure she never could have planned. Kate soon realises the old seacape, painted long ago by an eccentric local artist, is actually a puzzle. And with the help of some bizarre new acquaintances – including a museum curator's magical cat, a miserable neighbour, and a lonely boy – she plans on solving it.

And then, one morning Kate wakes up to a world changed forever. For the Lord of Winter is coming – and Kate has a very important decision to make.

£1.99 ISBN 978 1 448 14153 1

DOCTOR WHO

Plague of the Cybermen

JUSTIN RICHARDS

'They like the shadows.'

'What like the shadows?'

'You know them as Plague Warriors...'

When the Doctor arrives in the 19th-century village of Klimtenburg, he discovers the residents suffering from some kind of plague – a 'wasting disease'. The victims face a horrible death – but what's worse, the dead seem to be leaving their graves. The Plague Warriors have returned...

The Doctor is confident he knows what's really happening; he understands where the dead go, and he's sure the Plague Warriors are just a myth.

But as some of the Doctor's oldest and most terrible enemies start to awaken, he realises that maybe – just maybe – he's misjudged the situation.

A thrilling, all-new adventure featuring the Doctor as played by Matt Smith in the spectacular hit series from BBC Television.

£6.99 ISBN 978 1 849 90574 9

BBC

DOCTOR WHO

The Dalek Generation

NICHOLAS BRIGGS

'The Sunlight Worlds offer you a life of comfort and plenty. Apply for your brand new home now, by contacting us at the Dalek Foundation.'

Sunlight 349 is one of countless Dalek Foundation worlds, planets created to house billions of humanoids suffering from economic hardship. The Doctor arrives at Sunlight 349, suspicious of any world where the Daleks are apparently a force for good – and determined to find out the truth.

He soon finds himself in court, facing the 'Dalek Litigator'. But do his arch enemies really have nothing more to threaten than legal action? The Doctor knows they have a far more sinister plan – but how can he convince those who have lived under the benevolence of the Daleks for a generation?

Convince them he must, and soon. For on another Foundation planet, archaeologists have unearthed the most dangerous technology in the universe…

A thrilling, all-new adventure featuring the Doctor as played by Matt Smith in the spectacular hit series from BBC Television.

£6.99 ISBN 978 1 849 90575 6

DOCTOR WHO

Shroud of Sorrow

TOMMY DONBAVAND

23 November 1963

It is the day after John F. Kennedy's assassination – and the faces of the dead are everywhere. PC Reg Cranfield sees his recently deceased father in the mists along Totter's Lane. Reporter Mae Callon sees her late grandmother in a coffee stain on her desk. FBI Special Agent Warren Skeet finds his long-dead partner staring back at him from raindrops on a window pane.

Then the faces begin to talk, and scream… and push through into our world.

As the alien Shroud begins to feast on the grief of a world in mourning, can the Doctor dig deep enough into his own sorrow to save mankind?

A thrilling, all-new adventure featuring the Doctor and Clara, as played by Matt Smith and Jenna-Louise Coleman in the spectacular hit series from BBC Television.

£6.99 ISBN 978 1 84990 576 3

BBC

DOCTOR WHO

A History of the Universe in 100 Objects

JAMES GOSS AND STEVE TRIBE

Every object tells a story. From ancient urns and medieval flasks to sonic screwdrivers and glass Daleks, these 100 objects tell the story of the entire universe, and the most important man in it: the Doctor.

Each item has a unique tale of its own, whether it's a fob watch at the onset of the Great War or a carrot growing on the first human colony on Mars. Taken together, they tell of empires rising and falling, wars won and lost, and planets destroyed and reborn.

Within these pages lie hidden histories of Time Lords and Daleks, the legend of the Loch Ness Monster, the plot to steal the Mona Lisa and the story of Shakespeare's lost play. You'll find illustrated guides to invisible creatures, the secret origins of the internet, and how to speak Mechonoid.

A History of the Universe in 100 Objects is an indispensible guide to the most important items that have ever existed, or that are yet to exist.

£20 ISBN 978 1 84990 481 0